W E B   O F   D E S I R E #2
FLAME

ALEATHA ROMIG
New York Times, Wall Street Journal, and USA Today
bestselling author of the Consequences, Infidelity, Web of Sin,
and Tangled Web series

COPYRIGHT AND LICENSE INFORMATION

FLAME

2020 Edition License

SYNOPSIS

FLAME – book #2 WEB OF DESIRE

"*What matters most is how you walk through the fire.*" ~ Charles Bukowski

No longer simmering and crackling beyond our realm, the fire smoldering in the distance roars to life. The blaze has the capacity to scorch and destroy everything and everyone in its path.

All that I've known and believed was obliterated the moment Madeline spoke a truth I'd never suspected. With one sentence, one plea, my life has taken an uncharted turn. Through the smoke and soot, I search for answers.

A man, an outfit, and my brothers-in-arms have been my

solace, my calling, and my reason to live. Now that I know there's more, what will the future hold?

The Ivanov bratva wants Chicago. I want what they possess. With the Sparrow world at war, and Madeline's declaration, she and I are surrounded, trapped by the inferno.

What will remain when the flames cease and we are left surveying the ashes?

From New York Times bestselling author Aleatha Romig comes a brand-new dark romance, *FLAME*, set in the dangerous world of Sparrow Webs. You do not need to read the *Web of Sin* or *Tangled Web* trilogy to get caught up in this new and intriguing saga, *Web of Desire*.

FLAME is book two of the *WEB OF DESIRE* trilogy that began in *SPARK* and concludes in *ASHES*.

Have you been Aleatha'd?

PROLOGUE

The end of SPARK, book #1, Web of Desire

Patrick

"*M*r. Kelly."

I didn't draw it out. Instead, I turned my entire hand. 9, 8, 7, 6, and 5, all of diamonds.

"A straight flush."

Chairs moved as the room erupted.

"Ladies and gentlemen," Sparrow said loudly as he stood. "We will maintain order."

I reached over to Madeline, but she was also standing. Her

expression of elation was gone, replaced by what could only be construed as fear.

"I can help you."

She straightened her neck. "No one can."

I sat dumbfounded as she made her way through the crowd to Ivanov.

Why would she go to him?

There was no question by the Detroit kingpin's expression, he was upset. With the volume and commotion of the room, I strained to hear what they were saying. The uproar won. That was all right, I didn't need to hear his words. Ivanov's body language alone had the small hairs on my neck standing on end.

The dealer was collecting the chips.

Sparrow and Mason came my way. "Good job," Sparrow said. "Let's go downstairs and get this figured out."

"What about..." I looked over to Andros Ivanov still talking to Maddie.

"We have Sparrows here," Mason said, looking at Sparrow. "Both Ivanov and Hillman and their respective crew will be escorted off the property as soon as we are secure."

Our number-one job was keeping the boss, Sterling Sparrow, safe.

I looked from my friends to Maddie and back again. "I will explain this soon—I've tried already—but first I have to be sure of something. My gut is telling me something isn't right." I looked at Mason and tipped my chin toward Sparrow. "Get him downstairs."

The commotion grew louder around Ivanov and his men with Maddie right in the middle.

Sometimes it's safest in the middle of the fire.

Oh hell no. I couldn't stand by any longer.

Ivanov's voice came into range. "I told you what would happen if you lost."

"Get the other spectators out of here," I ordered, speaking to a Sparrow capo. "I want this hall cleared."

"No, no, you didn't say that," Maddie's voice cracked. "Andros, I'm sorry. I had a great hand. You saw it. It was dealt to me. I was so sure." With each sentence her desperation mushroomed, causing the words to come faster and faster.

I walked closer, leaving Mason and Sparrow with other Sparrows.

"Please...don't do this," she said, holding onto his arm.

He reached for her hand and roughly pushed it away.

I moved closer. "Don't touch the lady."

Ivanov's laughter resonated above the crowd noise. It wasn't only his. Now Hillman and his men were circling the others.

"Lady?" Ivanov asked. "You have the wrong woman." He eyed Madeline. "This one's a loser."

My fist came forward. Before I had time to think, it collided with his arrogant jaw.

"No," Madeline screamed as her hands came to her lips.

Ivanov staggered backward as his arms went out. "Wait," he demanded, holding back his men as they lurched forward, their eyes on me. "No, not yet." He regained his position as he rubbed his chin.

"Get out of my club—now. Your invitation has expired."

I knew the deep, commanding voice. It was Sparrow.

Fuck. He needed to get out of here.

"Your club? You think this club is yours?" Ivanov asked.

"You probably think the city is yours too. You're wrong. I have parts, and soon I will have it all."

"Get the fuck out now," Sparrow said, his words demanding yet his tone eerily calm, "and you will live to see tomorrow."

"Come," Ivanov said to the men gathered. "We'll be back." He nodded to Mason. "Better check on the man in the office. He was no longer useful to me."

What?

Mason's gaze met mine.

Was he talking about Beckman?

By the time I turned to Madeline, she was walking, her head down, following Ivanov's and Hillman's men as they exited the room.

"Madeline, stay here," I said, ignoring the way Sparrow and Mason were looking at me.

Her head shook. "I can't, Patrick."

"Man," Mason said, reaching for my shoulder, "whatever is happening, let her go."

Ivanov stopped and turned to Madeline. "I told you that returning required a win." His gaze came to me. "Keep her. Her usefulness is also done. I have the newer version." His lips curled into a smile. "She's something else...fresh, innocent, and even more beautiful."

"No, Andros. I'll do anything," Madeline called out as Ivanov and his men continued to leave.

"Make sure they are escorted off the property," Sparrow was saying.

"Please, you promised," she pleaded, her voice growing louder.

"And you promised me a win." Those were his last words.

My attention went to Madeline as I tried to make sense of what happened, what was happening. In the few minutes since the last game she had crumpled. I went to her as she leaned forward sobbing as if she'd been hit in the stomach.

Standing taller, she looked up at me with tear-filled eyes. "I told you I had to win." She looked at me, Mason, and Sparrow. "Please, if you can, stop him. I have to go with him."

"Maddie, you don't understand who he is," I said.

She nodded. "I do. I know exactly who he is."

"Patrick, what—?" Sparrow began.

"I've been trying to tell you—"

Madeline's gut-wrenching wail stopped my reply.

I reached for her arm. "I'm going to tell them."

"I-it doesn't matter," she muttered, sobs hiccupping her words. Mascara and tears covered her cheeks as blotches filled her neck and chest. "Y-you don't understand."

I reached again for Madeline's arms, no longer caring about Sparrow and Mason. "I *understand* you're my wife. I'll keep you safe."

"Patrick," she said, trying to catch her breath. "I have to go with Andros."

"You don't have to."

"I do. He has my—" Her glassy green eyes stared up at me. "Patrick, Andros has *our* daughter."

PATRICK

*D*aughter.

The word rang like an echoing gong repeating over and over in my head, each time demanding more—more thought, more consideration, and more understanding.

Though hell was breaking loose around us, such as the resounding shrill of a fire alarm, her declaration had my full attention.

Daughter.

The single word held too much meaning, and at the same time, not enough. The information—the bomb Madeline had just dropped—was difficult to process. My mind scrambled to compute.

"What?" I asked.

Madeline nodded, her fear-stricken gaze not leaving mine.

This woman had walked away, never giving me the chance to be a husband, and now she attested that I was more—that I was a father.

My grip of Madeline's arms tightened as I stared into the depths of her green orbs with the world around us erupting in pandemonium. Though others were present, the two of us were alone in the eye of the storm. "Say it again," I demanded.

"I never meant for you to know."

"You're saying there's a child and she's mine?"

"Yes, Patrick. But she's not a child, not anymore. She's sixteen years old..." Another sob erupted from her throat. "...I know who Andros is, what he is capable of doing, and we can't let him have our daughter, not without me present to keep her safe."

I have a daughter.

I am a father.

The volume outside our bubble continued to grow. Hurricane-force winds metaphorically blew as voices rose. Ivanov's show didn't go unnoticed as murmurs morphed to shouts of anger and fear. Sparrow capos worked to clear the poker hall as contenders and spectators alike were corralled and moved onto the landing and beyond. Elliott was in my peripheral vision.

My gaze left Madeline's as I searched for Sparrow and Mason. They were both doing what I should be doing, helping to clear the room. My eyes met Sparrow's. After a nod to Garrett, he came my way. "They're out of the building."

Madeline turned to Sparrow. "I don't know who you are, but you seem to know who Andros is, the kind of man he is. Please, I'm begging you. Stop him before he goes back to Detroit."

"Ms. Miller," Sparrow said, "as part of the Ivanov bratva, you're also not welcome here."

She gasped as she looked from him to me. "I have no one, no place, not without Andros."

"Then I suggest—"

"Excuse me."

We all turned to Marion Elliott.

"It's time you leave," Sparrow said.

"Yes." Elliott turned to Madeline. "I'm sorry to have overheard. You aren't without options, Madeline. Come to Texas. I have resources."

What?

I stepped in front of Madeline. "Goodbye, Mr. Elliott."

He took a step back but continued speaking to Madeline. "I hope you still have my number."

Madeline didn't reply as she clenched her handbag.

"Walk Mr. Elliott to his car," I called to one of the capos.

As Marion Elliott was escorted away, I spoke to Sparrow. "It's true what was said before. Madeline and I are married. She's my wife."

His dark gaze narrowed. "This weekend?"

"Seventeen years ago."

There was an almost imperceptible shake of his head as if I were presenting information he wasn't ready to hear. "Deal with her. You have ten minutes. We're clearing the building."

With the king's declaration made, Sparrow turned and walked away.

"Deal with me? What does that mean?" Madeline asked.

"It means you're a liability."

"I'm not. Yes, I have been within the Ivanov bratva, but not...in. Who does he think I am or what I know? Yes, I have heard things, but I don't know..." Her green eyes opened wider. "I'm not here for them. Please tell me you believe me. Tell me that you believe that I was here to play poker."

"Who financed your play?"

Her eyes closed and opened. "Andros."

"Who financed your travel? Your expenses." I motioned to her green gown. "Your clothes?"

Defeat and disappointment washed over her expression as her chin dropped. "You're right. I suppose that's the way it looks. I promise you that I never told him the name of my daughter's father. He couldn't have known."

"Birth certificate?"

Her head shook. "I didn't list a name, any name."

My neck straightened and teeth clenched. Not only had she denied me the experience but also the claim.

"Fine," she said dejectedly, "I'll leave."

She took one step toward the door before I reached out again. Grasping her wrist, I spun her back toward me. "How? How did you end up with him, part of *that* organization?"

Her neck stiffened. "Does it matter, Patrick? It seems you're rather familiar with the workings of the bratva. Organizations fall under many names." Her chin tipped toward Sparrow. "Who is he? How did you get involved with him, with the other men around here? Are you a family? A cartel? An outfit?"

Letting go of her wrist, I took a step back and exhaled.

Her head tilted. "Tell me, Patrick, is my sin that I'm involved with the wrong crime syndicate?"

Officially, Sparrows were an outfit. In reality, the definitions of the titles she spouted weren't dissimilar.

"Ivanov just declared war—war on my..." I fought for the

right word. Yes, we were an outfit, but we were more than that. "...on my *family*."

"I don't care. There are always wars and coups. There is always someone who Andros is threatening or who is threatening him. Don't you understand that I don't give a shit about what he does or what you do? All I care about is my family—my daughter—and keeping her safe. It's all I've cared about since..." She sighed. "...since I had her to care about."

"And you think she's safe in a bratva?"

"Sometimes the safest place is in the middle of the fire." It was the same thing she'd said earlier in the night.

"I'm not letting you leave," I said.

"It isn't your choice."

It was. I could keep her here. I could keep her locked away in our tower. Sparrow wouldn't be happy, but damn it, this was my wife, the mother of my child. My mind swirled.

A child.

A daughter.

No, not *a*—mine.

My child.

My daughter.

Scenes I'd never before dreamt—an infant in my arms, a child running about, and a teenager—swirled like ghosts through my mind. Their images were too fleeting and too transparent to grasp, yet like apparitions their presence was there.

As the different images materialized an unexpected reaction occurred. An unfamiliar sense of pride combined with a colossal desire to protect oozed into my circulation. In the time span for a drop of blood to leave the heart and travel back, I was fully affected.

Yes, I'd fought for my country. I protected Sparrow. I wanted to care for Madeline. Yet somehow, for a young girl who up until a few minutes ago I didn't know existed, whatever had been brought to life within me was different—stronger and more intense than I'd ever felt.

The knowledge of this unknown young lady created an overwhelming sense of duty such as I'd never known was possible.

I had to protect my daughter, save her from Andros Ivanov and the Ivanov bratva.

The concept was crazy. I didn't know this child. I couldn't pick her out of a lineup, yet suddenly, her well-being was paramount in my thoughts.

My eyes narrowed as I stared down at Madeline. "You drop a fucking bomb that I have a child, a daughter, and now you plan to leave?" When she didn't reply, I asked, "Why didn't you tell me before now?"

"Does it really matter? I'm not presenting you with a baby wrapped in a pink blanket. That ship sailed," she said defensively.

"You're saying it's too late. If you're telling me the truth and I have a daughter, it's not too late."

Madeline nodded. "I am telling you the truth. The last I spoke with her, she was well and happy. That was before I left for Chicago, but Patrick, this isn't like I'm telling you I'm pregnant. She's sixteen. She doesn't know you—"

"Doesn't know me," I interrupted. "How the fuck would she? She doesn't know me because you never gave me a chance."

"I-I didn't want to tell you. I-I couldn't. I always feared what Andros would do if he found out who her father was, how he would use it against me and her." Madeline's head shook. "Please, I have to get to her."

"To her...to *my* daughter."

"To *my* daughter," Madeline corrected. "I have sacrificed..." She took a step back. "It doesn't matter. I didn't know you were here in Chicago or anywhere. Hell, I didn't know until Thursday that you were still alive. Once I did, once I saw you again, I couldn't tell you. I didn't want you to feel obligated."

"Fucking obligated." My volume rose. "I am obligated. I was obligated seventeen years ago when you left me."

Her neck straightened. "This is not going to be settled here. As I said, I'll leave."

"And do what?"

"I'll do what I've always done, beg for his forgiveness."

The small hairs on my neck stood to attention. "Is this some game the two of you play?"

"No, Patrick, it's not a game. Nothing with Andros is a game. This is my life. It's my daughter's life. And for her, I'll do it. I'll take whatever penitence he deems sufficient for losing his money. I'll offer him anything and everything to be back with her."

What the hell was she even saying?

"Do you think he'll hurt—" It was at that moment I realized something fucking obvious. I didn't know my own daughter's name. "What's her name?"

"Ruby," Madeline said as more tears glistened in her eyes. "She's beautiful and intelligent. She's talented. She's also kind and naïve. I named her Ruby after the precious gem that is her birthstone and because the name reminded me of the color of apples."

Her answer twisted the knife in my gut. "Her last name?"

"Miller. I can explain that later. First, I need to get to her or get her to me."

"You said you know Ivanov," I said, not wanting to know the closeness of their relationship. "Is he a threat to Ruby? Does he know where she is?"

She swallowed. "He knows where she is. I want to say he wouldn't do what he insinuated, but because I do know him, I can't answer that for sure." Her head shook as she stood taller. "Ruby thinks of him as a..." She hesitated.

"Father," I said.

"Not fully. She knows he isn't. Maybe she considers him an uncle or surrogate."

Her words made me bristle. I was her father.

Madeline reached out. "Ruby doesn't think of him as..." More tears came to her eyes. "If he acted upon what he just insinuated...He can't mean what he said. I have to get back to her." More sobs bubbled from her throat. "My God, she's only sixteen. She doesn't know...I've done my best to shelter her. All I want is to hold her and tell her she's safe."

That was exactly what I wanted as I imagined images of Madeline at that same age.

Did Ruby look like her mother or did she look like me?

As I was about to ask more, the room shook. The reverberating blast of a gunshot rang out, rattling the walls and light fixtures and pulling me back to reality.

PATRICK

The windows rattled as a gunshot blast echoed within the walls of the poker hall.

Without hesitation I reached for the gun beneath my jacket. With the other hand, I pulled Madeline behind me and spun toward the door.

Suddenly, my mind wasn't on an infant, a child, or even a teenager. Instead, I was seeing the room around me, scanning the few remaining faces.

Terror showed in the eyes of the few remaining bystanders as they crouched to the ground. The other Sparrows had duty in their gaze, their guns drawn and backs against the wall.

Sparrow?

Where the fuck was Sparrow?

While Madeline and I'd been talking, he and Mason must have left the room. That was also the direction the shot had come from.

"Patrick?" Madeline said, her voice again quaking. "What's happening?"

I pulled her to the side wall near the windows and glanced down at the street. The red awning obstructed my view as a string of cars waited to pick up their waiting passengers. "Stay here."

With my heart beating at untold speed, I lifted my gun and nodded toward the other Sparrows. We stepped in the direction of the open doors. My eyes immediately met Mason's green gaze. His neck was taut, cords coming to life as he barked orders.

On the floor near his feet lay a man I recognized as one of our own. His name was Mattis. By the appearance of things, he was very much alive and in considerable pain. The cause wasn't only from the way the heel of Mason's boot pushed down on his lower back, but from the blood seeping from his right hand onto the floor.

I stepped out farther, my gun still drawn, and surveyed those present. In the last few minutes, the sheer number of people had dwindled. It now appeared we were surrounded by mostly familiar faces.

"There are some people in there," I said, "who need to be escorted out. We want only Sparrows here."

A quick turn to my left and I saw who I'd been seeking. The visual confirmation allowed me to release a relieved breath as I holstered my gun. Sparrow was alive and unharmed. In all his regality he stood near the wall, talking to Garrett, the epitome of control and power, appearing impervious to whatever had happened.

From the banister I peered a story below, into the club's

entry, where Sparrow capos were clearing the rooms. The restaurant, cigar room, and bar were all officially closed by order of Sterling Sparrow. Mutterings of discontent made their way to us, yet it appeared that the exodus was progressing smoothly.

"Ivanov?" I asked, stepping closer to Sparrow.

"He, Hillman, and their men have driven away."

I thought about Madeline's plea. "We could stop them before they board their planes."

Sparrow's head shook. "I told you to deal with her. You realize that no matter what she's said, she's a plant, a trap."

She could be.

I hadn't thought of that.

I didn't want to think of that.

"Tell me," he said, "what you said about her being your wife, is it true?"

"Seventeen years ago. The marriage is still valid."

"What about what she said about a child?" he asked. "If it exists, could it possibly be yours?"

It.

Ruby was a she, not an it.

I didn't say that. "Yes, she could. I don't fucking know if I trust Madeline now. I did a long time ago and I want to."

"I trust no one until they prove to be trustworthy."

"Sparrow, there was a time, she was. Up until Thursday night, I thought she was dead."

Sparrow lifted his hand. "One catastrophe at a time. We'll talk about that one later."

I wanted to argue, to tell Sparrow I'd get in a car and drive to the airport where Ivanov's plane was preparing to leave. Madeline may know which airport. However, that knowledge alone gave credence to his concern. I tilted my head toward the man on the floor. "What happened?"

Garrett, a trusted member of the Sparrows, joined the conversation. "Traitor."

I looked again, recalling the younger man from a few assignments and meetings. "Mattis, right?"

"Right," Garrett replied. "He's not talking, not yet, but he will. Thankfully, Mr. Pierce saw him draw his gun. Instead of asking questions, Mr. Pierce fired, hitting Mattis's hand and causing him to drop the gun. The timing was impeccable. It all happened before Mattis could shoot."

"His target?" I asked, knowing the answer yet needing the confirmation.

"Me," Sparrow said.

Fuck.

I should have been here at his side. "Sparrow," I began, "I should have been here. I tried to tell you..."

"Later," he said definitively, cutting me off again. "Go downstairs and check on Beckman."

Garrett spoke, "Sir, I sent a capo."

Sparrow and I turned.

"Do you have confirmation of his safety?" I asked.

"I have confirmation of his demise," Garrett replied. "From the sound of it, it was probably poison. There's a note. In it, Beckman confessed to Ms. Standish's murder and stealing the money from the safe. The note said he couldn't take the guilt. Yada, yada."

"You don't believe it?" I asked.

"I don't," Sparrow said. "I didn't know about this charade, but we know who killed Ms. Standish. It was your..." He inhaled, not saying the word *wife*. "...Ms. Miller's associate, Leonardo."

"Any news on Leonardo's whereabouts?"

"I'd put my money on a shallow grave," Garrett said.

My gut bubbled with the knowledge that we'd lost both Veronica Standish and Ethan Beckman in the course of twenty-four hours. They were supposed to be on our side. Leonardo was one of Ivanov's.

If Ivanov could order the death of an associate who had done his dirty work, what else was he capable of?

What would he do to Madeline if she returned?

What would he do to Ruby if she didn't?

"The capo who was guarding Beckman is being questioned," Garrett continued. "He seemed shaken by the discovery. This fucking place needs cameras. I've got men working to piece together a timeline. I want to know who brought Beckman food or water—well, everything."

"The safe." Sparrow said. "My money is in the safe." He looked at me. "The two of us are headed down now to confirm that it's still there."

$11,800,000.

I nodded, knowing I wanted to stay with Madeline, while at the same time recognizing my place was beside Sparrow. As we were about to leave, Madeline came into view, being tugged from the poker room. A Sparrow capo held onto her arm. When she came closer, her green stare came my way.

My descent stilled as I turned back and moved toward the capo. "Get your hands off of her."

"Mr. Kelly," the capo seemed to falter, "you said to clear the room. Mr. Sparrow gave the orders involving Ms. Miller."

What?

I spun toward Sparrow. "No one is touching her."

Sparrow's dark gaze met mine as he lowered his voice. "As I pointed out, she's part of the Ivanov bratva." His features hardened. "He's declared war. I told you to deal with her. Now we are."

My head shook. "I will. Things are—"

Sparrow stepped closer, blocking my view of Madeline as his volume lowered. "Look at me."

I fought the urge to look at Madeline and met Sparrow's dark stare.

"Listen closely," he said through clenched teeth. "We are at war. For all intents and purposes, she's as guilty as Mattis. Think about it, Patrick. For whatever history the two of you share, I would bet the entire twelve million we placed in the safe that it wasn't a coincidence she was here. Ivanov sent her here as your distraction. Yours personally."

I listened to his words.

"That means," Sparrow continued, "he's done his research. He knows what you're capable of and also calculated your greatest vulnerability."

If I were outside this conversation, I could agree with him. I wasn't outside of it. I was in the fucking middle, with fire raging all around me. I wanted to tell him he was wrong, but I couldn't form the words.

I believe you came to Chicago to fuck with me.

It was what I'd said to Madeline Thursday night.

Trust your gut.

It was Mason's advice.

My head shook. "I don't know what to believe."

"Believe this," Sparrow said, "she distracted you."

I nodded. "I tried to—"

"She's being taken for questioning."

My mind was a blur. My stomach churned with bile as I imagined our questioning techniques. "Where?"

"I need to know you're with me," Sparrow said.

"I am. I'm with you." I stood taller. "No one else questions her. It will be me."

"Currently, you're going downstairs with me to check the safe. This isn't a debate."

I stood dumbfounded as all eyes were on us. I lowered my voice. "We'll open the safe. Don't take her off premises. Not until..." I didn't finish the sentence. The decision would be his. The intensity of his stare told me that. All I could hope was that he'd see my point of view. "Sparrow, she's my wife."

"I need a fuck ton more answers," he said.

"You aren't the only one," I replied.

I turned back to the capo. "Lay one hand on her and I'll kill you right here."

His hands came up toward his chest, palms out. "Mr. Kelly..."

Sparrow stepped forward, speaking toward Madeline and the capo. "Ms. Miller, cooperate and no one will be hurt, not yet."

Madeline nodded. "Please, I need your help."

Sparrow spoke to the capo, "Confiscate her phone and handbag. Take her downstairs to the offices. Put her in Ms. Standish's office after you disconnect the phone and computer. Stand guard and for fuck's sake, no one brings her food or drink."

Madeline's eyes pleaded my direction. "Patrick, stop Andros from leaving the city. Once he's back in Detroit, he's unstoppable."

"Sounds like a setup," Mason said, stepping forward. He hadn't heard our earlier conversation as he had been dealing with Mattis. That traitor was now in the hands of other Sparrows.

My blood boiled as I looked from Madeline to Mason and Sparrow. I didn't want to admit it, but Mason was right. It did sound like a fucking setup. I spoke to the capo. "Listen to Mr. Sparrow. Take her down to Ms. Standish's office. Make sure she has no means to communicate outside this building. Stand guard. No one touches her. No one talks to her. No one brings her a thing. You won't fucking move from the door. Do you understand?"

"Yes, sir."

I spoke to both of them, "Stay there until I get there."

"Patrick, please. Ruby..."

"Madeline, don't make this more difficult than it already is." My jaw ached as I clenched tighter and stared her way. Without another word, I turned the other direction and headed toward Beckman's office. The safe was my first stop.

MADDIE

Seventeen years ago

With my head lowered and body crouched before the toilet bowl, I saw the bathroom door open inward. Very few spaces around the mission were private. This bathroom was one of them—if only I'd taken the time to lock the door.

The facilities were public, a one-person bathroom off a back hallway. Its location within the mission meant it served primarily for the use of the cafeteria workers. The mission had been constructed within an old elementary school. Classrooms were subdivided into apartments. The kitchen was mostly updated and the cafeteria was large enough to feed the current residents. The gymnasium was the all-purpose room, holding our church services as well as free-time area. The offices that had at one time been used by the principal and other administrators were used by the pastor, his wife, and a secretary.

Through watery eyes, I looked toward the opening door. A million thoughts and feelings were vying for attention. I was angry with myself for not locking the door behind me. At the same time, I was relieved to perhaps have a confidant.

The reality was that I hadn't had time to lock the door. I barely made it to the toilet before the breakfast I'd recently consumed made its way back up and out. My stomach constricted as I again gagged, my body retching from the internal assault. With the food gone, I was now left with dry heaves.

Kristine, the pastor's wife, entered and closed the door behind her. She was an older woman—older than me— probably in her thirties or maybe forties. She and her husband were the reason Patrick and I were here. Their vision was to help people like us, people who needed a nudge to move beyond the streets. When it came to all things around the mission, Kristine ran a tight ship, but no matter what the situation, she managed to smile and encourage.

Her expression held no condemnation, only concern. "Maddie, are you sick?"

More tears came to my eyes as I fought the rolling nausea. A slick layer of perspiration coated my skin, yet my limbs trembled as if the temperature had dropped to below freezing. My fingers blanched as I held on to the edge of the porcelain basin.

I inhaled and exhaled, waiting for the next bout of nausea. When it didn't come, I wiped my mouth on the back of my hand and shakily stood.

After flushing the evidence down the toilet, I went to the

sink. Cupping my hand under the running water, I brought a small amount to my lips. The fresh clear liquid cleansed and refreshed my mouth as I swished and spat, each round helping to remove the nasty taste. Finally, I turned to the woman who was responsible for our housing, who'd taken pity on me and Patrick, who'd helped provide us with a semblance of a life.

Kristine and I were nearly the same height. Staring into her eyes, I told her the truth. "I don't know if I'm sick. I don't think I'm contagious if that's what you're worried about. I can work. I can," I added the second confirmation as my sentences come faster, and fear added to my distress. Missing work would jeopardize our one-room apartment. "I'm sorry."

Kristine came my way, lowered the lid on the toilet, and directed me to sit. "Talk to me, Maddie."

"I-I don't think I'm *sick*."

"What do you think the problem is?"

Problem?

Was being pregnant a problem?

Wasn't it supposed to be a blessing or something corny like that?

Wrapping my arms around my stomach, I stared up.

As I did, Kristine crouched down until our eyes were again level. "Does Patrick know?"

Swallowing the new sobs, I shook my head. Finally, I shrugged. "I don't even know."

"Have you taken a test?"

"No."

"When was your last period?"

I tried to recall. My cycles weren't regular. After moving onto the streets, I assumed the irregularity had to do with nutrition—or lack thereof. It wasn't that I'd starved;

nevertheless, up until our relocation to the mission, the proper vitamins and minerals were often lacking. "I think it was just before we were married." I took a deep breath. "It was really short. I remember thinking it was weird, and I hadn't had one for a while before that. Like I said, I'm not regular."

"How short?"

"I don't know, maybe just a couple of days and not very much."

Kristine forced a smile. "Honey, you moved in here over a month ago, right after you were married. You could have already been pregnant."

My eyes opened wide. Part of staying at the mission was taking classes about righteous living. "I know it was wrong. We weren't married..."

She reached for my hand. "That's not important any longer. You made it right the day you two were legally wed. What matters now is finding out for sure if you're pregnant and taking care of you and the baby." Her light-brown eyes shone. "Are you going to tell Patrick?"

"I think that first I'd like to know for sure. After I get my weekly stipend, I will buy a home pregnancy kit. Unless you could maybe give me an advance?" I hated to ask. "And then I can go to the store today."

Her lips came together for a moment. "You know that Pastor Roberto and I are here for you, for everyone we take in. The tests from the store aren't always accurate. If you'll let me, I can help you."

My chest filled with a bubble of something like gratitude. Kristine and her husband Roberto had already helped Patrick and me more than anyone—ever. "I-I can't ask you."

"You aren't asking." Her head shook as she squeezed my hand. "We'll keep this between the two of us for a few more days. On Friday, after breakfast is cleaned up, I'll drive you to a place where they can help you."

"What about our room?" I asked, afraid she'd say we needed to move out. There were only a few children in residence and they'd moved in with their mothers or parents. Most didn't stay long, making me think they weren't welcome. "Will we be kicked out?"

"Don't you worry about that right now," Kristine said with a smile as she stood. "Go back to the kitchen and get yourself a piece of toast. No butter. Once you eat that, you need to get back to your duties. It's your turn to scrub down the stove."

"Okay."

"You won't let me down, will you, Maddie?"

My head again shook. "No, Kristine, thank you for helping me."

"Now, we don't know anything for certain. There's no need to jump to conclusions. After your appointment on Friday, you can better determine what the future holds."

"Why Friday?" I asked, wanting to get the test sooner rather than later. Friday was four days away.

"On Fridays, Roberto takes the boys to pick up supplies for the construction and remodel. With Patrick occupied away from the mission, he won't realize you've left. If it turns out to be a false alarm, then you can tell him when the time is right."

"Oh, that makes sense," I said. "I just don't know if I can keep it from him until then."

"You do what feels right," Kristine said. Her head tilted. "Do you want to get his hopes up and then be wrong?"

Hopes up?

"Do you think he'll be happy?" I asked.

"What do you think?"

"I don't know how he'll feel," I answered honestly. We'd never discussed children, which wasn't smart. Nevertheless, we hadn't.

"The place I'm taking you," Kristine said, "will help you with the pregnancy. Be aware that they won't help you terminate it."

My eyes opened wide as my heart thumped in my chest. "I don't want that. I know it's stupid and we're still kids ourselves, and we can barely afford to live with just the two of us, but I don't want to..." It was hard to say the word. I'd thought about it off and on over the last week as the sickness made itself more known. Thinking and saying were two different things. "...abort." Tears glided down my cheeks. "If we learn I'm pregnant, I want this baby."

"Of course you do. Why wouldn't you? A baby is a lot of work, though. Have you been around babies much?"

"Not really. I was an only child, and well, after my parents died, the foster homes where I stayed had mostly older children. Except one." The memory came back. "There were three babies. Miss Edith—that was how we had to address her—could house more babies and make more money. The thing was, she didn't take care of them She made it the older girls' responsibility."

"Did that include you?"

I nodded.

"Then you do have some experience."

"Not really." I sighed. "The babies cried a lot and when they did, Miss Edith would yell at us. I went out one night with a bit of cash and vouchers to buy diapers and formula. I wanted the break even though I'd only been in that house about a week."

"What happened?"

"I never went back. It was the last home I was ever in. I took the cash and used the vouchers for food for me..." I shrugged. "Miss Edith liked to drink vodka. She said you couldn't smell it on her breath—that's why she drank it." My nose scrunched. "I could smell it. That night I could smell a lot of it. I figured it was the right time. By the time she probably realized I was gone, it was too late. I boarded a bus and made my way here."

"What happened to the babies you abandoned?"

I'd never thought of it like that. I hadn't thought of them at all. "I don't know. I suppose the other girls took care of them."

Kristine nodded. "Do you think you can handle your own child, one you can't abandon?"

"I won't be alone. I have Patrick."

"You just said you aren't sure how he'll feel."

I had said that, but Patrick wouldn't abandon me over a baby. I knew he wouldn't. A slight smile came to my lips as I imagined him with a child. We may only be children ourselves, but we'd learned to lean upon each other, take care of each other, and look out for each other. Our life circumstances caused us to grow up faster than some. He was only eighteen, but Patrick was a good man. In my heart, I believed he'd be an equally good father.

We'd learn this parenting thing together, just as we already had learned so many other lessons.

"I won't know how he feels until I tell him," I said. "As for me, this baby will be different because it's mine, right?"

"I have never had a child," Kristine said, her voice sounding far away.

I was suddenly very self-conscious of the fact that I may be experiencing something she never had. "I'm sorry."

"Don't be. God had a plan for me. Even though I'm not the right person to answer that question, I believe I was put here for instances like this. You and the others are the children I've been given." She smiled. "I realize you're not a child, Maddie."

My head shook as I looked down at my stomach.

Had it grown?

I wasn't sure if it was the regular meals or maybe... "I don't feel grown up."

"No matter what you're feeling, on Friday be sure to voice your concerns. While I don't know what it's like to give birth to a child, I know that this mission and each person who comes here is special and valuable. I know I'm proud of all you and the others do. I couldn't imagine abandoning you or any of the others. There are too many possibilities for your future."

"Thank you," I said.

"Now..." She turned to the door and back. "Think about this. On Friday, they may discuss other options that you may not have considered." She waved her hand. "We're getting ahead of ourselves." She reached for the door handle. "Go eat a piece of toast and clean the stove. After that, until it's time to start working on dinner, you should rest."

"What about lunch? I'm on table duty."

"I'll take your place."

"No, I can't ask that."

"You didn't," she said with a grin as she opened the bathroom door and stepped out.

Standing, I stared at my reflection in the small mirror over the sink. My cheeks were gaunt with dark circles under my green eyes. Kristine was right about me needing rest. Over the last few weeks I'd been uncharacteristically tired—exhausted. I'd thought it didn't make sense, not since we now had a safe home. I figured it was my body taking advantage of the new situation, wanting rest I'd missed.

Now, I believed it was more.

The thought of Patrick tugged at my conscience. I wanted to tell him about the possibility of a baby. It was the right thing to do, but then again, what if I wasn't pregnant? What if I would just worry him—as I've been concerned—over nothing?

I turned on the water and cupping my hands, I splashed cool water over my face. The paper towel was rough on my skin as I dried my cheeks and eyes. I wasn't certain that the impromptu face-wash hid my pallor, but it did reduce the evidence of crying.

With a deep breath, I stepped back into the hallway near the kitchen.

"There you are," Patrick said as he came bounding down the backstairs. He reached for my hands. "Are you okay?"

"Yes," I answered more out of habit. "What are you doing?" There was something about his smile that appeared bigger than normal.

"Pastor Roberto said that soon I can run my own crew for demolition."

Demolition was what they did before remodeling—using sledgehammers and carting away the debris.

"I thought you liked the remodel better?"

"My own crew, Maddie." His blue eyes shone with the possibility.

I lifted myself up on my toes and kissed his cheek. "You're amazing."

"No, Maddie, we are. Don't you see? This will give me the experience to get a job—a real job with money. Pastor Roberto said he'd give me a good reference after I put in the time."

Time.

I had predicted that I was about five weeks pregnant. However, after what Kristine said, I could be farther along than that.

Three months?

Four months?

"How much time?" I asked.

"Whatever it takes, Maddie girl. We're going to get that house."

"With the white picket fence."

He kissed my cheek. "I'll see you tonight by dinner. Love you, Maddie girl."

"I love you," I called as he hurried past me the direction of the kitchen and cafeteria on his way to Pastor Roberto.

The building where the mission was set was still in the stages of demolition and remodeling.

I wasn't certain how they had the money to do what they were doing. Then again, the money was only for supplies. The residents of the mission provided the workforce. The men worked the demolition and remodeling while the girls worked the cafeteria and cleaned the common areas. We were all responsible for keeping our own apartments—rooms—clean.

As I stepped into the kitchen, the high rectangular windows caught my attention. From my angle, I saw only the gray sky and large snowflakes. It was late February in Chicago.

A smile came to my lips. We weren't cold. We weren't hungry. Patrick could take what he learned and use it for a real job, one with real money. My hand went to my stomach.

"Baby, we can make this work." My volume was almost inaudible, yet I heard it and maybe so did our baby.

MADELINE

Present day

I stood motionless as my last plea hung in the air, and Patrick turned and walked away. "Patrick," I called one last time.

My chest ached from the sensation that my heart had been ripped from my body. I looked down at the long emerald dress, the necklace, and shoes. My long hair fell forward as I once again gave into the unbelievable pain and loss.

It wasn't only Patrick walking away. It was also Andros's betrayal.

How could he walk away from me and abandon me after all we'd been through, after all of these years?

Did he really think he could begin a relationship with Ruby?

The thought made the concoction bubbling within my stomach churn.

Andros didn't have relationships.

Rage brewed under my skin.

I was eighteen when we met—when he...

I forced the memories away, concentrating on my age the night we met.

At the time, he had been nine years older than I.

Ruby was now sixteen.

That made Andros twenty-seven years older than her.

I looked to the men standing near me. "Please, I need to get to my daughter."

Instead of answering, the man who had ushered me from the poker room held out his hand and said, "Your handbag, ma'am?"

"I-I..." Without relinquishing them, I looked down at the small purse. "I need it back."

"That's not up to me."

I lifted my gaze to the tall man who had been talking with Patrick, the one with the longer hair. The dark-eyed one had left with Patrick. This man had his back turned my direction, yet I felt his power.

All of these men had it, a scary yet familiar aura, similar to that of the men within the Ivanov bratva. My gut told me I was right. This wasn't the Russian mob, but it wasn't legal either.

The tall dark-haired man who left with Patrick was the one who spoke to Andros, telling Andros to leave his city.

His city.

It didn't take a genius to figure out that that man was to Chicago what Andros Ivanov was to Detroit.

"It's up to him," I said, lifting my chin the direction Patrick and the man disappeared. "The dark-haired one," I clarified. "Isn't it?"

The other one with the long hair turned my way. His green gaze zeroed in on me and then to my escort. "Mr. Sparrow told you to take her downstairs."

Sparrow.

"Sir," I said, hoping I could get him to acknowledge me. "I didn't expect this—being left here." Every eye was on me. "Andros has my daughter." I sniffled back another sob. "I'm not sure who you are or who Mr. Sparrow is, but I need your help. I'll do anything to get to her."

The man's green eyes narrowed. In his gaze I felt the familiar edge of fear that came with Andros, and yet unlike the leader of the Ivanov bratva, there was life in this man's eyes. Within his orbs I saw a cyclone of possibilities: contemplation, calculation, and yes, power, but more. I prayed it was compassion.

Could men who lived in a world similar to Andros's have both power and compassion?

"Do you have children?" I asked.

I prayed he did.

He didn't respond.

"She's sixteen," I said, willing my voice to stay steady. "If you allow me to unlock my phone, I can show you her picture."

"Take her downstairs," he demanded.

The man beside me reached for my elbow. I pulled it away.

"Please, let me show you Ruby's picture."

The large man seemed to be considering my request.

I swallowed. "I know you heard what I said. I realize it sounds unbelievable, but if you'll just let me show you her picture, you'll know."

While Ruby had my dark hair, she had Patrick's blue eyes.

It was a beautiful combination, even as an infant. While I'd tried to forget Patrick, seeing his blue gaze every day made it impossible.

The man stepped forward. Some of his dark-blond hair had fallen loose from the tie near the nape of his neck. The tendrils framed his face, the locks coming to his solid jaw. He reached out his hand. "Give me your handbag and phone and go with our man. Eventually you may need to convince us of your story, but not yet. You have someone else who deserves to see that picture first."

Patrick.

Who were these men that they would respect Patrick's decision?

How was Patrick involved in this?

With new tears I handed my purse forward. "The phone is inside."

"Tell me, Ms. Miller, did you agree to distract us?" he asked. "Was that your plan or Ivanov's?"

"I came here to play poker."

He lifted the purse. "Will our people find a tracker on your phone, maybe sewn into your purse, or..." He eyed me up and down, "...your clothes? Is Ivanov leaving Chicago or is he waiting to see where you will lead him? Is he listening now as we speak?"

A bubble of dread formed in my throat.

Could he be listening?

My head shook. "I don't know what he planned. He doesn't confide in me. I came to play in the tournament. But you're right; my phone has one of those GPS things. I don't care if you turn it off. I just need to get to my daughter. I need to get to her before Andros does."

He handed my purse to another man. "Do what you need

to do to this. I don't want it leaving this building. We're not playing a fucking game of hide-and-seek. If that asshole is still in our city, we're hunting him, not the other way around."

The second man opened my purse and removed the phone. "Smashing it under my heel will take care of everything."

"No, my pictures," I cried. These men didn't seem like the sentimental type. Perhaps I could offer something else. "I also have Andros's phone number."

The two men looked at one another and back to me.

"My, the lady is quick to give in," the long-haired one said.

I stood taller. "Andros left me, not the other way around. He abandoned me. My only loyalty—for the last seventeen years—has been and continues to be my daughter. I'll do anything for Ruby. After all these years, Andros discarded me. I owe him a debt I can never repay, but nothing matters without Ruby. I wasn't sent as a spy if that's what you're worried about." I looked down at the dress. "Get me different clothes. I'll change. You can go through all my things. Just please leave me my pictures and phone book. I also have the number to reach Ruby."

"Take her downstairs."

My heart clenched. I was once again at the mercy of men without compassion.

My neck straightened. I hadn't given up seventeen years ago; I wouldn't now.

The original escort again reached for my elbow.

"Hey," the long-haired man said. "Lead her. Don't touch her. I'd like to avoid another dead Sparrow, and if you go against his direct orders, I'm not certain Mr. Kelly will allow you to live."

The young man sucked in a breath. "This way, Ms. Miller."

I would cooperate. I would do anything to get back to Ruby.

As we walked the hallway toward what I presumed were the back stairs, I wondered about what the man with the longer hair said.

A dead Sparrow.

And earlier, Mr. Sparrow.

I'd heard that name before. It was one of those times when Andros conducted business in my presence yet didn't reveal enough for anything to make sense. My mind scrambled.

Sparrow.

Steven?

No, the first name was more unique than that.

Sturgis?

I played with the platinum bracelet on my wrist, the one Andros gave me in the back of Elliott's car.

Platinum wasn't golden in color, but white, like silver. Then I remembered.

Sterling.

Oh shit.

The man who'd left with Patrick was Sterling Sparrow. I had heard of him. He was most definitely to Chicago what Andros was to Detroit.

How was Patrick in this mix?

We came to a stop at the entrance to the offices where Veronica had taken me just yesterday morning. How could so much have happened in such a short time? After a knock, the door opened from within. As it did, I heard the tenor of Patrick's voice reverberating through the hallways.

Patrick, please believe me.

I didn't say it aloud, but I did think it with all my might.

"In here, ma'am," my escort said as he opened the same door Veronica had opened for me on Friday morning, ushering me into Veronica Standish's office.

PATRICK

I couldn't think about Madeline at this moment even though she was forefront in all of my thoughts. Allowing her to infiltrate my mind was allowing her to do what Ivanov had sent her to do. She was somehow part of his bratva.

Was there a child?

Had she given birth to my child?

I refused to dwell on the possibility. Even considering it took my focus away from the crisis at hand. I'd already let Sparrow down, I wouldn't continue to do it. I had to think about the facts.

Veronica Standish was dead.

Ethan Beckman was dead.

Nearly fifteen million dollars had been stolen.

Hillman and Ivanov were making a show of working together.

Ivanov or Hillman had convinced at least one of our men to go against Sparrow.

Were there more?

The capo who had been guarding the safe since Sparrow went upstairs was currently being detained until the safe was opened. According to him, no one else entered the office. The way this night had been going, he better be right. If when we opened the safe, the additional nearly twelve million was gone, we'd be less another Sparrow.

My patience was worn thin—so much so, that it was fucking see-through.

Sparrow crouched down before the safe and entered the combination. Beckman had shared it with Sparrow earlier in the day. I doubted it had taken too much persuasion. At that point, Sparrow was supplying Club Regal with the funds it needed to complete the tournament.

"I changed it," Sparrow said as the beeps filled the room.

"You changed the combination?"

"Fuck yeah. Someone stole the money with the old combination. Whoever did that had access. I wasn't taking a chance."

He was no longer useful.

Ivanov's comment came back to me. "Beckman didn't have access," I said.

Sparrow's dark eyes came to me. "We need to figure out how Beckman communicated to Ivanov that he couldn't open the safe any longer."

There were too many unknowns. Beckman's communication and his murder didn't happen in a vacuum. "The capo guarding Beckman, I think he's the link." I held my breath as Sparrow pulled the handle, releasing the safe's door.

"It's here," he said.

I exhaled. "Thank fuck."

Sparrow stood. As he did, Mason entered the office. His eyes opened wide.

"Money is here," I said.

"We need to talk," Sparrow said. "Mason, get Reid on the computer on the secure network. The four of us need to be in agreement."

That was part of the reason we followed Sparrow. He welcomed our points of view. He believed that four sets of eyes and ears were better than one. Of course, the final decisions would always be his; nevertheless, he strived for agreement.

Mason nodded as he pulled out the laptop from earlier and after connecting, he hit a few buttons and Reid's face appeared.

"It's about fucking time. Tell me what's happening," Reid said.

Sparrow gave him the highlights: Andros Ivanov was here at the tournament. Hillman and his men appeared to be working with the Ivanov bratva. That also meant there was the possibility that other former McFadden men were working with Ivanov.

"Ivanov financed Madeline Miller," Sparrow went on, his gaze briefly meeting mine. "Ivanov tasked her with winning the tournament. If she had won and it was discovered that the money was gone, Ivanov would have had justification in causing an uproar. From what we can assess, Ivanov had more than her in the game. He had Hillman, and I believe Elliott, in the mix. In reality, Ivanov had three of the final six players working for him."

"Fifty percent chance to win," Reid said, "but he didn't count on Patrick."

"Or he did," Sparrow said, looking at me.

"I don't know how he would have figured out I'd be the one to play, but yes," I said to Reid, "it appears he had a plan to distract me."

With Reid through the computer screen, I had three sets of eyes on me.

"And it worked," I admitted.

"You won," Reid said. "Right? That's what Mason texted to me."

"I won. I was also distracted." I took a deep breath. "First, do you have tails on Hillman and Ivanov? Are you watching? Have they reached the airport?"

"They're at two different private airports. Their planes are fueled and ready, but they haven't filed their flight plans. They don't appear to be in a hurry to leave."

Sparrow stood taller. "They're waiting for a signal."

My eyes closed.

Mason looked up from the screen of his phone. "Garrett acquired clothes for Ms. Miller." He looked at me. "It's not enough to have her change on her own. Man, if there's a tracker or a microphone in her bra or...concealed in...fuck, you know what I'm saying? She has to be searched."

"What is going on?" Reid said.

"I'll do it," I volunteered. "I'll question and search her. If anyone else—"

Sparrow nodded. "Answers first."

I looked at the computer and concentrated on Reid. "The short version is this: you all know that before basic training I lived on the streets of Chicago, and I'd been there since I was young?"

I was only looking at Reid who nodded his response.

"When I was fifteen, I met a girl, also homeless." A thousand images came to mind. The apple and the police chase. Other stories I didn't have time to relate. "We became friends, more than friends. She was..." I inhaled. "When I was eighteen and she was seventeen we were befriended by people starting a mission. I wasn't anxious to get involved, but the more they talked, the more I liked the possibility. They offered housing—a roof, three squares, and even a weekly stipend for incidentals. At the time, it was as if they'd offered us the fucking Ritz."

I took another breath as my friends remained silent.

"The only catch," I went on, "was that that girl and I couldn't live there—living together—if we weren't married. Neither of us were against marriage. We just hadn't pushed it, but damn, it made sense, right? Get a piece of paper and get off the streets. The people at the mission helped us get IDs. Then, the day after Madeline turned eighteen, we went to the justice of the peace. And boom, I was married—we were."

"S-shit..." came from the computer.

I stood and paced to one wall and back. "Yeah, we were all happy and shit, and then one day I came back to the mission and she was gone. The pastor's wife told me she sent Madeline out for kitchen supplies. I can't remember her name —Kristen or something. Anyway, she claimed she gave Maddie—Madeline—a hundred dollars in cash. She made it sound as if Maddie had run off with the cash like she'd done when she was younger from a foster home. I didn't want to believe her.

"It wasn't that Maddie wouldn't steal. I'd heard the story about the drunk foster parent too. It was that she wouldn't have done it from the mission. She was too happy with what we'd done and held hope for our future. For some reason, I even remember that morning she disappeared that she was excited and maybe nervous."

I sat back in one of the chairs and sighed. "Maybe she had it all planned. Anyway, I spent the next weeks canvassing the city and asking questions. There were rumors about teens disappearing." I looked around the room. "Trafficking and the like. I couldn't believe that. We'd both known the dangers. Finally, someone told me they heard she was dead, that her body had shown up at the morgue. I went there. It took all day but I arrived. I had the marriage license. They told me there was a backup of Jane Does, to come back in a month.

"I enlisted the next day. A little over a month later I reported for duty. You know the rest."

"And you never heard from her?" Mason asked.

I shook my head. "No, I looked occasionally, but in my mind, she was dead. I never mentioned her because...why?"

"Because she showed up," Sparrow said.

"She did. I knew it was her on Thursday night."

"And you didn't think—"

I stood again. "To mention it? Yes. I tried a couple times. Did I think she was involved with Andros Ivanov? No. Did I think she had my daughter sixteen years ago? Fuck no."

"Wait, what?" Reid asked. "You have a daughter?"

"I don't know." I looked at the computer. "Her name is Ruby Miller. I would assume she lives in Detroit. Can you see what you can find?"

"Yeah, I can, but she's a minor and that name isn't unique. The search won't be easy."

It didn't matter. I didn't want my answers from Reid. I wanted them from Maddie.

"She offered to show me a picture," Mason said, handing a phone my way. "I thought you should be the one to see it."

I reached for the phone but my gaze went around the room.

Mason spoke first. "So far we've determined that the phone isn't transmitting a signal. The GPS has been disabled, and I did a quick check for spyware. The one I found is not high-tech. We disabled it from making calls and accessing networks for any kind of communication, but that can be easily rectified. You can still access her gallery without the phone transmitting to Ivanov or anyone."

"What about receiving calls?"

"They'll go to her voicemail. We're monitoring it."

I looked up from the phone to my friends. "I've let you all down. I'm sorry."

Mason continued, "Just because the phone isn't transmitting doesn't mean she isn't. Make sure she isn't wired. If Ivanov is waiting for a signal from her, he's not going to get it."

The idea that she was wearing a wire or a tracking device made my stomach turn. It was one thing to explain to these men that I'd married when I was eighteen. It was something else to admit that she'd returned as a member of a bratva, one who had just declared war on us.

"Where are the clothes?" I asked.

"Garrett has them in the hallway," Mason said.

I turned back to Sparrow. "What's going to happen if..." I had trouble vocalizing my thoughts.

"Your wife. Are you still married?" Reid asked from the computer.

"Legally, yes," I replied. "I still have the license." Not that the paper made it legal, but it was the documentation from the courthouse.

"And if there's truly a daughter," Reid went on, "a paternity test is no biggie. Hell, they sell them at the local drugstores. I can get you one more reliable than that."

"She's a member of the Ivanov bratva," Sparrow said again.

"Boss," Reid said, "I don't know this woman. I know Patrick and so do you. I also remember a night when he was the voice of reason about family, about my wife and Mason's sister."

"This isn't the same thing," Sparrow's voice rose.

"Family," Reid repeated.

Sparrow stood taller. "Fucking make sure she's clean and not relaying any information to Ivanov. Under no circumstances is she going to the tower. We'll deal with logistics after you question and search her."

I nodded. "I understand. I wish I was, but honestly, I'm not sure I can trust her."

"Until you are, she's not getting near our family," Sparrow said.

"I also don't think I can send her back to Ivanov. She said she..." I paused, recalling her declaration to beg forgiveness. "It doesn't resonate right in my gut. But fuck, if Ruby is out there and she's mine..."

"Then she's part of our family," Mason said.

I wasn't sure why that meant even more to me than Reid's

words, but it did. A few moments ago, Mason had considered Madeline an enemy, a member of a rival organization. His change of heart, even about Ruby, was a big step, one I wasn't certain her mother deserved, but one nonetheless.

"I'm going to find Garrett," I said.

Sparrow nodded. "One last thing, just a minor piece of this fucking puzzle."

We all waited.

"We're at war and that needs to be our number-one priority."

"Maybe Madeline can help?" I wasn't sure what I was offering.

"Or she could bring us all down in flames," Sparrow replied.

I stood taller. "I love her." Damn, that was hard to say. "I still do. I didn't want to. When I saw her Thursday night, I fucking wanted to hate her. My feelings aren't about Ruby. I knew I loved Madeline..." I took a deep breath. "...when I first spoke to her again. I also don't know her. A long time ago, I trusted her. As much as I don't want to admit it, I also fucking love this girl, this teenager I've never met. I know that sounds ridiculous and soft, but I can't stop thinking about her. I don't have answers, but I also don't want rash decisions that can't be undone. I need answers first."

"I do too," Sparrow said.

"You can take her to Montana," Mason offered.

"I'm not hiding from this war."

"It's not hiding if you're protecting an asset."

"Can I still count on you?" Sparrow asked.

I didn't hesitate. "With my life." I started to walk toward the door and stopped. "Sparrow, it's not that you're not my priority. It's that, whether this is Ivanov's doing or not, I now have multiple priorities. I don't want to let any of you down."

His jaw clenched as his dark stare was my only answer.

With a deep breath I turned toward the door.

Reid's declaration was the last thing I heard as I turned the doorknob. "We've got your back."

MADELINE

There was no way to measure time. The man standing guard outside Veronica's office disconnected the computer and telephone within, taking the cords with him before leaving me alone. My phone was confiscated earlier and I wasn't wearing a watch. The office where they were holding me was without windows, not that darkness in the middle of the night would be revealing. Nevertheless, I couldn't be sure if I'd been in here twenty minutes or two hours.

With the way my anxiety over Ruby was building, each minute was like an hour. And each hour uncertain of her fate was a lifetime. I peered around at the office, the one that only a day ago had seemed nice. The walls were closing in and there was nothing I could do.

Trapped like a caged animal, I did what the captured lioness would do. I paced.

My heels clicked upon the tile floor as I walked the length of the office and then the width. The large tile squares gave me an estimation of the size of my confinement. If I searched Ms. Standish's desk, I might be able to find a ruler or another actual unit of measurement and make an assessment. The truth was that I didn't care.

Ten by twelve.

Twelve by twenty.

It was irrelevant.

A cell was a cell.

My mind filled with my daughter. The puffiness of my eyes was the remaining evidence of the tears I'd shed. That was past tense. As I continued pacing, my eyes were no longer moist.

The men with Patrick obviously had their preconceived ideas about me.

They were correct in assuming that I was a part of the Ivanov bratva. I had been for nearly seventeen years. That didn't mean I held any loyalty to them or their ways. It meant that as much as I was a captive in this office, I had been captive within the Ivanov world. Andros didn't need locked doors or guards; his bindings were more restrictive while conveniently less visible.

He had Ruby.

Letting out a breath, I sat at the small table, the place I'd sat talking to Veronica only a few days ago. With my elbows on the surface, I held my head and closed my eyes. My chest ached with the visions I created in my mind.

My daughter's face appeared.

In the last few years she'd matured, losing her cherubic

childish appearance to that of a young woman. Slim yet fit, much to my chagrin, she had developed, her body morphing budding ladylike curves. Her breasts were no longer contained in the likes of a training bra as her hips widened. Even her facial features had changed. The round cheeks of the little girl she once had been were slimming as her face elongated.

At sixteen she was too beautiful. I worried that others would see her, not as the child they knew, but as the woman she was becoming. Her long dark hair was similar to mine. When left unattended, it cascaded in waves and soft curls over her shoulders. When her hair was styled, it lay smooth and shiny or fell in long ringlets.

For the first time in too long, I could honestly reflect upon her father's influence in her appearance. Where my eyes were green, Ruby's were a vibrant blue, much like Patrick's. There were other parts of Patrick in Ruby, parts I stubbornly refused to acknowledge as anything other than environment.

But now, seeing him again, I knew those qualities were more than the way I'd raised her. Ruby had Patrick's determination, his inquisitive nature, and his ability to see the good in people. She even saw good where it didn't exist and most certainly wasn't deserved.

Andros Ivanov.

She saw him as the man who helped and provided.

I was complicit in her assumption. I'd hidden the monster from her.

Little girls had nightmares about monsters under their beds. I couldn't tell my daughter that what she should fear most wasn't hiding in the shadows but visible in the light. In retrospect, I supposed I hadn't wanted her to live with the alarm that racked me day and night or to ever know the price I'd paid to stay by her side.

If she fell into Andros's hands—into his bed—it was my fault.

At the sound of rattling, I spun toward the door as the knob turned. My breath caught in my throat and eyes widened as I waited. The door moved inward.

As soon as I saw him, I pushed the chair away from the table and stood. My gaze searched his as Patrick shut the door behind him, closing us in. Within his grasp were clothes. They were folded, yet I was certain they were for me.

"Patrick," I said, his name both a statement and a question, for I was certain that my fate lay in his hands.

Patrick's head shook as he handed me a piece of paper.

Reaching for it, I opened the page with trembling hands.

Don't speak.
Come with me.

I wanted to argue, to ask about Andros, and remind him about Ruby. There were so many words vying to be uttered, yet I kept them all at bay, instead, closing and opening my eyes in resignation.

At least now Patrick was with me.

Taking a step forward, Patrick opened the door.

"Sir," a tall man said as the door opened.

He wasn't the same one who had been guarding me before. This one seemed to emit more power. I believed he'd been present upstairs. There were too many new faces to keep them all straight.

"Come with us and wait outside the conference room to collect..."

My gaze went to Patrick's, wondering what he'd left unsaid.

Collect...what?

Me?

I reached for Patrick's arm. Beneath my grasp his forearm, one that I knew to be both solid and strong, tensed. His icy stare looked at my hand and then to my eyes. Although he was silently telling me to let go, I couldn't. The turn of events had left me alone in unfamiliar territory. Like a kite that had broken free—or been discarded—after most of its life it had been tethered to a string and controlled by a master manipulator, I was unsure if without Andros I would fly or crash to the ground. I needed the connection to Patrick to keep me from a free fall.

Instead of releasing my hold, I gripped tighter.

With a shake of his head, he led me down the hallway and around a corner to a new door.

"In here," Patrick said, turning the knob and opening the door to a small conference room.

Letting go of his arm, I stepped in front of him, taking in the room. The table wasn't large and was surrounded by eight chairs. When the door closed behind me, I turned back.

Patrick handed me another note.

Sighing, I again reached for his next instructions.

. . .

Remain silent. Before we speak, you will strip yourself of everything —every piece of clothing, jewelry, and hairpins. Or I will.

When I looked up, his head tilted to one side.

Strip or be stripped, was that really a choice?

MADELINE

I crossed my arms over my chest as I contemplated my future.

It didn't take a genius to understand that these men wanted a guarantee that I couldn't contact Andros. If they only knew the depth of my hatred for the man, they wouldn't be concerned. Of course, they never would know if they forbade me to speak.

Instead of verbally responding, my lips came together in a straight line as I studied Patrick's expression. Within his set jaw and cool gaze, I saw the determination I once loved and admired.

Reaching out, I silently asked for a pen or pencil.

The look staring back at me was all the communication we would have.

Patrick laid the clothes on the table and walked back to the door. With a twist of his wrist, the door locked. Step by step, he came toward me. My mind told me to rebel, to let out my brewing emotions on him. Yet my body wasn't willing to push him away.

My eyes closed as he reached toward me. I imagined a caress of my face or the cupping of my chin. Instead, I opened my eyes as one by one he plucked hairpins from my hair. Before long, a pile formed in the palm of his large hand. Laying them on the table, he ran his hands through my long locks, his fingers combing and searching.

If this were another place—under different circumstances —the actions may be considered attentive and pleasurable. This wasn't another place or time; it was a conference room in the office wing of Club Regal and I was being searched.

My necklace was the next to go, followed by the platinum bracelet. My breath caught as Patrick lowered the zipper of my long emerald dress. Cool air met my back as the zipper descended. He brushed the straps from my shoulders, letting the material pool around my high heels. I spun toward him, meeting his stare with mine.

This may be a strip search and in Patrick's mind I may deserve it, but that didn't mean I would cower in his presence. This man had seen me naked when I was younger than our daughter. He'd tended my bruises and infirmities as I had his. Life on the street wasn't kind, yet we'd survived because of one another.

It wasn't until we were older that we discovered sexual pleasure. We found it in the warmth of togetherness and the way we enjoyed one another's touch. One would assume that without the oversight of others that we jumped into sex.

We didn't.

Like other teenagers, we experimented and explored.

Streetwise and sexually ignorant, we were each other's

teacher as well as pupil.

Patrick nodded toward my scant pair of panties.

My thumbs caught in the waistband as I pulled them over my hips and down my thighs, allowing them to fall to my ankles.

Without a word, he nodded his chin toward a chair at the conference table. As I sat, he crouched down and reached for the panties, pulling them over my shoes. Then he moved my feet apart and unbuckled each strap, releasing my high heels and removing them from my feet.

Our eyes met as his hands landed upon my thighs. The width of his body moved closer as at the same time, he applied pressure, pushing my legs farther apart.

Instinctively, I resisted.

His blue eyes snapped to mine.

Silently, they demanded my compliance.

Intellectually, I understood his next move.

A strip search wasn't complete until every crevice was explored.

Sitting taller, I complied by opening my legs.

This wasn't meant as a sexual experience, yet as one finger and then two searched, my core clenched. My body couldn't separate the meaning, instead, responding to his long fingers and knowing of what he was capable. I stifled a moan as his touch disappeared.

Helping me stand, Patrick turned me around, placing my hands on the table and applying pressure to my lower back, moving me to his desired position. This final search was the most demeaning and invasive. Tears threatened to return as he pressed a finger against my tight ring of muscles.

I wouldn't cry. I'd been through worse.

My eyes closed as Patrick verified that my last possible place to hide something from the Ivanov bratva was indeed clear.

At the loss of his touch, I stood, spinning toward him. Folding my arms, I covered my breasts and stood my ground as he disappeared into the small attached bathroom. The sound of water running filled the office. When he returned, he lifted the panties, dress, and accessories and took them to the door, opening it only wide enough to pass my belongings over the threshold.

"You know what to do."

I couldn't see the person to whom Patrick was speaking though I easily assumed it was the man from a few minutes before. Embarrassment flooded my circulation as I imagined facing Patrick's associates, knowing they knew what had happened in here.

As the door closed, I finally spoke. "I've never hated you until now."

He scoffed. "The opposite of love is not hate, it's indifference."

"Elie Wiesel."

Patrick made a quick nod.

"Tell me, Patrick. Is that what you now feel about me —indifferent?"

With one quick glance toward the door, he took a step closer and then another. I didn't back away. There was nowhere to go. Instead, my chin rose and my arms dropped to my sides, all the while keeping his blue stare in view.

When he came to a stop, we were close enough for me to feel the heat of his body as the lingering scent of cologne filled my senses. He reached for my chin.

"Indifferent? No." He stared down at me. "At this moment, I hate you too. I should fuck that tight ass to punish you for...for all of this."

I didn't back away from his grasp of my chin. My eyes stared into his icy blue glare. "Is that who you've become, Patrick, a man who uses his cock as punishment?"

A vein throbbed to life on his forehead as the muscles in his neck grew taut. "At this moment, I'd say yes."

Spinning from his touch, I resumed the position he'd placed me in, my breasts flattened on the hard surface and my legs spread. Craning my neck, I looked back. "Do it, and then I will have more reason to hate you."

Instead of taking my dare, Patrick reached for my arm, spun me, and pulled me back to standing. My motion didn't stop until I crashed against his hard chest. I sucked in a breath of relief as his arms encircled my waist, and he pulled my naked body against his clothed one. The hardness of his contained erection probing my stomach alerted me that he was capable of doing as I'd said. However, within his gaze, the ice from earlier was shattering before my eyes, crack by crack and fissure by fissure. Heat returned, a flurry of flames crackling as his blue orbs swirled with emotion.

"I fucking hate you," he said, "and God help me, I still love you."

My body melted against his as new tears filled my eyes. With a blink, one escaped and rolled down my cheek. "I never stopped...loving you. I did it every day through Ruby." I laid my cheek on his chest, too overwhelmed to continue our stare as I confessed, "I didn't know if you ever came back from the war."

With his heart beating in my ear and the scent of cologne in the air, Patrick stood taller.

Pulling my face away, I again sought his gaze. "Yes," I said, "I looked for you. It was only once. You see, I had a rare opportunity. All I could find was that you'd enlisted and gone off to fight."

"After I lost you, I wanted to get away from here." His arms loosened their grip until he took a step away. "How could you not tell me about her?"

I shrugged. "How could I? I didn't know where you were. I didn't know until I saw you Thursday night."

"It should have been the first thing you said."

I shook my head and again covered my breasts with my folded arms. The loss of his warmth left me chilled, reminding me of my lack of clothes. "I better get dressed."

One side of his lips curled upward. "I'd rather keep you like this."

"Whether you love or hate me, I'm begging you to please help me get to Ruby. I want to believe Andros isn't capable of doing what he said." I swallowed, debating my next words. When I looked back up, I concentrated on the eyes the color of our daughter's. "She's sixteen. I was eighteen." I inhaled. "He's capable."

"How do I know I can trust you? How do I know this isn't a ruse to bring down Sparrow? It could all be a trap. She might not exist."

"She does. If only I had my phone—"

My words were cut off by a loud banging as the door to the hallway rattled on its hinges.

Patrick nodded as he scanned from my hair to my toes. "Get dressed."

MADDIE

Seventeen years ago

*Q*uietly as possible, I turned the knob and pushed the door inward. Soft snores filled the warm air of Patrick's and my apartment. That term was deceptive. The space we had to call our own wasn't much. Like others in the mission, our apartment consisted of one room. Our furnishings were second- or thirdhand, but they were ours. We had a bookcase, a dresser, and a small table with two chairs. The sides folded down to a rectangle or came up for a circle. Our bed had a simple metal frame, mattress, and bedspring. The sheets and blankets were clean and soft. Once a week I'd take the sheets and our towels to the basement laundry room along with our clothes.

Despite its simplicity, it was more than we'd ever had and exceedingly more than I'd expected. At this early hour, the lights within were turned off and the large windows were covered with plastic blinds. While it was the middle of the night, the blinds helped to limit the illumination of streetlights below.

As I opened the door, a triangle of golden hue highlighted the bed and the man sleeping.

Unaffected by the hallway light or the opening of the door, Patrick lay stretched out on top of the blankets. His legs were covered by gray sweatpants and his widening chest was bare. The work he'd been doing with the pastor was affecting his body. Physical labor brought definition to his muscles. Regular, healthier meals also aided in our transformations from too skinny to healthy.

Even though he was eighteen, Patrick was still growing and maturing. With his one arm cast over his eyes, I couldn't help but notice that Patrick's biceps had grown as part of his transformation. Since our placement in the mission he was even a few inches taller. The change was increasingly noticeable in his jeans. Thankfully the mission received donations of clothes and household items. Kristine was generous when needs were brought to her.

It didn't matter that it was still winter in Chicago; the man before me was a furnace, radiating warmth. In his arms or simply in the same room, that warmth filled me in a way I was coming to recognize. Since our first meeting, there was a calm about him that kept me anchored.

In our world it was easy to get led astray. Patrick was my tether.

As I watched him, I contemplated climbing back in our bed, sliding under the covers, and curling up next to him. I didn't want to wake him by disturbing him. I also didn't think I would. Recently, he'd become a sounder sleeper. Within the safe walls of the mission, no longer did he need to protect us as we slept.

Oftentimes when I woke during the night, I enjoyed moving close, placing my head on his shoulder, and running the tips of my fingers over his toned abdomen. The memories brought a smile to my lips.

Closing the door, I waited in the dimness for my husband to stir.

Patrick was my husband.

I was his wife.

The titles broadened my smile.

After my parents died, I never thought I'd again be part of a family. The foster-care homes were filled with people, yet they weren't a family. Even this mission wasn't a family. To me a family was about acceptance and security. The concept had been elusive until now, but by some miracle or maybe stupidity, it was within my grasp.

Patrick, me, and our child could be a family.

My hands went to my stomach.

It had been four days since I spoke with Kristine. During that time my nausea had persisted. The waves hit me at all times of the day. Morning seemed to be the worst, but that didn't mean it went away later in the day. I'd found that keeping some small bits of food in my stomach helped. It didn't need to be a lot; even a few crackers would help. Surprisingly, I'd also been able to keep the news from Patrick. While having the bathroom down the hall from our apartment had its disadvantages, lately I'd come to appreciate the distance.

Taking a seat at the table, I pulled a packet with two saltines from the pocket of my robe. It was still too early for others to be awake, and yet I'd awakened with the urge to race to the bathroom and vomit. After I brushed my teeth and donned a robe, I tiptoed to the kitchen in search of what I now held.

The cellophane wrap crinkled loudly in the quiet darkness. I held my breath, again waiting for Patrick to wake. It wasn't that I was afraid of his ire. It was that I wasn't ready to tell him about our situation, not until I was confident.

Once I freed the crackers, I lifted one to my lips. My mind told me to eat, but my body wasn't on board.

Having food in our rooms was a violation of the rules, yet I hoped that Kristine would understand. Barely opening my lips, I nibbled on the salty edge. Bit by bit I ate, taking very small bites and waiting for the rebellion to rage within my stomach.

Once the crackers were consumed, I continued my wait. When the nausea didn't return, I removed my robe, revealing the camisole and shorts I'd worn to bed.

As I crawled to my side of the bed, the springs squeaked, echoing off the walls. I slid under the covers, and curled closer to Patrick. Even in his sleep, he wrapped his arm around my shoulder, tugging me against his warm chest.

"Maddie girl, you're cold." His voice was thick with slumber as he ran his warm hand over my bare shoulder.

"Go back to sleep. It's too early."

Lips came to my forehead. "Did you have a bad dream?"

That had been a problem when we first met. I'd wake in the middle of the night in a complete state of terror. Imagined images of my parents after their car crash. Rats and bugs crawling over them and me. Faceless people threatening.

There was never an actual abduction or assault. I would wake just in time.

I hadn't realized how vivid the dreams were until I moved into the hole in the wall with Patrick. He'd wake me as I thrashed and screamed, lulling me back to sleep with promises of fighting my demons.

"No," I replied.

His head lifted from the pillow as his eyes blinked away the sleep. "Are you okay?"

I reached across his toned abdomen and settled against his shoulder. "I am. I really am."

Laying his head back down, he sighed, still holding me close.

There were still a few hours to wait before it was time to wake. With the rhythmic sounds of his breaths as a backdrop, I drifted into a blissful sleep. Dreams weren't as vivid when they were happy. It wasn't actual scenes I saw or experienced but a feeling.

Warmth.

Safety.

Happiness.

It was so close.

The alarm clock on the bookcase squealed. Patrick jumped from the bed and silenced the noise.

"You always do that so fast. Have you ever heard of snooze?" I asked.

"I don't want it to wake anyone else." He sat on the edge of the bed. "Next week, Pastor Roberto is going to let me take a crew. It will only be two other guys, but he said I'll be in charge."

I smiled up at him, taking in his messed hair and shining smile. "I love you."

He leaned down and planted a kiss on my forehead. "You know I love you too."

I nodded.

"We're going to do this, Maddie. You and me. We're going to make it."

"You and me." *And baby*. The words were on the tip of my tongue.

Today was my appointment with the people Kristine knew. Maybe tonight I would be able to tell Patrick. Then again, maybe I wasn't pregnant. I wasn't certain why that possibility made me sad. If I was, we were in for big changes.

"What if things change?" I asked.

"Things always change." His lips curled upward. "That hasn't stopped us before."

I inhaled and stretched upon the warm sheets.

He was right.

PATRICK

Present day

*O*pening the door, I was met with a dark stare. I'd known Sparrow long enough to know his body language. Without his saying a word, I knew he was upset, something he rarely showed. Whatever had happened or he'd learned had him even more upset than he was earlier, or perhaps it wasn't something new but the accumulation of recent events.

With a quick glance over my shoulder, I confirmed Madeline's state of undress. Stepping into the hallway, I closed the door behind me.

"Anything?" he asked.

"I haven't heard from Garrett about her clothing, but on her? No."

"You're sure?"

"Are you asking if I thoroughly searched or if I would lie to you?"

His head shook. "Garrett came to me. The platinum bracelet was transmitting, audio and location."

I sucked in a breath. "Fuck."

"The office is clean. She didn't plant anything in there. The fucking bracelet was enough. Ivanov heard or has recorded every damn word upstairs and anything since. The guard said he never heard her speaking while she was alone, but she could have been. She could have been relaying every goddamned move."

"What about Ivanov?"

"He still hasn't taken off. Hillman neither."

"What are they waiting for?" I asked.

"If Ivanov didn't know about your relationship with Ms. Miller, he does now. That's a fucking jackpot when trying to infiltrate the Sparrow outfit."

"She's not trying..." I didn't finish. "This is his war, not hers."

Sparrow stood taller. "Start thinking like the man I know, the one who uses his brain, not his dick."

My neck straightened.

"We can't risk this," Sparrow went on. "I *won't* risk this. Ivanov is probably waiting for you to take her to our headquarters. That fucking bracelet would have led him there. She's a liability and if you were thinking straight, you'd agree."

She wasn't a liability. She was my wife—the mother of my daughter.

"I won't lead him there; I'll lead him somewhere else."

"What?" Sparrow asked.

"Give me the damn bracelet. I'll lead him away from here.

I don't want that monster around the other women any more than I want him near Madeline or Ruby."

Sparrow's large hand raked through his dark hair. "Does she exist?"

I pulled Madeline's phone from the inner pocket of my suit coat. "I was about to find out."

"We're at war and you want to abandon the outfit—us. Where do you plan to go?" He turned a circle. "You're...important to us."

"You have Mason."

"Fuck, you aren't interchangeable. That's not how this works."

I nodded as the lump in my throat grew larger. "Maybe not, but he's capable of doing whatever I do."

"Fuck no." His jaw clenched and unclenched. "You..." It wasn't easy for Sparrow to say whatever he was about to say. "...are the fucking voice of reason, usually," he clarified. "Mason is good. No, he's fantastic at what he does, but he's also more volatile."

He was right under usual circumstances. These weren't usual and I wasn't even close to being the voice of reason. "Sparrow, listen to me. You, Reid, and I ran this outfit. Hell, we took over the outfit with the three of us. I will come back. I'm not leaving you. I'm leading the Ivanov bratva away from here and away from the people I care about. That is reason. In the process, I plan to save my daughter from their clutches."

"Alone?"

I could take a handful of capos with me. Doing so would leave Sparrow with fewer men. "I won't take any men away from the war we have happening here. You need every single one. It's bad enough I'm taking me away."

"Take Garrett and two others. You can use whatever plane —whatever resources—you need or want. And here's what you're going to do." He inhaled as his nostrils flared. "You are going to take her." He nodded toward the door. "You're going to go somewhere not associated with us, not my cabin or Mason's. Those places are our safe houses. I don't want the Ivanov bratva to know they exist."

I nodded. "I need to learn where Ruby is."

"I'm not done," he said. "This place you're going, while you're there, you will maintain constant communication. I'm fucking pissed—don't think I'm not—but that doesn't get you off the hook." His eyes narrowed. "I want you back. Sending you away isn't some kind of fucking test. You will succeed and once you do, I expect you to get your ass back here. And while you're gone, if you learn anything and a way to bring them down, tell one of us." He again tilted his chin toward the door. "I don't trust her. I'm not sure I ever will just knowing who she's been associated with. That doesn't mean I don't trust you."

"What would you do if you learned you had a daughter?" I asked.

"I kept it wrapped."

"I was eighteen. Affording food was more of a priority than condoms."

"I don't know what I'd do," Sparrow said with a small inflection of empathy. "I'd want to know if it were true." He shook his head. "I remember overhearing conversations between my father and his men. It was probably Rudy. They fucked every female in sight. You know the stories."

I did.

"They didn't care who they fucked, but they did care that there were no kids." He scoffed. "No kids equaled no proof. They had a doctor—hell, I hope he was a doctor—who routinely provided abortions for their mistresses as well as the girls in the stables." He exhaled. "I don't know what made me think of that."

"The thing is, Sparrow, Madeline wasn't a mistress or caught in your father's or McFadden's trafficking. She was...she is," I corrected, "my wife. And if I had known back then I wouldn't have suggested termination. Even with no fucking money and living in a mission, I would have wanted the kid because it was part of Madeline."

His head shook. "Figure this out and get your ass back where you belong."

"Yes, Mr. Sparrow."

Unexpectedly, Sparrow's long arms came around my shoulders, pulling me into a back-slapping embrace. "I mean it. If you die out there, I'll kick your ass." He took a step away. "If this goes south, after giving my permission, that makes me fucking responsible. I lived through that once. I don't want to do it again."

"You won't."

"I'll talk to Garrett, and Reid will set you up with what you need."

"Hey," I shouted as Sparrow started to walk away.

He stopped and turned.

"Win this war," I said, "and the same goes for you. Stay safe. I don't want to find my family and lose one too."

"We've been to war before."

"We have. We also have more at stake." I was talking about Madeline, Ruby, and the women back at the penthouse.

Sparrow nodded and turned away. His footsteps echoed off the cement walls as he disappeared around a corner. For a moment I stood in the silence, wondering where Madeline and I would go. As I was about to reach for the door handle to talk to Madeline, Garrett came around the corner.

"Sir, which plane do you want ready?"

"Are you all right with this? Going with me?" I welcomed the assistance, but I didn't want a crew that would rather be back in Chicago.

Garrett stood taller and his eyes gleamed. "You mean taking this war to them, going into the enemies' city, taking one of their biggest assets, and showing those Russian motherfuckers that they can't threaten us...fuck yes, sir. I'm more than all right with it. I'm ready to kick Russian ass."

I liked the way he made it sound. "You're going to be my second. I want two more men, ones you trust with your life. Get two cars ready and we'll head to the airport west of the city." Sparrow's planes were not all in one location. The planes at the airport I requested weren't as big and ostentatious as the one Sparrow had painted like a bird. Even with the tracker, I planned to get in without fanfare. That reminded me. "You should know that we'll have the tracker bracelet. Once we're ready, it'll be like a fucking beacon telling the Ivanov bratva where we are."

With a bit of a grin, Garrett pulled a box from the pocket of his suit coat. It looked like a jewelry box.

"What's that?"

"A little thing Mr. Pierce thought would come in handy." He opened the lid. Lying upon the soft velvet was the platinum bracelet Madeline had been wearing. He closed the lid. "It's lined with a unique polymer agent that he's familiar with, sir. It blocks transmissions. No signal will go out until Sparrows decide."

Sparrow was wrong about Mason. He could be a level thinker, too.

I nodded. "Give us five. Oh, and...Ms. Miller..." I hesitated on her name. "...needs better-fitting clothes and she needs shoes."

"I'm on it."

As Garrett walked away, a renewed sense of purpose bloomed within me. Yes, this was about Madeline and Ruby, but it was also about the Sparrows. Garrett was probably correct that Ivanov saw my daughter as an asset. If he hadn't before, after hearing Madeline's announcement of my paternity, he did now.

Along with the sense of purpose came another feeling. I no longer questioned Ruby's existence. Even without proof, since learning of her, I knew in my heart and soul that she was real, a part of both Madeline and me. We'd been children learning to survive, and in the process, we'd created a life.

After seventeen years, mine was suddenly incomplete without Ruby in it.

Turning the knob, I gazed inside as Madeline turned my direction. I'd known the clothes I'd brought weren't her size, but I hadn't anticipated how fucking cute she would look. Her dark hair was free and tousled from my removal of the hairpins. The sweatpants and sweatshirt were designed for a man, one closer to my size, not a woman half my size. To try to make them fit, Madeline had the sleeves rolled up, creating large rolls near her elbows. The elastic at her ankles kept the pants from dragging on the floor or covering her bare feet. The pile of clothing hadn't contained any underclothes. That thought was suddenly in the forefront of my mind.

"Tell me what's happening," she said, reminding me that there were priorities at hand.

I inhaled and exhaled. "We're leaving."

"We?"

"Yes, we. Ivanov is still in Chicago, waiting for some signal. Do you know what that is?"

Her head shook. "I don't. I really don't."

"The bracelet you were wearing, where did you get it?"

Her eyebrows knitted together as she contemplated her answer. "Bracelet? Do you mean the platinum one?"

I nodded.

"Andros. He gave it to me just before today's—" She reconsidered. "—probably yesterday's, now—tournament play. He was in Marion's car when Marion's driver picked me up from the hotel."

"What? Ivanov was in Elliott's car?"

She nodded. "Yes. I didn't know until I got in. The windows were dark." She shook her head. "Anyway, on the way here, he lectured me on winning the tournament, implying that without a win I wouldn't return to Detroit. When he was done, he handed me the bracelet."

"Did he tell you to wear it?"

"He didn't have to. It is how he works—a lecture, a threat, a goodwill gift. Punishment, another gift. Sometimes it's the other way around, a gift and then the price for the gift."

I didn't like the way her eyes changed as she spoke about him. It was as if with each word or memory, another cloud settled, dimming the vibrant green.

Madeline came a step closer, still with bare feet. "Why did you ask?"

"It contains a tracker. Not only does the signal tell him your location, it also has an audible function. He's heard everything you or anyone around you has said until I took it away."

Her arm wrapped around her midsection. "Oh my God. That means that he knows you're Ruby's father."

"You never told him?"

"No, I told you I hadn't." Her expression darkened with what could only be described as unadulterated terror. "And you're part of the Sparrows, the organization he wants to take over." She didn't say it as a question, more like a play-by-play as the pieces fell into place. "He now knows that he has the daughter of one of the men in the Sparrow organization." She collapsed into the chair near the table. "We need to get to her."

"Do you think she's in danger?"

"I honestly don't know if this knowledge will help or hurt her." She looked up. "If you give me my phone, I'll show you your daughter, your beautiful daughter. Once you see her, I know you'll believe me."

I offered Madeline my hand. "We have time for that on the way to the plane."

"Plane?" she asked as she stood.

Her small hand fit perfectly into mine, just as it had nearly two decades ago. I gave it a squeeze. "Madeline, I can hate you for not telling me about her while at the same time, I can love you because you're you. And damn it, I never stopped. When it comes to Ruby, I don't need to see the pictures, though I want to. I believe you."

"You do?"

"Yes, and now you need to believe me."

"Okay."

"Ivanov hasn't left Chicago. We're going to save our daughter. After we do, you will need to make a choice."

"My choice is and always has been Ruby."

"She's not one of your options."

Ruby would never return to Ivanov with Madeline. I would make sure of that. I wasn't under an illusion that a sixteen-year-old girl would want to leave the life she knew. I also wasn't expecting a happy home in some suburb with a white picket fence where Madeline, Ruby, and I live out a happy ever after. No, my life had taught me that fairy tales didn't exist.

Madeline's choice wasn't if she'd stay with Ruby. It was if she'd help us take down Ivanov.

A knock came from the door.

"We'll discuss this later," I said. "Now, we need to get out of here."

PATRICK

*G*arrett drove the SUV toward the airport as Madeline and I sat silently in the back seat. She was still wearing the oversized sweatpants and shirt. On her feet were tennis shoes that Garrett found in Veronica's office. I imagined Veronica changing out of heels and into the more comfortable shoes when she wasn't on the club's floors managing events and employees, things she'd no longer do.

When Garrett handed me the tennis shoes, he promised to have appropriate clothes on the plane. I knew from experience that he'd made a call to the pilot or perhaps one of the flight attendants. Even in these uncertain times, the Sparrows had trusted employees who were capable of providing whatever we asked.

Two capos who Garrett chose to accompany us, Christian and Romero, were in an SUV driving behind us. I'd worked with both of them over the last seven years. They'd shown their allegiance to Sparrow time and time again. There'd been situations where I'd trusted them with my life. Now I had to trust all three of these men with Madeline's life.

In reality, it worked both ways.

I also had to trust Madeline.

It's a trap.

Mason's words lingered in my thoughts.

Was our destination a trap? Was Madeline setting the three Sparrows on this assignment up for an ambush?

A half hour ago back at the club, after Garrett gave me the shoes, I'd again closed the door on the conference room. When I turned, I was met by a more determined Madeline.

"What choices are you talking about?"

"First things first."

"First, you said Andros is still in Chicago. You also said we were going to save Ruby. We need to hurry. I know where she is."

"In Detroit?"

"Ann Arbor. She's in a boarding school not far from the university."

The university was the University of Michigan, Sparrow's alma mater.

"My daughter is in a boarding school?"

Madeline nodded as she began to pace. "She lived with me—with Andros—full time until she was in second grade." She turned toward me, her eyes filled with pride. "He had a tutor who worked with her...where we lived. Having her in a public school was too much of a risk. Oh, Patrick, she's so smart. Too smart.

"I tried to keep things hidden from her young mind, but she'd ask questions. Believe me, even with her living there, I'm with her or she's with me as much as possible. The truth is that having her go away to school was my idea. I begged Andros to let me move her away from the bratva. A little girl doesn't need to hear..." She brought her hands

together as her eyes momentarily shut. "...or see. Our apartment was separate for the most part, but she was a child, curious and adventurous.

"He thought he could speak in his native language and keep her from understanding. When she was very young, he'd say things in her presence...horrible things...orders to his men. I didn't understand much of it then, but I detested the way his words felt. He dismissed my concerns, saying she didn't understand."

"But she did," I said.

Madeline nodded. "She was around five years old and he said something mundane. It wasn't bad—my Russian had improved. I remember, Andros asked for something from one of his men, speaking in Russian. His man replied that he didn't know where it was. Ruby chimed in speaking fluent Russian and telling them where it was."

"What happened?"

"After that he was more careful."

There were so many questions I wanted to ask. The Sparrow side of me wanted to know more about the apartment and where the bratva was housed and operated. The newly found parental side of me wanted to know more about Ruby.

"Sir, the cars are ready," Garrett called from the other side of the door.

"I want to know more, but first, do you have an address in Ann Arbor for the school?" I asked Madeline.

"Yes, but it's late."

"It's early," I corrected. "There's always someone at a boarding school, correct?"

"Yes."

Taking Madeline's hand, I led her out of the room, through the hallways and to the back of the club. The hallways were mostly quiet. I wasn't certain what had transpired while I'd been with Madeline or what had been done with Beckman's body. The lack of knowledge confirmed my new reality. My concentration wasn't on Sparrow, the man, but on my wife and daughter and how they fit into this Sparrow puzzle.

In silence, we reached the back entrance. It was more difficult to see and monitor, if there was a chance that Ivanov was watching. Did he have the technology Reid and Mason had mastered? I glanced at the woman by my side. Would she know?

Now, as the SUV drove through the early-morning coldness and dark Chicago streets on our way to the airport, I turned to Madeline. We had a few minutes. Removing Madeline's phone from my suit coat's inner pocket, I handed it toward her. "I believe you. I'd like to see a picture."

Madeline reached out and took the phone. "Did they disable the GPS?"

"Yes."

"Good." When she looked up from the dark screen, her features were sad and thoughtful. "Has Andros left yet?"

"Not the last I heard."

Her eyes grew wide. "We're not going to the same airport, are we?"

"No, and currently, the signal from the bracelet is being disrupted. He doesn't know where you are or what happened to the signal."

Her head shook. "He doesn't like the unknown. He likes total control."

I huffed. "Too bad. He's about to lose it." When Madeline didn't respond, I asked, "Will the boarding school release Ruby to him?"

Maddie nodded. "Yes."

"And she'd go?"

"Yes."

Swiping the phone's screen, Madeline entered a code and as she waited, the sadness morphed to something happier. I could see it in her eyes and in the lifting of her cheeks.

"She really is beautiful," Madeline said. "It's not just a mother's bias." She extended her hand, offering me the phone. "I never thought this was possible, but, Patrick, may I introduce our daughter, Ruby Cynthia Miller."

I considered myself a strong man. I risked millions of dollars in a poker tournament. I'd killed other men and watched as they bled out. I'd re-appropriated excessive amounts of funds, stealing from people and corporations and even royalty without batting an eye.

Yet as Madeline held her phone, the screen began to blur.

My eyes filled with moisture as the smiling brunette came into view. She looked like Madeline as I remembered her, the same hair and cheekbones. I blinked away the wetness as I settled against the seat. Stretching the photo on the screen I enlarged her face. I could have gone my entire life and not known that I had a child, but now, staring at her blue eyes, I knew without a DNA test that they were mine.

I blinked again and looked over at Madeline. "She looks like you."

"With your eyes."

"Why?" I asked.

Madeline extended her hand. There it lay, palm up between us. It would be easy to reach out and take it, to intertwine our fingers and pretend we hadn't lost seventeen years, pretend she hadn't shut me out of my daughter's life. I didn't do it. I never was one to take the easy road.

Sitting straighter, I asked again, "Why did you leave me?"

"May I just say that I didn't? Please don't make me relive any of that, not until I'm confident that Ruby is safe from a similar fate."

My gut twisted with her answer.

She didn't.

"You didn't leave me?"

"Not the way you think. I know you deserve answers. Hell, Patrick, you deserve so much more than words, but right now all that matters is Ruby."

"How secure is the boarding school?" I asked.

"Their security is why we chose it."

I exhaled, returning her phone to my inner coat pocket. "We. Are you saying you and Andros Ivanov?"

"Yes, Patrick. I'm not going to lie to you. In truth, there is a long list of people..." She shrugged. "—some whose real names I'll never know or recall—who I should hate. I don't, not because they don't deserve it, but because I only had the energy to truly despise one man. It's Andros. I have also never needed someone as much as I needed him. At one time, I may have even been grateful for his appearance in my life. Sometimes, through the years, those positive emotions have emerged, but even then, they pale in comparison to my immense hatred for the man he is, what he has done, and what he's capable of doing. Andros is incapable of love. I know that better than most. However, he has cared for Ruby.

"I have always appreciated that. My life has been..." She paused. "I don't know if Andros saved me or secured my place in hell. I do know he has, up until now, never harmed Ruby. The threat was what kept me in my place. He knew from the first time we met that I'd do anything to keep her safe. I just don't know why this one poker tournament was so important."

"Because he wanted you here in Chicago. You said you didn't tell him about us. You didn't tell him you were married?"

"No."

"Somehow he must have known. He knew that you were a distraction for the Sparrows, for me."

The car slowed as Garrett drove us through the gate of the private airport. I looked down at my watch.

"It's almost four in the morning. Once the wheels are up, we can be in Ann Arbor by five thirty."

My phone rang. Pulling it from my coat I read the screen: *REID*.

"Arriving at the airport," I said as I secured our connection.

"Leave the bracelet in the car."

"All right. What's the plan?"

"Once you take off, Mason's going to take Ivanov on a wild goose chase around Chicago while you get to Ruby's school."

Yes, I'd filled my friends in on all Madeline had said. After all, one of Sparrow's last directives was communication.

"How long do you think you can delay him?" I asked.

"Not sure. We've got eyes on him. Hillman is still here, too."

I inhaled. "They have to know we're going to go after Ruby. Why are they waiting?"

"We'll tell you what we know, when we know it," Reid said. "You do the same. The GPS on your and Garrett's phones is secure. We'll be watching."

By the time I hung up, the SUV had come to a stop

outside one of the Sparrow hangars. The plane was already out and the steps were down. I couldn't guess at how many times I'd boarded one of Sparrow's planes or how many times I'd put myself at risk for the man and the outfit. Each time it was done without hesitation. This felt different.

I turned to Madeline. "If you're lying to me, I don't care if I love you, I will kill you."

"If we don't save Ruby, I don't want to live."

The door beside me opened. "Sir," Garrett said.

"What did that person on the phone say?" Madeline asked.

Instead of answering her, I scooted out of the car, turned and offered her my hand.

As the cool winter air blew about us on the tarmac, I placed my hand in the small of her back; the soft oversized sweatshirt was beneath my palm. "Let's go, Mrs. Kelly, and get our daughter."

MADELINE

$\mathcal{T}$he cabin around me was luxury at its finest. I didn't care about the white leather seats or the faux gold trim. The surroundings were insignificant as I mindlessly drummed the tips of my fingernails against the leather armrest. Their resulting taps floated away, engulfed by the hums and workings of the airplane as we neared Ann Arbor.

With each mile, my mind recalled snippets of our daughter's life while physically I stared out the small window. Beyond the rectangular pane was the still-darkened sky. Above us was a moonless canopy of jet-black velvet sprinkled with shimmering stars. Below us was a turbulent sea of gray clouds, billowing in peaks and swirling in chasms.

The sound of engines alerted me to the plane's descent. The scene beyond the windows changed as we flew lower and clouds engulfed us in varying shades of gray.

As if the swirling gray wasn't made of moist air but of solid particles, the airplane pitched one direction and then the other. I had the sense of being a silver ball inside an old-fashioned pinball game. No longer tapping my nails, my hands gripped the armrest.

"Ms. Miller, please fasten your seat belt," Millie, the flight attendant, said as she fought to remain standing. "Marianne said to expect some turbulence as we prepare to land."

Reaching for the seat belt, I forced a smile and latched the buckle. "Thank you, Millie. You should find a safe seat too." When she turned, I added, "Is Mr. Kelly...is he going to return for the landing?"

"I-I," Millie said, holding on to the wall for support as the turbulence continued. "I'm sorry, Ms. Miller. Mr. Kelly didn't say."

After we'd taken off from Chicago and reached a cruising altitude, Patrick led me to a private bathroom near the rear of the plane. Within its confines, along with the essentials, I found a shower and a rather large changing area. The space reminded me of a luxurious locker room, well, without the lockers. There were closets. Patrick told me to search for something that fit, something I wanted to wear when we entered Westbrook.

Westbrook Preparatory Academy was where Ruby had been since she was seven years old. Over the nine years she'd made friends and lived a life closer to normal than one in a bratva. I liked to tell myself that. It made sleeping easier.

Within the academy, the age groups were separated. At first I hadn't been keen on the idea of her being with the older children, especially at only seven years old. She wasn't. The campus was large and divided like a small community. There were individual dorms for all ages with house moms who oversaw the children in their care. There were also buildings with classrooms, laboratories, theaters, and gymnasiums. Elementary was separated from middle school and separate still was high school.

Beautiful and full of green space, it was the campus I fell in love with. Of course, this time of year—winter—it was more like white space. Westbrook even had an ice-skating rink along with other winter outdoor activities. When Ruby was younger, she enjoyed ice skating.

After Patrick left me alone in the changing area, I took a quick shower, washed my face, and using the makeup I'd found on the plane, reapplied less of a "poker face" and more of a "mother face." And then I changed into a pair of slacks and a sweater. The emerald dress I'd been wearing earlier was back somewhere at Club Regal, and the sweatshirt and pants I'd been given were a joke. The clothes I'd found here on the plane were similar to ones I would choose. Whoever had selected the contents of the closet had good taste. Thankfully, everything fit.

I'd even been provided with underclothes including socks and a pair of stylish boots. The final additions to my wardrobe were a long wool coat, gloves, and a cashmere headband to cover my ears. The person who chose the clothes was well aware of midwestern winters.

When I asked Millie where the clothes came from, she replied, "Mr. Kelly had requested them."

Asking Patrick how he came up with the closet of clothes was just one of the many questions on my long list. I also had stories I was eager to share. Despite the fact it was nearly dawn, my mind was a cyclone of memories and milestones of Ruby's childhood that I wanted to relive with Patrick. He'd missed too much that could never be brought back. Perhaps with time, pictures, and stories, he'd come to understand what an amazing blessing she has been and is. I'd been led down the wrong path before she was born, but I was proud of who she had become. Despite the world she'd been born into, somehow Ruby had thrived.

I hadn't seen Patrick since he left me in the changing room.

Turning away from the window, I peered at the partition separating the two cabins within the plane. The partition had been closed since I returned from changing.

I knew the other side was where I'd find Patrick. I could hear the muffled voices. I could also assume that the man he referred to as Garrett was also there. Garrett and two other large men had entered the plane after Patrick had ushered me up the stairs. I only saw them for a moment, but I'd been with Andros too long not to recognize reinforcements when I saw them.

The plane was now in a steep descent, the clouds beyond the windows swirling like smoke from a raging fire. My breath of relief as we exited the cloud bank was short-lived. Beyond the window snow fell, attaching to the window and wing. Leaning toward the glass, I searched for the ground beneath us. While we were still high, the altitude wasn't what obstructed my view. It was the darkness—time of morning combined with the swirling snow.

A gray mass with shimmers of light beneath us came into view. Streets lined with streetlamps and cars materialized. White headlights and red taillights were the only indication of their direction of travel. The snow continued to fly, reminding me of supersonic special effects in a seventies' movie.

Despite the inclement weather, my excitement blossomed. I'd soon be with Ruby. Her beautiful face came to mind. She'd be sleeping when we arrived or recently wakened.

I tried to recall the day. So much had happened.

It was Sunday morning.

A smile came to my lips. Ruby would still be asleep. I imagined entering her dorm room and waking her like I did when she was visiting and staying in Detroit. Watching her sleepy eyes meet mine and a smile bloom upon her face was one of my favorite activities.

I'd been honest with Patrick when I'd said I spent as much time with our daughter as possible. What I hadn't said was that the frequency and duration wasn't at my discretion. It never had been. Like everything else, Andros was in control. Even holidays weren't a forgone conclusion. My heart ached with the recollection of the year he'd taken her away, leaving me in Detroit. Of course, Ruby didn't know the truth—that I was being punished. She was told I was ill, a lie that I'd perpetuated on our phone calls. I couldn't ruin her holiday with the ugly truth.

For once, I was in control. Well, maybe it wasn't me but Patrick. That was all right. The sense of change was empowering and truly felt right.

How would Ruby react to an unscheduled visit?

Could I convince her to leave with us?

My pulse increased.

Did Patrick's men know for certain that Andros wasn't on his way?

As the sound of landing gear rattled the floor beneath my borrowed boots, I looked again to the closed partition. "Please come back here, Patrick." I hadn't spoken loud enough to be heard. We descended lower as the blue lights of a landing strip flashed in the distance.

Abruptly, the trajectory of the plane changed, throwing me back against the seat.

I gasped as the whine of the engines grew louder and noises echoed within the plane. Gripping the armrest, I inhaled sharply. Where we'd been about to land, we were now climbing back into the sky, through the swirling snow and into the clouds.

My tired mind tried to make sense of the sudden change.

We weren't landing in Ann Arbor. We were traveling away...away from Ruby.

"Patrick," I yelled, hoping he could hear me.

Panic raced through my circulation, thumping in my ears and combining with the roar of the engines as the plane's deceleration morphed to acceleration.

"Patrick," I called again.

Fighting with the buckle on the seat belt as well as the centrifugal force binding me to the seat, I freed myself and pushed off of the armrests. Though the plane continued to climb higher and higher, I made it to my feet. Like swimming against the tide, I pushed toward the partition.

As I reached forward, the door slid open, and I was met with an angry blue stare.

"Did you think we wouldn't check?" Patrick growled.

Behind him three sets of eyes stared my direction.

The plane continued its ascent as my footing slipped and Patrick reached out, seizing my wrist.

"I so fucking wanted to trust you."

PATRICK

$\mathcal{M}$adeline's beautiful green eyes opened wider as my grip of her wrist intensified. Like a vision, she'd appeared beyond the partition. No longer donned in oversized clothes, her every curve was covered by a soft sweater and black slacks showcasing her slim waist, round tits, and shapely ass. My gaze fell to where we were connected, seeing my fingers wrapped around her delicate wrist confirmed that unlike an apparition, she was real.

Damn.

With every shard of my shattered soul, I wanted to hate this woman. I longed to be unaffected by the tug-of-war that pulled tighter when we touched or the surge of energy and power that our union created. It was more than that. While physical connection increased the bond, it wasn't required. Simply being in her presence—no, knowing she was alive—did things to me I detested. I didn't want to feel the overwhelming sensations—covetousness love and desire.

I didn't want it.

But I couldn't stop it.

The feelings were there, bombarding my body and soul and radiating through me. Like the injection of a drug, my flesh burned as Madeline's being flooded my circulation.

I detested everything about it.

I couldn't hate her, even if I should, even if it was my desire.

Instead, I chose to hate our bond.

I chose to concentrate on the facts. That's what I did.

That's what had made me the man I was today. The facts were clear, crystal. Madeline had left me. She could claim it wasn't as it seemed or as I presumed. The semantics didn't matter; seventeen years ago when I lost her, I longed for my life to end.

Maddie had been more than my wife. We'd been together for over three years. I realized now that timeframe was hardly a lifetime, but to an eighteen-year-old, it was a fucking significant portion. She was my first love, my reason to live, work, and strive to be a better man. Madeline had been my everything—the reason I woke in the morning and came back to wherever we were living in the evening. Her sleepy morning smiles and the way she curled close under the blankets were my motivation to survive.

The night I returned to find her gone, my life as I knew it ended.

My reason to continue was gone—vanished.

"I don't know, Patrick," the pastor's wife said. "She went shopping earlier today for the kitchen, for food supplies. I should have gone with her." She reached for my arm. "You don't think she left you, do

you? It was only a couple hundred dollars. Didn't she do this before to a foster home?"

The memory of that conversation still gnawed at my gut.

Shock.

Hurt.

Disappointment.

Disbelief.

Loss.

And now within the last few minutes, faced with new deception, those feelings were back with a vengeance.

"What are you talking about?" she asked, trying to free her wrist. "And why didn't we land?"

Garrett, Christian, and Romero bristled in their seats, knowing the reason, knowing what we'd learned—what we'd barely escaped. With a quick look over my shoulder, I spoke to Garrett. "Confirm the fuel supply with Marianne and once the flight plan is set, let me know via text." I didn't need to say more. Garrett knew my new desired destination.

"Yes, sir."

"And," I cautioned all three men, "under no circumstances are we to be disturbed."

Their response was swift, three quick nods combined with mumbles of affirmation.

"Patrick?" Madeline questioned, looking up at me.

Without a verbal response, I continued my hold of her wrist as I stepped toward her, staring into her eyes and pushing her backward into the aft cabin. Once we'd both crossed the threshold, I closed the partition behind us as the whine of the engines and angle of the plane reminded me that we were still climbing to cruising altitude.

"What happened?" she asked. "You can trust me. You said you wanted to. What's stopping—"

"Seconds," I interrupted through gritted teeth. "We were seconds from a fucking ambush."

Her head shook. "I don't understand. You said Andros was still in Chicago. What about Ruby?"

My jaw clenched tighter as her pulse thumped beneath my grip.

I towered over her petite form. "Did you hear me? Seconds. If we had touched down, we could all be dead. All of us, Maddie. You, me, those men. Was that your mission, to go down in a kamikaze effort to take out Sparrows?"

"What?" She stared in disbelief. "No. I wouldn't. Ruby is my reason for living. I would never agree to leave her."

Releasing her wrist, I stepped back. "Then what exactly was your plan? Did Ivanov promise to spare you? You said you'd do whatever he wanted, whatever he decreed was your penitence. That was what you said—your words. Would delivering four dead Sparrows to his doorstep be enough of a penitence?"

"No. I didn't even know about Sparrows until tonight at the club. He never said...I told you there's always some fight—some war. I never listened or questioned. It wasn't my place. My concern is and has always been Ruby. Besides, I haven't spoken to Andros since he left me at Club Regal. You know that. How could I?"

Inhaling, I ran the palm of my hand over my hair. My bicep bulged beneath my shirt and suit coat as I attempted to rein in my frustration. Our gazes met. "Are you listening? The airport was a trap. Minutes before we were to land, my men in Chicago hacked into the airport's security. When they did, they saw Ivanov's men in position. Somehow, even without the bracelet, they knew exactly where we were going."

As the plane continued to ascend, Madeline stared into my eyes. With each passing second her expression hardened. "It doesn't matter what I say to you, does it?" With determination in her step, she came closer.

The soft scent of flowers preceded her arrival. Her hand landed on my chest. It took all my willpower to remain in place and not back away as the warmth of her touch transcended the fabric.

"Tell me, Patrick, will you ever forgive me? I've stupidly been sitting here..." She motioned to the seats. "...with visions of fairy tales that up until today I never allowed myself to imagine. But that's all they are, right? Stories. Make-believe. There's no happy-ever-after for us. You won't allow that."

"Me? You're turning this on me?"

"You will never see me as anyone other than the person who disappeared. The circumstances don't matter to you. Tell me, how do you see Ruby?"

"As my daughter. And right now I'm doing my best to not think about your betrayal or the fact that you've been part of a Russian bratva. Believe me, if I were concentrating on either of those, you wouldn't like where it would go."

"Is that a threat?"

"A fucking promise." As my reply came forward, I lost my will to fight, deciding instead to surrender to the connection, to take it, use it, and in doing so, hope it would extinguish.

Reaching forward, I snaked my hands around her waist, my touch connecting under the sweater, seizing her warm skin and pulling her against me. The softness of her tits smashed against my chest as my fingers splayed over her lower back, bringing her flush against me. The plane's pitch was on my side as she fell into my embrace.

I stared down, searching her gaze as her face tilted upward and her long hair cascaded down her back. Her plump painted lips parted, yet no words came out.

"You're my wife."

Her lids fluttered as our hearts beat against one another's.

"Fucking say something," I demanded.

"What do you want from me?"

The list was endless, and while our flight time would be a few more hours, at this moment, I had no desire to verbalize any of it. Instead, I reached higher under the sweater, releasing the snap of her bra. With one hand still holding her against me, the other skirted her warm flesh until it cupped her breast, tweaking her nipple as beneath my touch it hardened.

"Patrick," she moaned. "Is that all I am, a fuck?"

"No, Maddie, it's not all." Releasing her, I reached for her hand and began to lead her.

"Wait." She stopped. "Where are you taking me?"

"We're on a fucking plane. How many options do I have?" I asked as I once again led her back to the dressing area, all the while wishing we'd brought a different plane.

At least the dressing room would give us a bit of privacy.

MADELINE

$\mathcal{A}$s the door behind us shut, the cushioned round settee in the center of the room came into view. An hour ago, I'd sat there to don the boots I was now wearing. Suddenly, it appeared bigger. Maybe it was the closed closet doors or maybe it was the palpable sexual tension reverberating through the air.

"What about—?" I began to ask.

Patrick's finger came to my lips. "No talking, Maddie. I'll tell you what's happening, but first, I want my wife."

I took one step back as my skin tingled at the primal intensity within his searing gaze. Wordlessly, his blue orbs held me in place, forbidding my refusal of his claim or further dissent. Perhaps it wasn't he who forbade; maybe it was me who didn't want to refuse, who wanted the connection we shared, the fire in his eyes, and to be his wife.

My mind told me I was crazy, that in the last few hours I'd learned that regarding his chosen lifestyle, Patrick was no different than Andros. Like the Ivanov bratva, the Sparrows were their own piece of organized crime. Patrick may not be in charge, but he obviously held significant power. The evidence was visible with the way the others listened to his orders and respected his ideas.

Did Patrick kill people?

Did he relish their pain?

Did he involve himself in illegal activities?

Were people hurt, addicted, or killed because of what he promoted or allowed?

Was the answer yes?

I should care.

Had a lifetime in the Russian mob allowed me to wear blinders?

Somehow, it felt the opposite. Staring at Patrick as he removed his suit coat, tie, and cufflinks, my heart knew that any similarities with Andros ended with their profession. That wasn't to condone what either of them did. Nevertheless, I believed there was more to them than their profession. In that more, the two men were on opposite ends of the spectrum, maybe not good versus bad—but day versus night.

It was the life and vibrancy behind Patrick's eyes, as well as the way his wide chest, now devoid of his shirt, heaved and abs grew taut with each breath. Unlike Andros's eyes that were dead and calculating, Patrick's shimmered with a predatory hunger.

A lion sizing up his prey.

As Patrick neared, my lungs struggled to inhale as my skin warmed and core clenched.

"You're mine," he growled as his manly scent filled my senses.

I didn't protest. As my hands went to his strong arms, my fingertips roaming the indentations of his muscles, I tried to reason with myself.

This, here and now on this plane, felt different than the times we'd made love in the hotel.

Life had taken a drastic turn since then.

Before, I was bound to Andros; truly as long as he had Ruby I was. And yet high in the sky with Patrick's bare chest before me, his hands roaming beneath my sweater, and lips peppering my neck, freedom was within sight.

Closing my eyes, my head fell backward, and I gave into the rush of endorphins his lavished attention stirred within me. No longer a young boy, Patrick had become a skilled seducer. His nimble long fingers pried latches and buttons as he removed each piece of clothing from my body.

Sweater.

Bra.

Boots.

Socks.

Slacks.

Panties.

While his actions weren't the threat he'd uttered, there was still a message within each distinct deed. Unapologetically, Patrick was taking what he deemed his, reclaiming and conquering what had been his before anyone else's.

"My wife. Mine."

The words came with different emphasis as I surrendered to his touch and manipulation until he had me where he wanted. Lying upon my back on the settee, supported by my elbows with my nipples hard and core wet, I was exposed and bared to him.

Patrick took a step back. With his trousers still in place, I became aware of a pattern of inequality. One I was most certain he enjoyed—me completely nude, him not.

He scanned me from head to toe until our gazes again met. "Tell me your name."

"Patrick."

He reached for the buckle of his belt. My reaction wasn't voluntary. Yet the moment was shattered as I tensed and my eyes widened.

His gaze went from me to his own hand upon the buckle. "What? Fuck no, Maddie, don't ever fear me."

I wanted to object, to tell him it wasn't him. My reaction had only been a momentary lapse, but he'd seen it. He had an uncanny ability to see what I could successfully hide from others. That realization made me vulnerable in an uncustomary way.

I couldn't understand how Patrick could so easily read my emotions. After all, I was a poker player. I'd worked almost a lifetime to keep them in check and yet with Patrick, each one was flashing like a neon sign.

"I don't want to," I admitted. "You said...you said I wouldn't like where this was going and so far, I do."

Undoing the belt and button, and lowering the zipper, Patrick allowed his trousers to fall. Reaching for the waistband of his black silk boxer briefs, he freed his impressive cock.

I fought to look up at his face as I took in the beauty of his manhood. Hard and thick, the tip of his cock glistened as he fisted the length.

"You asked me," he said, his voice thick with passion and laced with desire, "if I was the kind of man who punished with his cock." His hand continued moving as he stroked the velvety taut skin. "I fucking want to be. I want to take you over and over. I want to prove you're mine. I want to erase whatever has ever happened to you, and furthermore, I want to hate you with every thrust. Every time your pussy contracts and you're on the brink of orgasm, I want to deny it. I want to punish you for leaving, for not telling me I had a daughter, and for not giving me a choice." His hand moved faster as the cords in his neck grew taut and his shoulders pulled back. "I want you to hurt just a fraction of the way I have."

A strike of his belt would have been less painful than the power of his words.

Patrick's insight made me see myself.

My past.

The things I'd done.

I saw the woman I'd allowed myself to become, the one he now saw. The one he wanted to deny pleasure and even harm.

My chin fell forward as I swallowed, fighting the bubbling tears of self-loathing.

Through the years I'd faced worse words, threats, and even physical punishments. I'd faced them and moved on for the next round and the next. I told myself each time that I'd done it for Ruby. I still believed that. However, through Patrick's eyes, I also now believed I accepted my fate because deep down, I believed I deserved it.

Warmth covered my legs and torso as his solid body crawled over me. His erection probed against my tummy. Patrick reached for my chin, bringing it up until our lips met. Gently his tongue danced with mine as we both fell to the settee. Deeper and deeper he probed. The actions of his lips and tongue radiated warmth like the flame of his gaze. When his kiss ended and I opened my eyes, his blue stare was right in front of me as our noses touched.

"Don't," he said.

I sniffed back the tears. There were too many things to say and too many memories vying for the chance to take away any pleasure. I took a deep breath. "You should hate me."

"I said I wanted to. I didn't say I did."

I shuddered as his words settled over me.

"Don't give in to those clouds," he said.

Arching my back, I moved my legs until his hips were between them and his hard cock poised. "Do it," I said with confidence. "Punish me this way. Get it over with and then maybe we can move forward." When he didn't move or speak, I reached between us, fisting his erection and lifting my hips.

"Stop," he demanded.

"You don't understand. I want you to do this."

His forehead furrowed as he moved my hand away. "Maddie, you deserve better than an angry fuck."

My head shook. "I don't." My shoulder shrugged. "I don't, but for the first time in seventeen years, I want a man. I want the same man I wanted then. I want to feel you. Be angry. Punish. I don't care. You make me feel. It's something I haven't...not in so long."

Patrick's palm gently came to my cheek as he pulled my gaze back to his. "You know that now I can't."

I could still feel his erection between us. The tips of my lips curled upward. "I am confident you can."

"I'm not saying that I'm incapable," he corrected. "I won't. I want you back, Maddie—all of you. When I fuck you...when we make love, it's not because I hate you or am punishing you. Yes, I'm mad and fucking hurt. I don't know if I can trust you, but I damn well know that when I'm inside you, it's because you're mine. The thing you need to accept is I want more than your body. I want all of you. Every damn piece."

"I don't understand. Patrick, I want this. I do. I don't care if it's because at this moment you love me or hate me. I want to feel you, to know you're real, that I'm real."

He took a deep breath and pulled away, the absence of his wide chest and warmth left me cold and alone. I reached for a blanket or cover, but there was none.

Standing at the end of the settee, Patrick's gaze again seared my skin as he slowly moved his sight over my exposed skin. "You're fucking beautiful. Exteriorly, you're more gorgeous than I remember." He offered me his hand.

Exteriorly?

He saw the ugliness beneath.

With a sigh, I laid my hand in his open palm. He tugged until I too was standing.

Patrick again cupped my cheek. "I saw them that first night at the hotel—the clouds. I guess I wanted to hurt you for hurting me. I wanted to not be the only victim here, but I can see that I'm not."

"Patrick, I made choices..."

"You're so fucking strong and at the same time, you're the fifteen-year-old girl I pulled into a literal hole in the wall."

"No, you're wrong," I said. "I gave that girl up to survive."

He shook his head. "You may have tried to hide her. I bet it worked when you were dealing with people who never knew her. And oh God, when you're playing poker or seducing a Texas oilman, you keep her covered. But, Maddie girl, I see you and the clouds when you lower your defenses, when you allow me the immense privilege of seeing the real you."

"The real me isn't beautiful."

"The real you is stunning and sad. Seeing the clouds helps me realize that I don't hate you, Maddie," he said with an inhale. "I hate what I see." He exhaled. "I've never said this aloud to anyone. Losing you hurt. Fuck, I joined the army to die."

His confession wounded while at the same time gave me strength. Honesty. We had that once. He was offering it again.

"You were gone," he went on, "and I wanted to be gone too. I didn't care if I came back from war because there was no one to come back to. I served two tours over there. I took ridiculous risks when it came to my own safety. Along the way, I found a family. I can hate you for leaving, no matter the reason. But where I am, where I was when I saw you again for the first time since your disappearance, it's not a bad place to be. But you..." His words trailed away.

"I have Ruby," I said, mustering the strength I could. "I don't regret—"

His kiss stopped my words—the lie I'd been telling myself forever.

When our kiss ended, Patrick released my face until we were holding hands, mine in his and his in mine, like we used to. "I want every piece of you. I want to know what happened, what you did, and even what was done to you. I need that and you need to tell someone who will love you unconditionally."

My head shook. "You won't. I promise, you won't."

"I will, but I'm asking you to please wait. Don't tell me yet."

Nodding, I sniffled with relief.

I would tell him if he wanted. I'd tell him the horrible truth because he deserved to know. Yet in doing so, I would ensure the end to any hope of a future. What I would tell him would be a flame and fireball leaving our hopes and dreams in ashes. After all, what man would want a woman who had done what I had?

"Maddie, I'm a fucking shambles right now."

I smiled as I scanned his naked Adonis form up and down. "If this is you as a shambles, I'm impressed. I've been rejected, but I'm impressed."

"You weren't rejected. I want you. I'm still fucking hard. I want you. Know that. Tell me you do."

"I guess."

"Not fucking you is more difficult than bending you over that stool and taking you."

The emptiness he'd left between my legs ached. "Then do it."

He kissed my forehead. "I want more than your body. You need to know that. I want what's here." He kissed my head again. "And here." His hand came to my chest. "The thing is, I'm too fucking messed up at this moment with you, Ruby, and the war. If you confirm the information that I suspect about what's happened to you, just like in the war in the desert, I'm liable to put all my personal safety aside and act recklessly. The difference now versus then is that now it isn't all about me. It isn't even all about you. I have a family who needs me to think straight." He huffed. "With my head and not my dick, quoting a friend."

Patrick sat on the edge of the settee and pulled me to his lap. I came to rest upon one of his strong thighs. "You are my wife, whether you admit it or not. I want to hate you and maybe that would be possible if I had ever stopped loving you."

My head fell to his shoulder as more tears filled my eyes.

I had to be dreaming. Maybe I died back at the club or perhaps we both died at the Ann Arbor airport. After all I'd been through and what life had thrown my way, how was it possible that this strong, handsome, caring man could be back in my life?

I didn't deserve him.

Patrick's arms wrapped around me, pulling me against him. I was still nude, but so was he. We were both vulnerable. He'd shared something with me that he said he'd never vocalized. Knowing that filled me with as much warmth as his caresses.

I closed my eyes as he gently rubbed small circles on my back and down my spine. His touch was neither punishing nor demeaning, instead a gentle reassurance of overwhelming support.

"I never stopped loving you either," I mumbled against his warm skin. I looked up. "I'm not sure I can ever say what you want to hear." He wanted me to admit to his last name. If I did, I would relinquish Miller, a reward I didn't deserve. My name was a daily reminder of what I'd done. Like a chain around my neck, it reminded me of my past and of my worth.

"I'm not giving up," he said. "I want all of you. Admitting to our name is only one part."

He joined the army to die.

As that thought resonated I said a silent prayer of thanksgiving, thankful that his wish hadn't been granted. Even

if we would never be what we'd dreamed a lifetime ago, there was still hope that one day he could be a part of Ruby's life.

Ruby.

"Patrick." I stared into his eyes. "The ambush...I hope you believe I didn't know."

"I believe you wouldn't willingly leave Ruby."

"You're not questioning her existence?"

"No, it's been confirmed beyond what you've told me."

"How?" I asked. "We were promised security and anonymity at Westbrook."

"I'm sure you know that there are ways."

I shook my head. "If you or your people could find her, anyone could. I have to get to her." I almost said I needed to tell Andros. Depending on him was a difficult habit to break. I feigned a smile. "You're right, I wouldn't leave her." I sat up. "Tell me where we are going—and how will we get back to her? We have to get to her before Andros does."

"It's too late for that, but the war has just begun."

MADDIE

Seventeen years ago

I looked out the window of Kristine's van as the streets of Chicago passed by. It wasn't often that I rode anywhere. Mostly, Patrick and I walked. If I gave it a lot of thought, since meeting him, our world had been pretty small. Seeing the tall buildings of downtown Chicago on the horizon filled me with hope for our baby—if I were pregnant. There was a great big world out there and Patrick and I would show our little one the way.

"How have you been feeling?" Kristine asked as she navigated the highway.

I pulled the sleeves of an oversized sweatshirt over my fingers to try to get warmer. It had snowed earlier in the day. When I saw the giant flakes falling out the window, I was concerned Kristine would say we would need to postpone the appointment. She didn't. Despite the earlier accumulation, the streets and especially the highways were clear. The sheer volume of traffic was probably the reason. Well, that and the temperatures were hovering in the high twenties. With the addition of sunshine, the melting was underway.

"I had early morning sickness this morning," I replied to her question as the van filled with music I recognized from our church services.

"Early?"

"Yeah," I said, "it was before everyone was awake. It woke me up."

Kristine looked my way. "You were sick in your room. Does that mean Patrick knows?"

I wrapped my arms around my midsection as the heat continued to blow. "No. I made it to the bathroom. He doesn't know yet. I wanted to say something this morning, but I figured what difference would a few hours make."

She smiled. "You know what, let's stop first and get you something to wear."

I looked down at my blue-jean-covered legs. I'd acquired them from Kristine's supply of donations. The t-shirt I was wearing beneath the sweatshirt was also from her donations. The clothes were even loose. Besides this was just an appointment with a doctor. "What's wrong with what I'm wearing?"

She reached over and squeezed my knee. "Maddie, there's nothing wrong with what you're wearing. When was the last time you had new clothes, brand new from the store?"

I sat straighter. This was why I avoided food pantries and homeless shelters in the past. I didn't want handouts. I didn't want pity. I'd made my choices and was willing to work to improve. "I don't need new clothes. I'm grateful for the clothes at the mission. Before we came to you I had the clothes I wore and one other outfit. Now, I even have a robe."

"I would love to do more for everyone at the mission. It's God's work. Let me get you something special for your appointment."

I looked at the clock in the dashboard. "I thought my appointment was at eleven. It's already 10:15 a.m. and I don't know how long it will take to get there."

"I do. Hey," Kristine said excitedly, "have you ever had your makeup done at the mall?"

"N-no. I don't wear makeup."

"Then it's settled. We're making a day of this. The office called this morning and said they had to change your appointment to three this afternoon. Let's go downtown to the Magnificent Mile."

The idea of being in such an expensive area wasn't appealing. The people there looked at me like they'd walked on better things. I didn't want their charity either. "We don't have to."

Kristine didn't give up. "We can go to Water Tower Place. I know the perfect department store that can show you how to apply some makeup. Oh, and if we hurry, we might be able to have your hair done."

"Done?" My nose scrunched. "I can't...I don't have enough money. I'm not sure I have enough for the appointment and test."

"Maddie, stop worrying. The Lord has blessed Pastor Roberto and I. Please let me share."

"Why can't we wait? If we find out I'm pregnant, I'll need things for my baby. I don't need new clothes, makeup, or my hair done."

Kristine's smile faded as she made her way toward one of the downtown exits. "I understand. It's that I don't have children and I guess I wanted...you know, for you to be all done up to tell Patrick the news."

Her disappointment was palpable. Leaning back against the seat I thought about all she'd done and what she'd offered.

Was it fair for me to reject her offer if it made her happy?

What would it be like to have new clothes?

I'd never before worn makeup. I remembered watching my mother apply mascara and lipstick. I'd always thought that one day I would be like her. She had dark hair, green eyes, and the brightest smile. I turned to Kristine. She was too young to be my mother, but I looked up to her, as I would my own mother. "Okay."

"Okay?" she asked.

"If you think it's a good idea. I feel funny being spoiled. I mean, the money could go to the mission."

"Oh, Maddie," Kristine said, "thank you for letting me do this. And we'll get lunch too."

I fed off of her excitement, allowing the possibility of an unplanned adventure to tingle through me. Shopping at the Magnificent Mile, being pampered at a cosmetic counter and a hair salon were unimaginable to me. I tugged my lip in anticipation. And then I thought of Patrick. I turned to Kristine, "Thank you for this. Patrick will never believe all I have to tell him tonight."

"We can park in a garage downtown and walk. Are you all right with that?" she asked.

"I haven't been downtown in a long time."

After the van was parked and we were on the sidewalk with the sun streaming down, Kristine looped her arm through mine. "Come on, Maddie, let's have a fun afternoon. I say we start with clothes, then makeup, and hair just before a late lunch. How does that sound?"

My eyes opened wide. "Crazy," I said with a giggle. "It sounds crazy."

By two o'clock, we were sitting in a restaurant within one of the big stores. For once, I didn't feel completely out of place among normal people. I was wearing a dress that made me look older than I was. It was white with long sleeves and a neckline that went lower than I'd ever worn. When Kristine brought it to the dressing room, I couldn't stop my complaints about how impractical a dress was for me. I mean, when would I wear it again?

However, after I tried it on, Kristine said it looked too good not to buy. The shoes she picked out were heeled. She said I needed the entire outfit and even bought silky pantyhose and new underwear—panties and a bra.

I couldn't describe the feeling of wearing all the new clothes, all the way down.

The woman at the salon was very nice. She and Kristine decided to have my long hair trimmed and highlights added. After it was washed and dried, the lady curled it, the long tresses hanging in waves. At the department store, the woman at the makeup counter spent nearly twenty minutes talking about my skin tone, cheekbones, and eyes. I'd never thought about any of it before. By the time she showed me the mirror, I hardly recognized myself.

"What will Patrick think?" was my response.

"He'll think he's a lucky guy," Kristine responded.

Now eating lunch, I sipped water and ate the most delicious cheeseburger I'd ever had in my memory. It wasn't only a burger. The French fries were giant, not like McDonald's, but thick and long. "Kristine, thank you," I said as I finished the burger.

"Oh, Maddie, I'm so happy you let me do this. You're absolutely beautiful."

I looked down at the dress. "I hope Patrick thinks so."

"Of course he will. What do you think?"

My cheeks warmed as my smile bloomed. "I feel like this isn't me."

"It is you. You're a beautiful girl with so much potential. I'm sure they'll agree."

"Who?" I asked.

She looked down at her wristwatch. "Well, it's about time to go to your appointment."

I let out a long sigh. "I don't know what I want to learn."

Did I want to be carrying a baby?

"Well, no matter what you learn, you can't do it here."

I took a deep breath. "How long will it take us to get to the appointment?"

"Not long. The building is just a few blocks away."

"Really? Downtown?"

Kristine laid cash on the table to pay for our lunch before looking up at me. "Yes, wait until you see the office. It's beautiful with a view of the park."

"Okay, let's do this."

After a short walk and an elevator ride, we were standing in an office waiting room with only four chairs. The sign outside the door simply read Miller Inc. "You're sure this is a doctor's office?" I asked.

Kristine went to the small window and spoke to the receptionist. When she came back she had paperwork for me to complete. "They just want you to answer a few questions."

"Do I need to tell them all of this stuff?" I asked, reading through the form. "I don't really know my family history or Patrick's."

"Just answer for yourself. It might be better to not put Patrick's name on there, since you don't know for sure."

"I know he's the father," I said.

"Oh, sweetie, that's not what I mean. I meant that you don't know his family history."

I looked at the form. "Should I use my maiden name?"

"They will want to see your ID."

We'd not made it to the license branch to get new IDs after our wedding. Mine still read Madeline Tate.

"Okay, I'll just fill this out about me and what I know."

Kristine smiled.

"Miss Tate," a lady called not long after I'd turned in the clipboard and pen along with my identification.

"That's me."

The older woman smiled at me and Kristine. "I'm Wendy. Do you mind if your sister joins you?"

Sister?

Oh, she meant Kristine.

"She isn't—"

"I'd love to since they only allow family," Kristine interrupted with a grin.

"Yeah, she can come."

Wendy looked me up and down in my new clothes. "You sure are pretty."

Though it made me a bit uneasy, I thanked her.

After confirming information such as my last period and

sexual history, Wendy showed me to a bathroom and asked me to urinate in a cup. After that, I joined her and Kristine in a small examination room.

The sight of the table and stirrups made my skin cool as a clammy perspiration came to the surface. "Um, I've never..."

"It's not that bad, Maddie," Kristine said. "I'll stand up by your shoulder and even hold your hand. Wendy just needs to confirm that you're pregnant."

Wendy handed me a paper gown. "Just put this on, sweetie. You can leave your bra on."

I stared at the blue folded paper. "Everything else off? Won't the pee tell you if I'm pregnant?" I was well aware that I sounded as unsure as I felt.

"Yes, but according to the dates you provided and your history of irregular menstruation, you could have become pregnant sooner than you are assuming. I want to check your uterus and see if we can get a better hold on how far along you are."

"Are you saying you know I'm pregnant?"

"Change into the gown while Kristine and I talk in the hallway."

"Kristine?" I asked.

"This is all routine, Maddie. Don't worry."

Nodding, I waited until the two left me alone. The drab room was small with the exam table, a light on a stretchy long thing, a stool, a chair, and a small counter with a sink attached to the wall. It had been a long time since I'd been seen anywhere that wasn't a free clinic. I supposed my unease was due to simply being out of my element.

Once I had the new clothes removed and neatly folded, I

donned the gown as I'd been instructed, climbed onto the exam table's edge, and called to Kristine and Wendy.

As they entered, Kristine was putting something into her purse that looked like an envelope.

"Is that my medical records?" I asked.

"What? No. Yes. I'll show them to you later."

I stared up at the ceiling as Wendy donned gloves, instructed me where to place my feet and legs, and began her exam. It didn't hurt as much as it was uncomfortable. Obviously, I wasn't a virgin, but having this woman look at me and place things into me was different and invasive. She pushed from within and without.

"Is that tender?" she asked.

"Yes."

"How many sexual partners have you had?"

I looked up at Kristine. The answer was one, but if I said one, wouldn't they expect me to know his information?

"I'm going to assume that means you're unsure of the number."

My stomach dropped at her theory. I wanted to scream that it was one, only one, and he's my husband. Before I could, I sucked in a breath, wincing as she placed something new inside me and scraped. "Ouch."

"We're checking for STDs."

The two women continued talking, but I wasn't listening. I only wanted to know the result of the pregnancy test, and it seemed as though she was saying it was positive. I didn't care about her assumptions. All I wanted to do is leave and get back to Patrick.

"Beautiful girl," I heard Wendy say. "At this point I'd estimate her to be fifteen weeks into this pregnancy.

Assuming she's clean, the baby alone will be sought after. Adding her could net quite a bounty."

I heard their words, but they weren't making sense.

"I'm pregnant?" I asked again for clarification.

Wendy stood and removed her gloves. "Yes. The last step is the interview with Dr. Miller."

"Interview? I didn't understand. And fifteen weeks? How could I be that far along?"

Kristine's hand came to my shoulder. "Don't you understand? That's great news. You're past your first trimester."

"But shouldn't I be showing?"

She looked at my exposed stomach and legs. "I'd say you are."

My hands went to my stomach. She was right. It wasn't much. I'd attributed it to the food at the mission, but there was a bump.

"You change back into that new dress," Kristine said, "and then you can meet with him."

"Why?"

Wendy nodded as she stepped from the room.

"Why am I being interviewed?" I asked again.

"All very normal protocol. I mean, Dr. Miller only takes on so many pro-bono cases. This is a great opportunity for you and your baby—prenatal vitamins and a healthy pregnancy. You want that, don't you?"

"Yes, I guess. I just wish Patrick were here."

"You change into the dress and knock when you're done."

Though my heart was racing, I agreed, the whole time wishing to be back at the mission, wishing I'd told Patrick the truth.

Once I was dressed again, I did as Kristine said and knocked on the door.

When it opened, Wendy scanned me up and down. "I think you will work out well."

I looked up and down the hallway. "Where is Kristine?"

"Not to worry. Please follow me."

Worry was an understatement as I walked on the unfamiliar high heels along the quiet hallway. When she stopped at one of the last doors, she inserted a key and opened the door. "Dr. Miller will be along shortly."

The door opened wider and my steps stalled as my heartbeat tripled in time.

"What is this?"

The room within was decorated like a cheap motel room. Basically, there was a bed and a chair. No windows. How high were we? I couldn't remember.

"I think I need to speak to Kristine."

"Step inside, Miss Tate. Learn to behave and the future is full of endless possibilities for you and your baby. Assuming Dr. Miller approves, your rewards and punishments are at my discretion as long as you're here. I suggest you accept that."

"Wait, no, I need to get back to my husband."

Her lips curled upward. "Girls like you don't have husbands." She nodded to my hand. "No wedding ring and an untold number of partners. The fact that I don't see any obvious disease is a positive. Enter the room, Miss Tate."

I peered back the way we'd come. The hallway was empty.

"Don't make me repeat myself again," she said.

When I stepped in, the door behind me shut. The clicking of the lock echoed against the plain walls.

What was happening?

What had I done?

I paced back and forth, wishing there was a bathroom or anything attached. There wasn't. The room was a box consisting of four walls and one door. The only light was overhead, and I didn't see a switch. Avoiding the bed, I sat on the chair and then stood. I paced and then sat. There was no sense of time.

Did Patrick know I was missing?

My breathing caught as I turned within the chair toward the sound of the opening door.

My beating heart thumped in my ears, echoing, as an older man entered. He wasn't dressed like a doctor. He wasn't wearing a lab coat or carrying a stethoscope but instead wore a nice suit. His black loafers were covered in water droplets as if he'd recently been outside.

After locking the door, he placed a key in the pocket of his trousers. My nose scrunched as he came closer, preceded by the strong odor of cologne and cigars.

"Stand up and turn around."

"I really think there's been some mistake. I don't belong here."

Immediately, my chin was in his painful grasp. "You were not given permission to speak. Take off the dress, the hose, all of it and turn around."

Tears came to my eyes. "Please."

The strike came out of nowhere. I didn't anticipate the blow to my cheek or what would happen next.

How could I?

MADELINE

Present day

"Too late?" I repeated as I stood and reached for the clothes we'd discarded to the floor. "What do you mean? Why didn't you tell me?"

With my mind now on Ruby, the lost opportunity for sex was quickly forgotten.

Could it be possible that by not having sex, I somehow felt closer to Patrick than if he had done as he threatened?

I truly wasn't certain. This was uncharted territory for me, the idea of someone wanting me for more than pussy.

Patrick too reached for his trousers and secured them in place. He straightened his shirt and one by one placed his long arms into the sleeves. Instead of replacing the cufflinks, after leaving the top button undone, he rolled each sleeve to just below his elbows, and tucked the length of the tails into his trousers before latching the belt.

From my little bit of recent exposure to this man, it seemed dress trousers, no tie, and rolled-up sleeves was about the extent of his casual wear.

Why were men's forearms incredibly sexy?

When our eyes met, my cheeks warmed. Still standing in my panties and bra, I'd been enjoying the show too much to continue dressing. "Um, I probably should dress."

"I'm not complaining, but you're not leaving this dressing room unless you're covered." He took a step toward me and pulled me close. "I don't want even a chance that anyone else sees what belongs to me."

I lowered my forehead to his broad shoulder, wishing that what he said could be true.

He pulled me out to arm's length. "I meant it about those clouds."

"Patrick, when I do tell you won't—"

"Stop."

"But—"

"Maddie, we have choices to make in our life. My choice is between spending the rest of mine upset that we missed out on seventeen years, or I can spend the rest of my life moving forward with my wife and daughter. You aren't the only one who has done things that don't make for a good story time. I'd rather look forward. What about you?"

I nodded. "You make it sound easy."

"No, it's fucking hard. For this to work we're going to go against some insurmountable odds." His cheeks rose as a grin came to his lips. "But I figure having one of the best gamblers on my side is a good thing for beating the odds. Are you on my side?"

"I want to be."

"Good, because we'll be better as a team. We always were."

"Right now my biggest concern is my...*our* daughter."

He cupped my behind and squeezed. "Then cover this sexy ass so I can concentrate."

With a stupid, giddy grin trying to curl my lips, I pulled the sweater over my head. After stepping into the slacks, I sat on the edge of the settee to don the socks and boots. Once I was done, I looked up to Patrick's adoring blue gaze. "I want you to trust me, Patrick. Of all the things I'm not proud of, sacrificing for Ruby isn't one of them. Losing you is."

He offered his hand. "I want to trust you and vice versa."

It was such an effortless move—Patrick offering me his hand to stand—and yet as I placed my palm in his, it felt like more. There was something invigorating at the dichotomy in size, how his fingers easily wrapped around my entire hand. His actions didn't feel threatening, as if he would overpower me. Electrifying was a better description. When we connected it was as if bursts of energy sparked, igniting a flame, not only in my core, but in my heart.

Except for Ruby, I'd closed off that organ for so long. Patrick's presence was like an AED to a dying heart. With the simplest of moves, he generated resuscitating shocks, bringing it back to life.

Inhaling, with my hand in his, I stood and said, "Tell me everything you know. What happened back in Ann Arbor?"

"I told you. Ivanov's men were ready to take us out. They would have riddled the plane with bullets. I'm not sure you could have negotiated surrender."

My head shook as the reality sank in. "He's really done with me." I sighed. "I suppose I knew there'd come a day. I always hoped it would be after I had Ruby away. I imagined university abroad."

"She isn't in Ann Arbor, not at Westbrook."

"Of course she is. Her next break isn't until—"

Patrick stood taller, stopping my words. "I'm telling you, not debating. She isn't there."

"You're wrong," I said as my deepest fear threatened to come true.

"When did you last talk to her?"

"Thursday, before going to Chicago."

"Are you sure?"

I tried to think back. I planned to call her before I left and then... "No, it was Wednesday. I remember it was Wednesday afternoon. Her classes were done for the day. Andros told me to call her then, saying I'd be too busy on Thursday."

There was a knock on the door. I looked to Patrick.

"I left strict orders not to be disturbed," he said as he walked to the door and opened it inward.

Millie was on the other side.

"I said we were not to be disturbed."

"Excuse me, Mr. Kelly, Ms. Miller. I apologize for the intrusion; however, Marianne just called and requested that you both be seat-belted."

Patrick inhaled, looking back at me.

"We're approaching our destination," Millie went on, "and Marianne said to expect turbulence. If you'll both reenter the main cabin, I'll be happy to bring you anything you need—a drink or something to eat?"

I saw the way Patrick's back straightened and neck grew taut with each of her offers. Patrick may be able to see me in a way others couldn't. I saw him too. Walking to the door, I stopped beside him. "Thank you, Millie. If we need to be seatbelted, you do too."

A smile came to her lips. "Thank you, Ms. Miller. I don't mind. It's my job."

I turned to Patrick with a tilt of my head. "We can continue this out there. It's better to be safe."

"Thank you, Millie," Patrick said. "Listen to Ms. Miller. She's right; we should all be secure if there's turbulence."

When Millie walked away, Patrick turned and reached for my hands. "You know, I'm usually the voice of reason."

"Apparently, now you're in shambles."

"I'm preoccupied, that's for sure."

I shrugged. "I'm partially responsible. Besides, I have a soft spot for people, especially women who do their job or try to help and are rebuked for it." Too many instances with Andros came to mind. I wouldn't have dared do with Andros what I just did. Instead, I did my best to support his staff when he wasn't around.

"I wasn't rebuking her," Patrick replied.

This wasn't the time for that discussion. "I want to know about Ruby. You're scaring me with the information that she's not at school. Let's sit out there."

Together we walked back to the main cabin. While we'd been in the dressing room, the day had begun to dawn and the sky to lighten. Taking the seat by the window facing the closed partition, I leaned against the leather and fastened the seat belt. To my surprise, instead of sitting across from me, Patrick took the seat to my side and squeezed my hand. "I don't blame you for being scared. I was too.

"Ruby was checked out of the academy on Wednesday night at around seven o'clock."

My head shook. "Only Andros or I can check her out. We were both in Detroit."

"And you know that for sure?"

My chest grew heavy. "I know where I was. He was there too. I saw him earlier in the day. I guess..." I tried to recall. "...Patrick, I have—I had—my own apartment within the compound. I did my best to stay out of his and others' way. If I were being honest, unless I was instructed otherwise, I kept to myself. I spent Wednesday night packing for the tournament. After my call with Ruby, I was notified that I'd be eating in my apartment, which was fine by me. It meant that Andros was preoccupied with something else. I read for a while before falling asleep." My neck straightened as I thought about my answer. "I don't know where he was—I assumed."

"So after he told you to call Ruby, you didn't see him again until...?" Patrick asked.

"Until he arrived in Chicago on Friday in the early afternoon."

"You said it wasn't a long drive to the academy from where you lived."

"No, less than an hour."

"According to the academy's computer system, Ruby Miller was not only checked out but removed from Westbrook Preparatory Academy indefinitely. The notes said that she was transferring schools."

Letting go of Patrick's hand, I ran my palm over the top of my slacks, up and down, the friction helped me think. "Oh, please no." I looked out the window. The sky above was blue as the early sun's rays cast pinks across the clouds below.

Gone?

Where was she?

Was she alone?

"She must be frightened." And then I thought of something. "You said that your people hacked into the academy's files," I said, trying to make sense of what was happening. "That wasn't supposed to be possible."

"I have some incredibly talented people on my side."

"Do you know where she transferred? I mean, they would have wanted her records."

"There was no information."

"Oh my God. My daughter."

"I told you my people are talented. Using a series of satellite images, they were able to follow Ivanov's motorcade."

I inhaled. Andros was paranoid. He always had been. He rarely traveled alone. "Where?"

"He took her to his plane."

I fought off the images vying for space in my head. "Where did the plane go?"

"It landed at a private airport outside Corpus Christi."

I fought against the seat belt to stand. "I know where he took her. He has a retreat on the north end of Padre Island. It's well protected. He goes there off and on during the winter. Maybe he told her it was a surprise vacation."

"I don't know what he told her. Would he leave her there alone?"

"Yes. But she wouldn't be alone. She only is at school because we thought...At the island house there's staff that stays there year-round. They know her and I'm sure she has Oleg."

Patrick sat back. "Who is that?"

"He's...I guess you would say...her bodyguard." A smile came to my lips. "He's big and scary-looking and she loves him. He's been around since she was a baby. And the others at the retreat know her too."

"We need to know exactly where the compound is. Now that it's daylight we can search satellites."

"I remember it was the north end, away from all the people."

"Tell me about the security."

"Walls surrounding the property except to the east. The beach is restricted, but Andros didn't want his view obstructed."

"We should be able to find it."

I let out a long breath. "At least she's safe there."

"Are you sure?"

"If Andros isn't there, she's in good hands."

"According to my men, Ivanov left Chicago after we didn't land in Ann Arbor."

My stomach twisted. "He's on his way to her."

"He already landed in Dallas."

My nose scrunched. "That doesn't make sense.

"I agree. Why stop there? Why not fly closer to the island?" Patrick asked. "I'm confident that Ivanov believed you'd go back to Ann Arbor for Ruby. He heard you tell me that she's my daughter. You were wearing the bracelet. Even with my people distracting him in Chicago, his making the assumption that you'd get to Ann Arbor as quickly as possible made sense. The reason he wasn't in a hurry to leave Chicago was because he knew you wouldn't find Ruby. He'd already moved her while you were preparing for the tournament. There's no way for him to know we followed him to Texas."

"What would I have done without you?"

"Maddie, I don't know how Ivanov knew you'd receive help from the Sparrows, but I believe he did. I believe this is all part of his bigger plan."

"I never told a soul," I said, thinking back to all that occurred before Ruby's birth. "No one but Kristine knew you were the father of my baby."

Patrick's forehead furrowed and eyebrows came together. "Kristine?"

"Pastor Roberto's wife at the mission."

"I'd forgotten her name."

Even the thought of the woman turned my stomach. "I never will," I said.

"She knew you were pregnant?"

"You said not to talk about this, not yet," I reminded Patrick as the plane began its descent for the second time.

Patrick looked down at his phone. "It turns out that Hillman landed in Dallas before Ivanov."

"That man gave me a weird feeling."

"He's a snake and I need to learn why they'd both fly to Dallas."

The cabin was silent for a moment. The closer we came to the coast, the sparser the clouds became as the sun continued to rise. Through the window the Gulf of Mexico shimmered beneath us. I was about to ask where we were landing when I had a thought. I turned to Patrick. "Marion Elliott lives in Dallas."

PATRICK

arion Elliott. He had to be a piece to this puzzle. I stood. "Madeline, I need to go to the front and talk to my men."

"We're about to land."

"This can't wait."

"Patrick," Madeline said as she reached into the purse she'd been given. "Here's my phone. I don't know how to check after your people did what they did, but there may be messages. I'm being totally transparent with you. I feel like I have seen Antonio Hillman before. I don't know, but it may have been in Detroit."

"With Ivanov?"

I shrugged. "Like I said, I tried to remain unseen. It's been easier of late; however, there are always exceptions."

Listening to her tone and seeing her sullen expression sent a chill through me. Memories of what she was saying overflowed with pain, regret, and sadness.

The latter was an overused term that was often said flippantly. Its overuse didn't lessen the impact of the much deeper-rooted emotion. Hearing her anguish made me want to pull Madeline into my arms and uncover every last stimulus for her sudden change in mood, expose them to light so bright that it evicted them forever from the dark recesses of her mind. I would. Not now.

Now we needed to concentrate on Ivanov, Hillman, and Ruby. "You're saying Hillman may have been in the bratva in Detroit?"

"Not as a regular—a visitor. There were...I guess you could call them parties. Large rooms with lots of food, alcohol, smoke, music..." She shrugged. "I suppose it's the same with the Sparrows."

It wasn't.

Sterling Sparrow was a private man. From what I'd seen, Andros Ivanov enjoyed showboating and splashing his name and the names of wealthy associates all over social media.

"You'd be surprised," I replied. "Under the veneered surface, those of us at the top of the Sparrow outfit are just regular people."

She smirked. "That would surprise me. To be *people* is to be human." Her head shook. "That doesn't describe Andros or his top men."

I reached for the phone that she'd now dropped to her lap. "Maddie, you gave me an idea. I'll let you know when I have more."

"Patrick."

"Maddie, I need to—"

"I don't want to say this, but I have to." She unfastened her seat belt and stood, her gaze meeting mine. "If what you say is true. If Mr. Sparrow and others—like the men up there..." She tilted her chin toward the partition. "If they're people, if they have a semblance of human qualities and decency..." Her lips thinned as her head shook. "They won't defeat Andros. He has no affiliation that supersedes his ambition. None. I'd like to think that Ruby could be the exception, but I can't be confident. Andros would sell his mother..." She huffed. "...or give her to his men if it would help his cause."

"What about the woman at his side?" The question came out before I could stop it.

She stood taller and lifted her chin. "Without batting an eye."

Yes, I was human.

I could also kill or maim. I had and would again.

I was fucking human because at this moment I knew I wouldn't rest until Andros Ivanov was no longer on this earth. I could blame myself for not searching harder or blame Madeline for her ending up with such a cruel man, but that wouldn't help us or Ruby. My blame, my hatred, my seething rage was only good if it spurred results, if it helped a cause. Otherwise it was a useless emotion that would be detrimental rather than advantageous.

It was my turn to lift my chin and square my shoulders. "Thank you for the warning, but you're wrong."

"You don't know him."

"No, I don't. I do know my men—my family. I know that right now the human qualities within me vying for supremacy are unadulterated rage and at the same time, overpowering love. I can't right the wrongs of the past. I can't erase memories. I can set the future straight, and if I have to burn down the entire Ivanov bratva to do that, I will."

"I don't want you to."

My head tilted in question.

"I don't want to lose you again. Let's get Ruby and let the rest work itself out."

"That's not an option, Madeline. The rest is a war. The rest threatens everyone and everything I love and have worked for."

"I never loved him," she said as she retook her seat. "Besides Ruby, I've never loved anyone...anyone but you."

"I have to get up front," I said, unable to face more of this conversation. Turning, I left Madeline alone with her thoughts and memories. It was a shitty thing to do; however, on the list of shitty things she'd experienced, I doubted it came close to the top. One day I'd put her first. Now was about rescuing Ruby and ending this war.

Two goals.

I wouldn't sacrifice one for the other.

I pushed open the partition and stepped into the anterior cabin. As I did, three sets of eyes came my way. "Marion Elliott," I said as I closed the door behind me.

Garrett nodded. "We've been watching. He landed in Dallas during the night. Traffic cams have him entering his ranch around three this morning."

"Why did Hillman and Ivanov both come to Dallas? I'm betting it has to do with Elliott," I replied, happy that they'd been watching Elliott.

"That's what we—"

"Sir," Romero said, interrupting Garrett, "there's a transmission coming through from Mr. Murray."

We all turned to the screens before us.

"Reid," I said, looking at his face on the computer. "There are four of us here." I wanted him to know I wasn't listening alone. Then again, if these men weren't trustworthy, we were already fucked.

Reid nodded. "First things first. There seems to be a fucking convention in Texas."

"Could they have found out where we were headed?" I asked.

"I don't believe they know you're there. Listen to this: we thought Hillman and Ivanov were waiting for a signal from Madeline. Instead, they both received a call from Elliott while he was on his way to Dallas."

"I would like to know what they discussed."

"I can only see the calls," Reid said. "If I could get closer to their networks or phones, I could add malware to hear future conversations. In the meantime, Elliott called both men and their flight plans suddenly diverted to Dallas."

"Tell me that we know more," I said.

The table and screens rattled as the airplane's wheels found the landing strip.

"We just landed in Corpus Christi," I informed Reid.

Reid began, "We know that no one has come or gone from Ivanov's island retreat since Friday morning when he left for Chicago."

"You found it?" I asked. "Madeline said it was on the north end."

"It is. It's a fucking small castle behind a wall. To locals, it's off-limits. They probably think it is a private hotel and resort. It's also well guarded."

The small hairs on the back of my neck stood to

attention. "Madeline said that Ruby is familiar with the retreat. She seems confident that Ruby's safe there."

"Then it's our opinion..." The *our* would be comprised of Reid, Mason, and Sparrow. "...that before you storm his castle on the beach, your attention should be on this meeting of the minds from the poker tournament." Before I could speak, Reid went on. "Marianne has been instructed to refuel and fly back to Dallas."

I bristled. "I want off this plane. If they're in Dallas, now is the chance to get Ruby."

"Or walk into another ambush," Reid replied. "If Madeline says Ruby is safe, take care of Ivanov and Hillman. If we want to kill this snake, then we need to cut off its head. I'll see what I can learn. Mason and a few more men plan to board one of the planes and head down in a few hours."

"No," I replied. "Mason can't leave Sparrow."

"I'm here," Reid said.

"And you're capable of protecting him, but we need you doing what you're doing. What about the money that was stolen? Any indication of who reaped the benefit of a fifteen-million-dollar infusion?"

"No, I'm watching transfers."

"What about Beckman? Standish was found by the police. It would look suspicious if he was found too, even with the fake suicide note."

"He won't be found," Reid said. "Mason took care of that. Club Regal is closed until further notice, and we have men working on finding new management." He shrugged. "Sparrow said to do an unplanned remodel to make the closure seem more legit."

"That seems like a priority," I said.

"Remodel with cameras."

A smile came to my lips. "See, Reid, you're needed there doing what you do. We all know Sparrow won't stay put in the glass tower. Lockdowns don't work on him. The four of us and Madeline will fly to Dallas. Get us a safe place to stay. See if we can gather Sparrows from the area. We need to know that whoever is contacted is one hundred percent behind us."

"Speaking of that, Mason spent a good part of the night with the top capos. He learned that Hillman has spent the last month reconnecting."

"Why the fuck are we just learning about this now?" I asked.

"You're asking nicer than Mason did. Our ranks will be cleaned."

I didn't like learning that we'd be losing men. We needed every one. Then again, one trusted man was worth a hundred traitors.

"Look at that," Reid said, his attention diverted.

"Talk to me."

"Ivanov and three of his men were just picked up by two of Elliott's cars. I don't know who is flaunting this, Ivanov or Elliott."

I shrugged. "Not sure what Elliott gains, but Ivanov gets to be seen around wealth. From what I've heard, he likes that."

"Heard? Are you learning anything from Madeline? Can you trust her?"

My neck straightened. "Yes, from her and I do." I remembered her phone. "Did Mason say that any calls to her phone would go to voicemail?"

"Yeah."

I pulled the phone from my pocket. "I have it. Can you access it to see if she has messages?"

"Sorry," Reid said, "I should have thought of that. I don't need her phone. I can access it from here."

"Glad to know I'm still good for something," I replied. "Get back to us if there's more news."

The plane began to move slowly over the tarmac. As it did, the door to the cockpit opened. "Sir," Marianne said, "we're being tugged to the fueling area. We should be back up in the air in twenty minutes."

"Are you still good to fly?" I asked, seeing her for the first time since we left Chicago. It had been a longer night than planned.

"Yes, sir. Dallas is only an hour and a half flight. My flight time hasn't been exceeded."

"We'll get you and Millie each a room so you can rest. Our schedule is unclear."

She nodded and turned back to the cockpit. Marianne had been with the Sparrows for many years and knew the drill. She wasn't our only pilot, but she was one of our most trusted. That job came with responsibility, uncertain schedules, and worthy compensation. It didn't matter if this detour was in her plans or not; she and everyone else aboard would conform to our schedule.

"I'll look into her voicemail," Reid said.

We all waited as Reid typed away on his computer. It was early Sunday morning and to look at my friend and associate, I couldn't tell he'd been awake all night. We were used to these hours, but I would guess along with Marianne and Millie, Madeline wasn't.

The plane came to a stop. Garrett rose from his seat and moved to one of the windows. "We're being refueled."

"Here we go," Reid said through the computer, garnering all of our attention. "Apparently, Elliott didn't call only Ivanov and Hillman."

"Madeline?" I asked.

"Yes."

"Tell me you can access the message."

Reid's smile filled the screen. "I can."

Taking a deep breath, I sat back against the seat, my gaze meeting Garrett's, Christian's, and Romero's as Elliott's voice came through the speaker.

"Madeline, I have been thinking..."

A few minutes later, I opened the partition to the rear cabin. Madeline was no longer seated. Her green eyes met mine.

"Why haven't we disembarked?" She scoffed, gesturing toward the long wool coat, gloves, and headband. "I guess I don't need those."

"No, but you need to sit back down. We're about to take off again."

"No. We're so close to Ruby." Her eyes widened. "I know where she is. If you activate my phone, I'll call her." She looked at the watch she must have found amongst the clothes. "I don't suppose she's even awake."

"You said she's safe," I reminded her.

Her face fell slack as she collapsed back into the seat. "Patrick, please. We're here and I figured out a way to get her. Can you get us a boat?"

MADELINE

"*I* fucking hate this," Patrick said. "There has to be another way than by putting you in danger." His complaint ended with a resigning sigh as he bent his long legs and perched on the edge of the large bed within the hotel suite's bedroom.

I watched him through the mirror, his reflection behind me as I secured the platinum earrings in place. "We talked about it since we left Corpus Christi. Marion mentioned Ruby in his message. I have to go."

Patrick stood and paced to the floor-to-ceiling windows and back. "You don't think he knows that? You don't think Elliott knows your Achilles' heel? He invited you to his ranch. He didn't mention that Ivanov and Hillman were also there. You're walking into a setup."

I spun on the high heels, the skirt of the green dress I wore pitching in kind. It wasn't as formal as the clothes I'd wear for a tournament. I'd found it among the clothes on the airplane. It was flattering yet not pushy, accentuating my womanly curves while keeping my assets covered. This may be winter, but this was also Texas, not Detroit. I had a lightweight wrap to keep my arms covered and my pumps were tall. Wearing them flattered my legs.

This wasn't my first attempt at flirting, and not even my first with Marion Elliott. He was an older man with more wealth than common sense. I'd done far less respectable things to protect Ruby. Meeting with a rich Texas oil baron wouldn't even make the front page of my list.

"What kind of a setup, Patrick? You can argue all day, but Elliott won't stand there and let Andros or Antonio kill me. The men poised with guns in Ann Arbor were there for you and your men, not me."

"And you know that?"

"I don't. I'm making an assumption just as you did. I wouldn't be as confident if this meeting was alone with Andros." I inhaled, refusing to allow that chilling thought to register. "Elliott said on his message that he heard my distress at Club Regal and wants to help."

Patrick came closer. Seizing my waist, he pulled me flush against his wide chest. "That's my job."

"I'm not the center of a pissing contest. This isn't about your ego. It's for Ruby."

"Don't go. We'll send a decoy."

I took a step back. "A decoy? I'm certain they would know it's not me."

"Not until it's too late. We implode the ranch. Tragic. A gas main break. Hillman and Ivanov are gone. Problem solved. We go back to Padre Island and retrieve Ruby, by force if necessary. I know how these chains of command work.

They're all behind Ivanov until he's gone, and then it's a dogfight to see who can take control. The bratva will be so concerned about the next king they won't notice Ruby."

I stood taller. "Or they will see her for the asset she is and her future will be even more unclear. I can hate him and so can you, but Andros has accepted responsibility for Ruby since before she was born. That's afforded her his protection. I don't know what the future holds, but I want to believe that he moved her to Padre Island not only to hide her from me, but also to hide her from others."

"Others?" Patrick asked.

"That power struggle you describe. Only Andros or I could have officially checked her out of the academy, but that doesn't mean people who work for him didn't know where she was. She isn't his daughter, but he treated her like the bratva's princess. I'm sure his men heard about what happened at Club Regal. A part of me wants to believe he moved her to keep her safe."

Patrick's hand cupped my cheek. The fresh scent of bodywash and cologne filled my senses, reminding me of the time we'd shared under the sprays of warm water within the large shower in the hotel suite. The water refreshed us while we allowed passion to momentarily replace our anxiety. Staying true to his promise on the plane, we didn't have sex—not intercourse—but that didn't mean either of us went unsatisfied. Fingers and tongues provided pleasure, as for a few minutes our cares were replaced by moans and whimpers of satiation.

Memories of being on my knees as warm water rained over us and Patrick came undone heated my skin. The feeling of the muscles in his thighs growing taut beneath my palms as he came closer to the edge empowered me to continue. It took the right partner to make a person feel empowered while kneeling. Patrick was the right man. I'd keep that memory with me as I faced whatever the future of the evening held.

I went on, "I am simply meeting Marion on his ranch to hear his proposal. I'll wear this..." I lifted the necklace dangling from my neck. It appeared to be a small pearl within a gilded enclosure. In reality, the pearl contained a transmitting device broadcasting audible as well as global location.

"I will be listening to your every breath." He once again reached for my waist, his long fingers splaying over the material of the dress. "I control when it broadcasts."

"You do?"

His grip tightened. "Like right now, it's silent. I don't want everyone in the Sparrow outfit to hear how fucking terrified I am of letting you out of my sight."

A smile lifted my cheeks. "Patrick, being back with you has meant more to me than I can say. I forgot what it was like..." I changed the direction of my thoughts. "You are all man." I leaned back and took him in, from his freshly washed hair to his clean button-down shirt, the one that covered his broad chest and defined abs, lower still to his expensive suit trousers and shiny leather loafers. "Handsome and powerful. I feel it when we're together. You're an anomaly."

"I am?"

I lifted myself up on my toes and gave his freshly shaved cheek a kiss. "You are. I feel your strength and power, not because you flaunt it or hold it over me and others. It's actually the opposite. Your demeanor demands respect and submission, even from those other men. They trust and respect you. I sensed it back at the club with Mr. Sparrow. It's his name, but he reveres your opinion, the big guy with the ponytail too. When I'm with you, I want to give in to you and relish your presence. I want to. That's different than being forced to. It's the difference between you and him."

"I'd like to think there are other differences."

"What I said before about not being able to beat him, I have a differing thought."

His long finger caressed my cheek. "What is that thought, Mrs. Kelly?"

My heart fluttered at the use of the name as well as his willingness to listen. I was tired of fighting my attraction. Just as I'd said, I wanted to give in and submit to Patrick in every way, not only sexually, though that was appealing. I wanted to be his wife again, different than before, in a way that consenting adults agree to become one.

Wanting didn't make it possible, not without Ruby.

"Human qualities," I said, "don't have to be your downfall or the downfall of the Sparrow outfit." I took a breath as I stared into Patrick's blue eyes. This man was all I'd said, and in this moment, he wasn't minimizing or dismissing me. He was listening. "Your men, they more than respect you. As well as the others who appear to be in power in Sparrow, they also respect you and dare I say, care about you. You've called them your family. Capitalize on that."

"I'm not sure I follow."

"Because you're too good of a man. What you were saying about the consequences if Andros was eliminated is true. Something has been brewing under the surface for a while now. I don't know what happened in his world or maybe beyond, but there's been dissension among the ranks. I don't ask for details. I wouldn't be told. But I listen and I hear things."

"You're saying when we take out Ivanov to watch for his successor?"

"I'm saying that some of Andros's most dangerous enemies may not be the Sparrows." I exhaled and shrugged. "But I'm sure I don't know or understand what's at work."

Patrick reached for my hands. "I will agree to disagree."

"About?"

"Madeline Kelly, you have always been intelligent."

"You don't know the poor—"

"Choices," Patrick said, finishing my sentence. "Poor choices and decisions rarely come about based on our knowledge or intellect. Usually, they reflect our heart's desire or emotions. You are alive, Ruby is alive, and you are within my grasp again because you have been smart enough to survive. Didn't you say that you're bilingual?"

That was an interesting change of subject. I answered anyway, "Yes, as is Ruby."

"Russian is a difficult language, one I've never mastered."

"Patrick."

"I know we both missed having a normal education."

We had, but like Patrick, I'd received mine later in life. "I need to be going."

He held tighter to my hand and looked me in the eye. "Don't let anyone diminish your abilities. I would suspect there is a lot of truth in what you just said about dissension in the Ivanov ranks. I'll talk to the Sparrows. If there is discontent in the Ivanov bratva, Hillman may not be the leech we suspected. Maybe he's in the market for a takeover."

"I don't know."

"And it's not your job to find out." He offered me a strained smile. "I'm turning on the receivers for your necklace. Do not take it off. It charges via body heat. It's also water-resistant, not -proof."

My lips curled upward. "I've already had one shower."

A satisfying growl resonated from Patrick's throat as his simmering gaze brought heat to my skin. The way he was staring was as if the dress had disappeared. With a sigh, Patrick pulled his phone from his pocket and after swiping the screen, he said, "You're now live."

My gaze fell to the necklace upon my breastbone as it rose with my deep breath. I suddenly wondered if it could detect my heart rate. If the answer was yes, I suspected that someone somewhere would see how fast my heart was beating.

"Find out what Elliott says about Ruby and come back to me," Patrick instructed, lifting my chin. "Know that Ivanov and Hillman are there on the ranch. If they leave, we'll monitor them."

"Can you tell me?"

"Not without raising suspicion."

Patrick's phone vibrated.

He looked at the screen. "I should answer this."

I stepped back, wrapping my arms around my midsection and preparing myself for whatever was at hand. I'd walked into more dangerous situations than Marion Elliott's ranch and lived to tell about it.

Patrick's voice stayed steady. "Hello. Yes, I can tell her. Has Garrett gotten her car ready? Okay." When he disconnected, he looked my way with a grin. "Apparently, an advantage of being overheard is being corrected."

"What do you mean?"

"An email address, unknown to Ivanov, has been added to your phone. We will only use it in emergencies, but we can contact you via that email. Your password is birthstone."

My cheeks rose as a grin came to my lips. A ruby is the gemstone for the month of July—Ruby's birthstone and name. "That's good. I can remember that. Please keep an eye on the island resort. Just because Andros is in Dallas doesn't mean he won't move her or have her moved. I need to know where she is, even if I can't see or talk to her."

Patrick planted a kiss to my forehead. "Let me walk you down to the car."

MADDIE

Seventeen years ago

I couldn't comprehend the amount of time that had passed. It could have been days or maybe weeks. The room where we were kept was below ground with no windows and one door. A single low-watt light bulb hung from the ceiling, enough to illuminate the shadows, similar to a nightlight that never turned off. Every few hours warm air blew from a vent in the ceiling. It didn't last long. With the cold concrete walls and floor, we should appreciate the warmth; however, its presence did less to heat and more to elevate the putrid odor of human waste.

One large bucket in the corner was our only toilet.

Running water wasn't present nor were beds.

Our clothes were our only blanket and the dress Kristine had bought however long ago was in shreds.

The first time I entered—what I'd overheard as *holding*—

there were seven other girls. I could say women, but that would be a stretch considering at eighteen I was one of the oldest inhabitants. Wearing what was left of the white dress, now stained with an assortment of bodily fluids, I walked barefoot into what could best be described as a cell.

The number of inhabitants varied over time. Today there were nine of us.

While new ones came, others disappeared. Only a few of us had been here since I arrived.

Thinking beyond the moment was impossible. Common concerns no longer existed.

Shower.

Brushing teeth.

Sleep.

The latter came in waves of exhaustion, times when maintaining wakefulness was beyond my ability. One need that didn't wane was hunger. Food was a reward if we behaved, if we performed to the customer's satisfaction.

With my back against the cold concrete and my knees drawn up to my chest, my wandering thoughts went back to the hours and days after Kristine left me.

Dr. Miller was the first to interview me.

I had no way of knowing that an interview meant rape.

Before I met Patrick, I kept my hair short and wore baggy clothes. I knew what could happen to girls on the street, and I did my best to stay invisible. And then one afternoon, the change began. It wasn't instantaneous but gradual. Patrick would run his fingers through my hair, innocently saying he liked it long. Over time, he'd hold me against him as his hands skirted my body, finding curves that I could no longer hide. His approval and appreciation gave me strength to embrace my femininity—not flaunt but accept. His presence allowed me the bubble of safety to become a woman.

When any thoughts of Patrick came to mind, my eyes filled with tears until they rolled down my filthy cheeks, creating a pathway through the dirt and grime. I sometimes wondered how I had any tears left.

Dr. Miller was the first to interview me the day Kristine left. Not the last.

After he was done, Wendy escorted me to the bathroom, and then to another room furnished with a similar cheap bed. I begged and pleaded. I told her I had family who would miss me. My initial pleas were met with reprimands and threats. Threats became action and my begging ceased.

By the time I closed my eyes that night, there had been four different men.

Thinking about them brought bile from the depths of my stomach. They were men I wouldn't approach on the street. Not because they appeared scary, but because they appeared old and normal. They were the men who came and went from high-rise offices, ritzy restaurants, and theaters with elegantly dressed wives on their arms. They wore expensive suits and held an air of superiority. I would have avoided their condescending expressions.

As they entered the rooms, their expressions held the same sense of supremacy.

Now they had purpose. Each one knew the outcome and what he would do. Each one instructed, dominated, and demeaned me. In a matter of hours, my illusions of family men were shattered.

Before the terrible awakening, I'd imagined these men as fathers or grandfathers presiding over a long table filled with children and grandchildren and smiling at their wives. How could I have imagined a world where they dispassionately did what they had done to me, each leaving me with bruises along with their semen? From the first interview, I realized the cold reality that simple gratification wasn't their goal. These men found immense satisfaction in not only vaginal but also oral and anal.

Dr. Miller had been the first to take me there. No amount of time or distance could make me forget the pain and burn as he forced himself into that virgin area. It was as if my cries fueled his speed and determination. It wasn't enough for them to come inside me, but also on me. Throughout that night, my face, skin, and even hair was doused.

When he left the room, I vomited. It was a combination of the pain, odors, and pregnancy.

Instead of helping me, Wendy made me wash the floor. After that, I was told to change the sheets for the next interview.

It wasn't until the third or fourth man was about to enter...it was difficult to recall...that I heard the conversation.

"How much did she cost?" the man asked before entering the room.

"Three hundred for her. Five for the baby."

"Five? What if it doesn't survive?"

"She's beyond the first trimester. I'm certain, sir, that not only will she bring you a profit, but a healthy baby will bring you twenty times what was paid."

The man scoffed. "I heard she's a fighter."

Wendy laughed. "They all start out that way. That's why I called you. I know how much you enjoy breaking them in."

"Next one, call me first. I'm not a fan of sloppy seconds or thirds."

"Of course, sir. I told her to wash, but if you'd rather not—"

"Wendy, you know me better than that. I like them tight. Next time, call me first."

"I will. We have more coming in a few days; one of our people in St. Louis said he has three targeted."

"Let me know when they arrive. Maybe I'll throw a party."

More.

Party.

Breaking.

As I now sat in the same filthy dress and imagined that others would endure what I had, I was thankful it wasn't me. That realization confirmed their success. I was breaking or maybe broken.

I wasn't sure.

Did the broken continue to fight?

A sob came from my chest as I hugged my legs tighter, my hand going to my stomach.

It was confirmed. I was carrying a baby—Patrick's and my baby—and it was to be sold as I had been.

I yearned to fight, flee, and get back to Patrick.

What must he be thinking?

I'd lived on the streets. I had experience. What I didn't have was opportunity—none of us did.

All of us stilled whenever the door to the hallway opened. The woman who appeared from the other side was Miss Warner. I didn't know if that was her real name. Reality didn't matter in this world. Miss Warner was how she was to be addressed. When she called your name, you were wanted upstairs. The appropriate response was 'Yes, Ms. Warner. Thank you, Ms. Warner.'

Inappropriate responses were met with force.

The punishments weren't completely wielded by her though she was quick with her crop.

"Walk faster, girl."

"Show your appreciation for this reward."

Each instruction came with a swift swat to a leg or arm.

That wasn't the same as punishments for misbehaving. For those, she had two large men who willingly obliged with belts and paddles. From what I'd heard, she enjoyed watching.

Though we weren't allowed to speak to one another, like mice hiding in the cellar, we whispered and at times, huddled close together for heat. Such as a children's game of telephone, there was no way of knowing if the retold stories were accurate or enhanced.

The positive aspect at hearing one's name called was that after the customer was done, we'd receive food. If my name wasn't called, food didn't appear. Three times a day water was delivered. If only I'd kept track of the water, I might know how long I'd been here. While I would have liked to use it to wash, I couldn't not drink it. Along with hunger came thirst. The bottles weren't new. After we were done, they were collected in an old milk crate, refilled and brought back. The water wasn't always cold, but it was wet, a valuable commodity. Not returning a bottle was a punishable offense.

Considering the squalor, the cell was kept neat.

The responsibility of carrying the bucket up the stairs alternated between girls. It was the only non-sex job that received an edible reward. Though admittedly, it was difficult to maintain an appetite when faced with the contents. Nevertheless, food was food.

There was a strange contradictory sense of wanting and

not wanting to be requested. I wasn't certain how the men knew to request us.

Did they say give me a blonde or maybe a brunette?

Did they have pictures of us and descriptions?

Was it like going to a restaurant and we were on the menu?

No one knew.

Each door that I'd seen within this building had a key lock. The door out of this room led to a concrete staircase—again no windows, no means to escape. The door at the top of the staircase led to a hallway with four locked doors. Over the time I'd been here, I'd only been led into two of the rooms.

That wasn't to say I'd only been upstairs twice. In reality, I'd lost count of my number of visits up the stairs. It was my observation that an assigned room didn't matter. The two I'd been in were exactly the same—four walls with no windows, containing a mattress upon a frame with one sheet and a chair.

Once led to the room, Miss Warner would instruct us to strip and determine the position we were to lie in upon the bed. The next instruction was to wait.

Could it be possible that the wait was the worst time?

So many questions came to mind as I waited for the door to open.

Who would enter?

What would they do?

Would it hurt?

Would I bleed?

I always did with anal.

I didn't know if that was normal or if I'd never had time to heal after the first night.

Would the customer be satisfied?

Would I be fed?

In the basement, I'd heard whispered stories about violence for no other reason than to inflict it. In the stories it wasn't punishment, but something the customer enjoyed. Until the first night, I'd never imagined such a thing.

Did it make me lucky that the only time that happened was the first night?

Was I a quick learner, easily broken, or simply complacent?

On each trip up the stairs, I considered the notion of fighting and fleeing.

And then my next thought was of the baby within me.

Round after round of unprotected sex hadn't caused me to miscarry.

What would happen if I tried to escape and was punished? What if I was hit or kicked in my stomach?

I wanted to believe it wouldn't be allowed to happen. After all, these people wanted to sell my child; however, I refused to have faith in their plans.

"How far along are you?" a blonde girl asked in a whisper as she sat beside me.

In the dimness I noticed the stringiness of her hair and the tears in her ragged dress.

Were we all bought dresses for our sale?

Her question took me out of my thoughts.

"I'm pregnant, but I don't know how far for sure."

"Me too," she said.

It was difficult to see in the dimness. "Are you showing?" I asked.

"Yeah. Some of them upstairs like that. How about you?"

"Not very much."

"Oh, once you do, your name will be called more often.

Sick bastards like the idea of screwing a pregnant woman. I don't know why. Some mommy fantasy I guess. At least it results in food. I'm always hungry."

"Yeah, me too." My skin peppered with goose bumps. "How long have you been here?"

"I don't know."

The common answer led to the hopelessness of our situation. I squeezed my legs tighter against my chest. "I'm Maddie and I'm always scared." It was a brave confession and true.

She reached toward me. I flinched.

My mind told me this was a friend and confidant. My body recoiled at any contact.

She sighed. "We all are. I heard Miss Warner a few days— or hell, weeks ago—saying that everyone here is pregnant. It's easier she said. No periods. No need for condoms. We can work for them every day and night without exception."

"I don't even know if it's day or night."

"I saw a customer's watch once. I didn't know if it was a.m. or p.m., but I tried to keep track. It didn't last long. I doubt anyone in here knows."

Sighing, I laid my head back. "I hate it. Their hands on me, their bad breath, and the way they smell." I turned to her, keeping my voice low. "The way I smell."

"Just pray that the customers don't complain. If one does, they'll make you shower."

"Why? A shower sounds heavenly."

"Not here. I've had two. I don't know how many times I've been screwed or the time of day, but I won't forget the showers."

I sat taller. "Tell me."

"There's a room up there, beyond the door at the end of the hall. You know where one of those big guys always stands?"

I nodded.

"It's them."

"What is?"

"Those men that sometimes help Miss Warner?"

"Yeah," I answered trepidatiously.

"It's them. They make you strip and they use a garden hose. The water is freezing. There's no shampoo or soap, just water, and they like to be sure we're really clean—everywhere. A cold-water enema, it made my stomach hurt and I kept using the bucket. It was awful."

My empty stomach twisted as her words became pictures in my mind.

"Once they're done," she went on, "they take turns. It's their chance to get in on the action around them."

"I feel sick," I said.

"Try to resist it. Puking in that bucket is the worst."

I knew from experience she was right. "Do you ever think about dying?" I asked.

Her shoulder shrugged against mine. "I bet we all do. You know they use the baby to keep us going." Her hand went to her stomach. "I felt mine kick the other day."

"Really?"

She reached again for my hand. This time I didn't resist as she placed it over her stomach. Her body beneath her dress was rounder and harder than mine.

"Just wait," she said. "And press down. You won't hurt me."

I did as she said.

"Did you feel it?" she asked.

"I don't think I did."

She let go of my hand. "I did. When he gets stronger you'll be able to. You'll probably be able to feel yours soon. I'm like you. I hate this, but I love my baby."

"Do you know yours is a boy?" I asked.

"No, I just like the sound of him or he over it."

More tears made their way from my eyes. "I heard them say they're going to sell mine."

"All of them."

"I don't want to go on without my baby." I'd lost everything else.

"Then get sold together."

I turned toward her, my volume increasing. "What? Is that possible?"

"Shh." She looked around. "I don't know. There were two girls here before you got here. They were close to their due dates. Both of their names were called and neither one has returned." She let out a long breath. "We have to have hope. In my head, they're both with their babies. Maybe it's some rich couple and they buy the mom too. You know to feed the baby. Hell, I'll do whatever they want. I'll let the guy screw me, give him head. It would be better than here and maybe I'd be clean or have my own room. Anyway, it's better than imagining any other outcome."

Get sold with my baby.

The seed had been planted.

The door opened and the room became deadly still.

Only Miss Warner's profile was visible with the light from the stairs. She tapped the small crop against the palm of her other hand, maintaining our attention.

We all waited.

The anticipation built, yet no one spoke.

"Cindy."

I exhaled, thankful it wasn't me while at the same time my empty stomach filled with disappointment.

The girl next to me stood. "Yes, Miss Warner. Thank you, Miss Warner."

I hadn't known her name.

Cindy, I'm sorry. Please come back. The words weren't spoken aloud.

The door closed blanketing us again in the dimness.

MADELINE

Present day

I wasn't certain what they had done, but since the bracelet Andros gave me was still in Chicago, Patrick's men decided it would be better if it appeared as if I was still there. Somehow, they inserted my name on a flight manifest, making it look as though I'd caught the first flight from Chicago to Dallas after receiving Marion's call.

I'd been to this city before for a poker tournament and knew that Dallas-Fort Worth Airport was large. Hoping that Andros wasn't able to access airport security, we had a plan. After I left Patrick, Garrett dropped me off at one gate and Marion's driver would retrieve me at another.

The only thing missing for my charade was a suitcase or luggage.

The reality was that Andros's people had cleared my hotel

room. I had no clothes or belongings, none not provided to me by Patrick and the Sparrows.

Did this association make me a double agent?

Was this like a spy movie where I'd be forced to pledge my allegiance to one or the other?

Or was I about to enter the scene where the heroine was tied to a chair and tortured at length until she gave up her secrets or her life?

The thought sent a shiver down my spine. Like the scattering of insects, the chill spread down my limbs, leaving goose bumps in its wake. Shaking it off, I stepped into the Skylink and reached for a silver pole as other travelers joined me. Following Patrick's plan, I disembarked at the same gate with the arriving flight from O'Hare. The timing was incredibly close. Soon I was falling into the crowd of passengers who had only hours ago been in Chicago.

At last I came to the baggage area. As I rode the escalator down, I caught sight of a gentleman, all in black, holding a sign.

MS. MILLER

I nodded as I came forward.

"Ms. Miller?" he asked.

"Yes. You're with Mr. Elliott?"

"I am. I work for him, ma'am. My name is David. May I help you with your luggage?"

When I returned Marion's message, he'd told me to expect a man named David.

"No luggage today," I said. Not only didn't I have anything to pack, I wasn't planning on a long stay. Marion had asked me to his ranch for dinner to discuss my unfortunate situation. He wanted to help not only me but also my daughter.

"Very well," David said, "please come with me."

I appreciated the distance he maintained. I wondered if this was the driver who wasn't able to join Marion in Chicago. No matter what, he was professional and efficient.

Walking through the glass doors, I inhaled the afternoon air. Dallas in January was pleasant, if even a bit chilly; however, in comparison to Detroit or Chicago, it could be considered balmy. A long black limousine caught my attention, bringing my nerves to alert.

"This way, Ms. Miller," David said.

Once we reached the car, he opened the door.

For a moment, I stood rooted to the sidewalk as the breeze blew strands of my hair about my face and the skirt of my dress. I wasn't ready to encounter Andros after the spectacle in Club Regal and I wasn't prepared to do that alone. I looked to my escort. "This is a large car. Is there anyone else inside?"

"Ma'am, this is Texas. Everything is big."

That wasn't an answer. "Anyone else?" I asked again.

"No, ma'am. It's only Nicholas, the driver, and myself. Mr. Elliott thought you might want an opportunity to rest after your flight. This is his favorite car and there's plenty of room and refreshments for the drive."

I let out a relieved breath. "Thank you. That was very kind of him."

Ducking lower, I stepped into the back of the car. To my

delight, I was alone. The man had been correct about the space. The seats lined three walls and to one side was cabinetry. Within minutes after the door closed, we eased into traffic, leaving the airport property and picking up speed on the highway.

From where I was seated, I couldn't see ahead of us but instead to the side. Through the darkened windows the scenes were similar to what I'd seen on the drive to the airport. Buildings of various sizes were on both sides of the interstate as cars and trucks vied for their lanes.

Within my purse, my phone buzzed.

Taking it out, I swiped the screen and entered my new password. An unfamiliar icon resembling an envelope appeared with the number one in a red bubble. I clicked it.

The email came from 'Customer Service Professionals'—a nice generic identity.

ARE YOU ALONE?

A smile came to my face. The sender was hardly generic. No, he was an incredibly handsome man who had rekindled a part of me I'd long forgotten. With a spark in his blue eyes, he'd resurrected a flame.

I replied.

YES, ONLY THE DRIVER AND ONE OTHER OF MARION'S MEN.

. . .

The email chain continued.

WE CAN SEE YOUR LOCATION. I'M WITH YOU.

"Ms. Miller." The voice came through the speakers.

I looked around for a button to push or a way to respond.

"On the armrest."

Finding the button, I pushed. "Yes?"

"The bar is fully stocked. There is champagne, a variety of wines, and of course, water."

"Thank you."

"With the current traffic, we should arrive at Mr. Elliott's ranch in forty-five minutes."

"Thank you," I said again, releasing the button and relaxing against the seat.

Reaching into the small refrigerator, I removed a glass bottle of water, and located a glass. I poured myself a small swallow. The cool liquid was refreshing. Refilling the glass, I took another drink.

As I did, I contemplated my current thoughts. I should probably be nervous or frightened, but I wasn't. I'd been through too many things to be either. And this time I wasn't alone. I had Patrick and his men within earshot.

In reality it was the length of the day that was catching up to me. It was early Sunday evening, and I hadn't slept since waking Saturday morning. My head shook as I watched the scenes change out my side window. The urban setting was waning, giving way to open landscapes as beautiful colors of dusk filled the sky.

Removing my shoes, I tucked my feet under my legs. As I did, I began a mental rundown of the last thirty-six hours. In all reality, it seemed as though I'd lived a lifetime in that span. The different scenes came back to me.

Waiting for Mitchell to arrive to my room.

Marion's car and Andros's surprise visit.

Progressing to the final round of the poker tournament and having dinner with Marion.

My gut twisted with the recollection of my failure, at losing everything in the final hand.

Everything.

The money.

The game.

The tournament.

Ruby.

Even Andros.

My skin bristled as I recalled the scenes in the tournament hall. After declaring war on the Sparrows, Andros dismissed me, leaving me high and dry and alone at Club Regal. Not alone. I had Patrick. I told him the truth. He had a daughter —we had a daughter. His demeaning search concluded that, in fact and unbeknownst to me, I was wearing a wire, one that transmitted to Andros. And through that transmission, I'd revealed a secret, one I'd held in my heart for seventeen years. Andros Ivanov now knew my secret: I'd always known the identity of Ruby's father.

I'd flown with Patrick to Ann Arbor only to abort the landing, fly to Corpus Christi, and then to Dallas.

Even recounting the day and a half was exhausting.

The car swayed gently, the tires humming below us on the

open pavement. One blink and then a longer blink, my eyes closed.

"It's only for a short rest," I told myself as I settled against the soft seat.

PATRICK

$\mathcal{T}$he suite next door to mine and Madeline's was larger, taking up a significant portion of the hotel's top floor. Reid had both suites secured under the name of one of our hundreds of shell corporations. The space was our new satellite command center—our home in Dallas. It contained four attached bedrooms, three in use for my associates: Garrett, Christian, and Romero. The main portion held a kitchen, a large living room, and attached dining area. No longer resembling a hotel room, my men had procured and set up multiple computers, screens, and other equipment. It now looked like a mini version of what we had in Chicago.

With our secure network, we had communication with the Sparrows back in Chicago as well as the ability to utilize much of the software located 950 miles away.

The unused bedroom was my private area, a space to speak to Reid, Mason, and Sparrow or call on my current associates one-on-one. It wasn't that I didn't trust this activity around Madeline. It was that I wanted to spare her what we were doing, allowing her to concentrate on Ruby.

As soon as she returned from Elliott's ranch, that was where I wanted her, in our suite, safe and sound.

One screen upon what was once a dining table was subdivided with different live views of the perimeter of Ivanov's island retreat. "I'd do anything to get footage inside," I said to no one in particular. "You know he has the place monitored and can probably see in every damn room."

"So does Mr. Murray in the tower," Garrett replied. "Yet footage within Sparrow can't be accessed. I'd like to think we have the best of the best..."

"We do," I interjected.

"We do," Garrett went on, "and technology changes daily. Ivanov wouldn't be in his position if he didn't have good people too. I know Mr. Murray is working on accessing it, but right now he's running into firewall after firewall, blocking his access."

I knew that what Garrett was saying was correct. I may not be as technically adept as Reid and Mason, but I was better than the average hacker or perhaps more efficient than the people employed by our government—well, the ones on actual payrolls. The organization Mason had been a part of was an entirely different level of intelligence.

Staying a step ahead of law enforcement agencies took constant work and understanding.

For some reason my mind went back to the trafficking operation Sparrow closed down nearly eight years ago when he took over Chicago. The repercussions were widespread, rattling the country and world with aftershocks and still occasional tremors.

Of course, it was the latest twist to the McFadden side of the business that more recently reinvigorated the tectonic-plate shift.

Seeing the technological ability in this suite reminded me how the way Sparrow's father had done business wouldn't work today. The human trafficking/involuntary servitude taskforce, with or without the help of the FBI, would have it closed down and everyone indicted before breakfast. We'd found proof of their operation occurring when Sterling Sparrow was a young boy. No doubt at the time, they thought they were cutting edge with private online chat rooms and live feeds. That didn't even scratch the surface of the operation. There were also the tried-and-true rings of forced prostitution involving minors and non-minors alike. There were parties and auctions as well as sales chains.

The Sparrows—before our current leader wiped out the old regime—and the McFaddens agreed to share the market. We'd worked to close down the Sparrow side. While we weren't the ones who uncovered all of Rubio McFadden's dirt, we simply exposed it to the world and let the authorities do their job.

Sometimes it was nice to remind ourselves that while we didn't play by conventional rules, we also didn't advocate the sale of women and children. I realized it wasn't a high bar, but it was one we exceeded—Sparrow's passion. He'd come into wealth because of his parents, his mother's money and father's business sense. That didn't mean he approved of all his father had done.

Closing down the Sparrow side of trafficking in Chicago had been Sterling Sparrow's mission since he was young. When we all met in basic training, we found we had similar desires. Mason lost his youngest sister. It's never been proven that she was placed in that horrific world. Of course, it was never proved that she wasn't. Sometimes the unknown is worse than the known. While I never told the others about Maddie, I would suspect that losing her when I did and believing she was dead helped shape my longing to end that particular corruption involving women and children. Reid had his own reasons, and together, we vowed to stop at nothing.

The ripples Sparrow's abrupt shutdown created exceeded our expectations, creating an even more dangerous world involving others who were determined to take back Chicago and reinstate business as usual. It's easy to concentrate on the victims. They should be the focus. Currently, that was Sparrow's wife's mission. She began a foundation centered on helping victims of sex trafficking. Mason's wife's mission was more scientific, a drug to suppress traumatic memories. She was fucking brilliant, and while her formula had awakened turmoil, she was still determined to succeed. Now with the help of the Sparrows, she was closer to her dream.

We were prepared for what would happen in Chicago, we thought. In reality the shock waves occurred throughout the merchandising chain. Shutting down the core outfit, the stables—as Allister Sparrow's men referred to them—were the first dominos in a long line to fall.

Anger and violence flared up all around the city and country. Customers lost their ability to act upon their sick-as-fuck desires. Finders and suppliers lost their source of income. Managers who ran the facilities where people paid a price to live out their sick fantasies, as well as those who transported the victims to willing customers, were affected.

We uncovered that victims were typically used until their

usefulness expired. According to some of the records we found in Allister's safes, the reasons for their dismissal varied. It ranged from mental instability to physical infirmity. Often, he or she was damaged by a customer or sometimes despite the attempts to stop it, pregnancy occurred.

Sales channels for all of the various situations had been established. A healthy baby could be sold for a profit above that of sustaining the pregnancy. When it came to selling the victims, most channels led beyond the border of our country. Again, it was a network of people, transporting and delivering.

Truly the fallout mushroomed larger than we'd anticipated.

For years it was a tempest, waxing and waning with the focus on retaliation against Sterling Sparrow. And through it all, we prevailed, keeping Chicago under Sparrow reign.

That wasn't to say Chicago was without crime or to insinuate that the Sparrow outfit didn't profit handsomely from illegal activities. It simply meant that as a young boy, the leader of our outfit sought to right one wrong, and while he— we—were guilty of a million sins, that one point of redemption still remained.

"Mr. Kelly," Romero called from the dining room, "are you watching Ms. Miller's GPS?"

I had been earlier, but since confirming her safety in the car, I'd been concentrating on other things. "Why?"

"I wasn't watching or listening," he said. "I've been watching the island retreat. I'm sorry."

My skin bristled beneath my linen shirt. "Why are you sorry?"

He pointed to one of the screens. "It's no longer recording a heart rate."

I took a step closer. "What about the audio?"

"It's muffled, sir. Like it's been placed inside of something."

Did she take it off?

Would she do that?

Why?

I reached for a pair of earphones. "I want the recording and keep monitoring the live feed."

A few hits on the keyboard and I was able to go back in time to before the necklace stopped broadcasting. Closing my eyes, I listened as I followed the GPS indicator en route to Elliott's ranch. I'd listened to most of this in real time. There was nothing to hear as Madeline's heart rate remained steady.

The corresponding map showed the car entering the ranch. According to satellite footage, the road to the house was rather long. Finally, the car came to a stop. A minute passed and then another.

Why wasn't she getting out of the car?

After nearly four minutes, the sound of a door opening could be heard.

"Madeline." Even with only one word, I recognized Elliott's drawl. "Madeline, dear."

I sat taller, my eyes opening wide as I waited for her response.

The voices were now farther away, coming through a vacuum. There was more than one, some raised and others steady. I couldn't make out their words as I waited for Madeline to speak.

"Lift her carefully." Again it was Elliott. "Take her upstairs."

"Sir, is she all right?" It was a woman speaking.

"Eloise, as I mentioned, Ms. Miller has undergone a difficult time. I'm sure she's simply exhausted. Follow David upstairs and help her to rest comfortably."

A difficult time?

I sat taller. Without confirmation, I could assume Madeline was unconscious, most likely drugged. Yes, you asshole, that was a difficult time.

Madeline wouldn't take off the necklace of her own free will.

"Yes, sir."

I paused the recording. "They fucking drugged her. She's unconscious."

All three men were standing near me. Garrett had his phone out, relaying my findings to someone in Chicago.

The next few minutes were nothing more than footsteps and breathing. I could only assume she was in this man David's arms.

"You may go now," the woman said. "I'll help Ms. Miller."

The heart rate upon the screen stopped. A few minutes passed, and the sound grew muffled as it had been when I listened live.

Unable to stay seated, I threw off the headphones and stood. "Goddamn it. She's unconscious and a woman removed the necklace."

"Do you think she knew it was a transmitter?"

"I don't know. She didn't say. I heard Elliott, but he wasn't alone. I don't know if the other voices were Ivanov and

Hillman or maybe his drivers and staff. Whoever is responsible for this has her now at Elliott's ranch."

"Sir," Garrett said, handing me his phone, "Mr. Pierce would like to speak to you."

I reached for the phone and putting it to my ear, I stalked into the fourth bedroom. "What? Tell me you're still in Chicago."

"I am. You're right. I'm staying with Sparrow, but you need to get your fucking head on straight."

"Come again," I said as the muscles in my bicep tightened as did my grip upon the phone.

"Someone removed the necklace," Mason said too calmly.

"That's not a newsflash. If you were fucking listening, you know that's what happened. She's also unconscious."

"Right, I was listening. Were you?"

"What the hell do you mean?" I asked.

"Did the woman sound nefarious? Was she harming Madeline?"

My head shook. "Nefarious, no. Harming, I don't know what the fuck she was doing."

"We pulled the recording here," Mason said. "We all listened as you did. The woman's words were that she would help Madeline. *Help*, Patrick."

"She's been drugged or something. She's not asleep." I ran my free hand over my head. "I'm going there, now."

The voice on the other end changed; no longer Mason, it was Sparrow. "No, you're not. If you do, you'll give away your location. Ivanov and Hillman are still on the ranch. Ruby is still in the island retreat. We have a photograph from a drone of a young woman we believe is your daughter. She was out by the pool near the gulf. Does that sound as if she's in danger?"

Sighing, I sat on the edge of the bed. "Madeline was right. Ruby's safe at the retreat."

"It appears that way. And with the picture we have confirmation."

"We'll keep an eye on everything from here and you from there," Sparrow said. "I'd be fucking irate if this were Araneae, but think about the positives."

"They aren't exactly clear at this moment," I replied.

"We have known locations for both of them. We have both places monitored. No one is coming or going who we don't see."

Though he couldn't see me, I nodded. "Send me the picture," I said.

"We think it's her."

"Madeline showed me a few different shots. I'll know. Send it."

"Stay fucking put," Sparrow said. "Let us work on this. We need to know Ivanov and Hillman's plans before we make a move. Right now, we're still putting out fires around the city. Stupid shit that is meant to distract us."

Fuck.

"Concentrate on that," I said. "I've got this."

"Oh fuck no. Distractions mean something big is coming. We cleaned house. Word is out that either they're with us or they will end up in a barrel. Hillman's losing his contacts, which means so is Ivanov. We have eyes everywhere. You aren't storming into another ambush. Besides, we've been talking about Madeline's theory."

I'd called Mason and filled him in on Madeline's thoughts about Ivanov's enemies from within after she left for the airport. We both agreed there was merit in her observations.

"Reid is searching Hillman's history over the last six months. We'll let you know if we come up with anything."

I appreciated that they hadn't dismissed the idea simply because it came from Madeline.

My phone vibrated. "Is that the picture?"

"Yes," Sparrow answered. "Tell me you won't go in guns blazing, not until we know what's happening."

"I..." I wanted to say fuck it. I was getting Madeline back, but I didn't. "As long as I know they're both safe."

"Wait for my word." It was the last thing Sparrow said before the call ended.

I switched to text messages and opened the picture.

My daughter was a woman. The resolution was poor, but I could see her. She was wearing a large hat over her dark hair. There was a book in her lap, and her long legs were stretched out on the lounge chair near a pool. From her position she could see the gulf beyond the pool's water. It was hard to determine it was her, yet I felt it. Those were Madeline's legs, healthier than we were at that age, but I knew in my heart it was Ruby.

Something else caught my eye as I tried to zoom in further. The grainy quality didn't help, but nonetheless, I was certain that the faint image to her side was a man—I'd guess a rather large man.

"Ruby, is he protecting you or a threat? Is he the man Madeline mentioned?" I shook my head and sent a text to Reid.

SEND MORE PICTURES.

MADELINE

My eyelids felt heavy as I moved against the soft sheets, snuggling within their warmth. The sensation filled me as I woke, my thoughts wandering as I wondered when the last time was that I'd slept so well.

Suddenly, I recalled Marion's car.

Where was I?

My hand went to my neck.

Nothing.

My necklace was gone—my communication with Patrick.

My eyes opened and my head turned from side to side as I looked all directions.

A cold chill settled over me, causing me to pull the covers closer as I tried to make sense of where I was and what had occurred.

I had no memory after the car.

It was as if I were an actor in a theatrical play. The curtain had fallen and I'd missed the next act.

As the reality of my situation consumed my thoughts, my pulse rate escalated to the point of dizziness.

"Stop," I counseled. "You're not back there. This is a bedroom."

Peering under the blankets, I saw I still wore the bra and panties I'd donned back at the hotel. Looking up, I listened. The soft purr of air conditioning was all I could hear as an overhead fan silently circled. Lifting the sheet to my chest, I sat up. With the movement, I evaluated myself—my skin and muscles. Nothing ached or felt sore or violated.

What happened?

Expanding my view, I moved my attention beyond the bed where I'd slept, seeing rays of sunlight shining through slats of plantation blinds, striping the room in golden lines. In the car the sun had been nearing the horizon.

How long had I been asleep?

I took in deep breaths, continually reminding myself to not panic.

As my eyes adjusted to the lines of sunshine, I took inventory of every corner of the room. Soft gray walls and white trim surrounded me, one wall lined with bookshelves and built-in cabinetry. Along with the bed where I sat were the normal bedroom furnishings, bedside stands, lamps, a dresser, and a chest of drawers. Over the dresser was a large mirror. Upon the shelves were spines of books—hundreds of books as well as colorful vases and other knick-knacks.

There was no question in my mind that this was Andros's doing. After all, there was no reason for Marion to drug me. I'd willingly agreed to visit his ranch.

Was that where I was?

Patrick.

My hand again went to my neck.

Oh my God, he isn't with me. He doesn't know where I am or if I'm safe.

What would that mean?

What was happening between the bratva and the Sparrows?

Ruby?

Fighting the bubbling anxiety, I continued my search, and with trembling hands, slowly folded back the blankets.

To my left was a door, slightly ajar.

Tentatively, I moved from the bed. Beneath my bare feet was a soft rug, an island upon which the bed resided. The floor beyond was shiny hardwood. Step by step, I walked toward the door. As I did, I scanned all around, wondering if I was being watched or maybe overheard.

Beyond the doorway, I entered a large attached bathroom. Switching on the lights, the luxurious contents came into view as the surfaces glistened. I ran the tips of my fingers over the hard surfaces of the vanity as I saw my reflection. Though my hair was tousled, I didn't appear worse for the sleep. It was then I noticed that my earrings were also missing.

There was a large glass shower with multiple showerheads and a long tiled bench. Within a corner, surrounded by opaque windows, was a soaking tub, the kind that looked old-fashioned but wasn't. The shelves were filled with various shampoos, conditioners, bodywashes, and lotions.

Hanging upon an ornate hook was a pale green cashmere robe.

After taking care of business, I reentered the bedroom and scanned every surface, hoping to find the necklace. Opening the closet led to the discovery of empty racks. I searched the dresser and chest of drawers next. One by one, I opened and closed each drawer to unfilled spaces. Other than my underclothes, everything I'd worn was missing. Not only worn, but had with me.

My phone.

My handbag.

Still wearing only my underclothes, I walked to the window and peered beyond the blinds.

What would I find?

If I was back in Detroit, it wasn't in the bratva nor anyplace I'd seen before.

I was obviously on a second floor.

The scene beyond revealed I wasn't in Detroit or even Chicago. The sky above was bright cobalt blue and below, green grass filled the space circling the building and going out to an iron fence. Beyond the fence the ground was covered with drier grasses, shades of tan and brown. Farther away, I saw scattered structures in motion. They reminded me of giant hammers, moving up and down.

Oil wells.

I was at Marion's ranch.

Of that I was confident.

That realization gave me strength to learn more.

Whether this was Marion's or Andros's doing, I wouldn't find answers while staying in this room. With the pale green robe as my only option, I went back into the bathroom and removing the soft material from the hook, wrapped it around my body and tied the sash.

The last door begged for my attention.

The small hairs on my arms stood to attention as I moved closer.

What if it didn't open?

What if I were locked inside?

A grumbling sound came from my stomach, its growl echoing within the walls of the bedroom. I couldn't wait much longer. I had to try.

Reaching out, I grasped the larger-than-normal knob and turned.

As the mechanisms within clicked, I let out a breath and opened the door, pulling it inward. The hallway I'd found was empty, no sentry keeping guard or anyone watching the door.

Like wandering a maze, I continued down one hallway and then another. Closed doors lined the walls as I continued, my bare feet upon a soft carpet. Between doors were photographs, large and stunning and mostly of landscapes and oil fields. Nothing mattered but finding an escape.

Finally, I came to the top of a staircase.

It wasn't as grand as I'd expect for this large home.

Sandwiched between walls on each side, the stairs descended to a landing and then turned. Slowly, I stepped down one tread and then another. My ears were on full alert as I listened for anything.

As the staircase made its third bend, voices and clattering came into range.

The bottom of the stairs came to another hallway, and to the right was a large kitchen complete with a staff of three. A large center island dominated the room with oversized appliances. It was a working kitchen, not one where families gathered but industrial. The women wore aprons over their clothes. For a moment, I stood silently watching as one woman cleaned counters, another tended to something on the stove, and a third came and went through another door.

As the third woman reentered from across the room, our

eyes met. She was a bit older with gray hair, a round face, and a growing smile.

"Oh, Ms. Miller," she called, coming toward me and wiping her hands on her apron. "You nearly frightened me to death. For a moment I thought you were a ghost."

A ghost?

Coming to a stop before the stairs, she looked me up and down. "Mr. Elliott asked me to press your dress. I apologize it's not ready. I'll have it up to you after breakfast."

"You have my dress? Do you have my other belongings?"

"Other belongings? I'm not sure what you mean."

"My handbag, shoes..." My hand again went to my neck. "My jewelry."

"Yes, miss. Mr. Elliott asked me to...well, I'm the one..." Her cheeks grew rosy. "I'm Mrs. Worth, but you may call me Eloise."

I took the last step down. "Eloise, are you trying to say you're the one who undressed me?" Perhaps it was my affinity to make people comfortable, but without much knowledge of her, I liked this woman.

"Yes, I did. I'm sorry. You were...a bit incoherent. Very tired," she corrected. "Mr. Elliott explained that you'd been overwrought with recent events."

"I think it was more than that, but I'm not upset to learn it was you and not..." I didn't finish.

Eloise's shoulders came back. "Mr. Elliott, he's a good man. He wouldn't..."

A smile came to my face as my stomach again rumbled. "I guess it's obvious that I'd like some of the breakfast you mentioned." As she started to lead me away, I asked again,

"My jewelry? You see my necklace has sentimental meaning. I would hate to lose it."

"I'll bring it to your room along with your dress, shoes, and other belongings." Her voice lowered. "I can also bring you some fresh undergarments."

"Thank you, Eloise, I would appreciate that."

She stilled. "If there's anything you need, please don't hesitate to ask. The bathroom is fully stocked and your clothes are to arrive this afternoon."

What?

"My clothes?"

"Mr. Elliott hired a personal shopper, but I am certain he won't mind if you decide there are other items you'd like."

"Eloise, I'm not following you. Why would Mr. Elliott be supplying me with clothes?"

A closed-lip smile came to her lips as her head tilted. "I understand. I know nothing has been announced yet. Oh," she said excitedly, "as you probably guessed, the stairs you found are the back stairs for the staff. After you eat, I'll be happy to give you a tour."

Why did I need a tour or clothes?

"Eloise, I'm not staying here."

She leaned closer. "Yes, dear."

This wasn't making sense.

Eloise turned away and began to walk. "Now, come with me. Mr. Elliott is out on the patio this morning. I'm certain he'd like you to join him. Do you want coffee...?" Her questions continued as I followed her away from the kitchen, through a large dining room, a sitting room, and another, until we reached a wall of windows. On the other side, a glass rectangular table with eight large wrought-iron chairs and plush cushions were visible. In the distance were large barn-like structures and miles of fencing.

As Eloise slid the door open, Marion's eyes met mine.

Immediately, he stood, forgetting his iPad and coffee. "Madeline."

Marion was dressed more casually than he had been at the tournament, wearing a light-blue button-down shirt, open at the collar, with sleeves rolled up revealing his tanned forearms. It was tucked into blue jeans and his belt was secured with a giant buckle. His cowboy boots were covered in dust as if he had worn them for working in the corrals I could see, and not for show. Small lines formed around his eyes as he smiled my direction, making me aware of my clothing, or lack thereof.

Tightening the sash on the belt, I took in the fresh air and sunshine streaming through a pergola covered in flowering vines. Looking about the patio, I searched for Andros and Antonio.

"Are you looking for someone?"

I wasn't supposed to know they were there. "I'm just looking. Your home is beautiful."

"I'm so glad you approve," he said as he pulled back the chair to his right. Before I could respond, he rattled off a list of foods for Eloise to bring. Once I was seated, he returned to his chair at the head of the table. The entire time, his blue eyes stayed fixed on me. "I can't believe you're here."

With my hands in my lap, I looked down at the robe and sat taller. "Marion, we need to talk. What happened last night? And what is going on?"

MADDIE

Seventeen years ago

My baby was getting bigger. I hoped I was eating enough for its nutrition. Cindy had been right about my name being called more frequently as my midsection grew. I tried to block out the things the men said. I wasn't certain that they all had mommy fantasies as she'd mentioned. My theory was that it had more to do with an outlet for multiple wants. They had fantasies of what they could and would do to a woman who was pregnant. Perhaps they felt their own wives wouldn't approve or would realize what sick fuckers they married.

That's what we provided. We were their opportunity for the men to live out what they couldn't elsewhere. I even had repeat customers. That sounded ridiculous, but their patronage assured my baby a bit of food.

I'd never been a big fan of peanut butter and jelly as a

child, yet here I craved them. They weren't readily available when I lived on the street. Sometimes shelters and even the mission had them. At the mission I learned it was an economical and yet nutritious option. I remembered Kristine talking about protein in the peanut butter.

I guess it was weird to think of her without dwelling on what she'd done, that she'd sold me. Maybe it was because despite that, for a brief time, she had been my best maternal influence since my own mother. It was hard to remember my parents.

With each passing day, memories of what life had been like before this cell or hopes of what it could be faded farther and farther away. Things like a life with Patrick and a house in the suburbs with a fence seemed ridiculous when food and living to the next day were now my goals.

Miss Warner didn't always provide peanut-butter-and-jelly sandwiches. Sometimes it was bologna or cheese. The bread was always white and chewy, and everything was always cold; a cold piece of yellow cheese or a cold piece of bologna or peanut butter and jelly between two pieces of bread. If we were lucky, if she was in a giving mood, or maybe if we'd especially pleased the customer, there was an extra bottle of water. If that were the case, the water had to be completely drunk upstairs just like the food eaten. Nothing was allowed back into the cell.

Food attracted mice.

That alone, even without the threat of physical punishment, was enough motivation for me. I'd hated mice and rats since moving to the street. They weren't only thieves; they were dirty.

Speaking of which, I'd now experienced a shower. Three

in total. It was everything Cindy had warned. Maybe it was because I was prepared, but of all that had been done to me, it wasn't the worst. That list was too long to rank.

When I was downstairs in the cell, I kept my hands on my stomach. The butterfly flutters had given way to full-out kicks. It was probably because as the baby grew, I didn't. Yes, my midsection had grown, but my circumstances made me a less-than-perfect host.

Some days I'd lay upon the hard concrete and pray for my name to be called, for food and the hope of more water. My needs had become so simplistic. Each movement within me reminded me that taking care of that little being was my only priority.

I vacillated on preferred gender. It didn't matter to me—I just prayed for health. I dreamed of holding a small baby in my arms and counting the fingers and toes, staring into eyes like mine or Patrick's, smelling the sweet baby scent.

I dreamed about that, but with each passing day feared it wouldn't happen.

My baby was to be sold.

It wasn't a secret.

We all knew.

Would a boy bring a higher price or a girl?

I didn't know how any of this worked, but my hope was that the more someone paid, the better chance my baby had of having a good life. Maybe he'd live in one of the big houses downtown or perhaps out in a suburb, like Patrick and I had talked about.

The two of us wouldn't have the white picket fence, but perhaps our child could.

The girls in the cell were now up to twelve in number. I

knew names because I heard them called. I knew faces because what else was there to see? I even knew the color of dresses. My white one was hardly white any longer. Everyone's was in varying states of tattering. Showers were not accompanied by clean clothes or even cleaning the ones we wore.

I knew all of this. My thoughts didn't linger on any of it.

Call it a defense mechanism. Over time I'd grown close to Cindy. She was easy to talk to and it helped to know I wasn't alone. We were all scared. We all hurt physically from what the men did to us and from sitting and sleeping on the cold, damp concrete. We were all hungry and thirsty all the time. We would talk about an entire loaf of bread as if it would be the greatest thing in the entire world. More than that, we all hated everything about here and these people and at the same time, we all loved our unborn babies.

A week ago, Cindy's name was called. She squeezed my hand before answering.

"Yes, Miss Warner. Thank you, Miss Warner."

By the time my name was called she hadn't returned. I wasn't too concerned. Some customers were quick while others liked to take more time. And since our food came in the same room where we'd been taken, I knew I wouldn't see her again until we were back downstairs. When I returned to the cell, I scanned the faces. I didn't have to ask. The other girls simply shrugged and looked away.

Finally, I asked one. Her name was Jules. She'd arrived after I had. She was quiet and kept mostly to herself. I sat down beside her. "Jules, did Cindy come back?"

At first I wasn't certain she heard me and feared speaking louder. We'd both be punished if we were caught talking. I laid my hand on her leg and she immediately withdrew. The action tugged at my heart. I understood her reaction. I had the same one, yet somehow, Cindy and I'd overcome that.

"No," she said curtly. "Please don't talk to me."

I nodded and moved away as new tears bubbled in the depths of my throat.

The next few hours, as I stared out at the other girls, I tried to recreate the fantasy Cindy had once told me. I imagined her, not as she'd been, but clean with washed hair and a warm, fuzzy robe and slippers with a baby in her arms. There would be another couple, the ones who had purchased her child, but they were good with kind hearts. They welcomed not only the baby but Cindy too. She would breastfeed and comfort the infant and then relinquish the baby's other care to the woman who'd purchased that right to be called mother. The man didn't require more of her. She was a nanny, a part of her baby's life.

I'd never know what happened to Cindy, and my future was still unwritten.

Nevertheless, I could dream of a better world for someone who I had considered a friend.

Time had passed since then. I had no way of knowing how much other than the growth of my baby within me. In my normal position against the wall, I alternated between sleep and detached reality.

"Maddie."

My head popped up from where it had been lying upon my updrawn knees. Even with my baby's growth, I was able to sit this way. Maybe I considered it a way to protect my child.

I hadn't heard the door open. In the light from the hallway I saw her silhouette.

"Yes, Miss Warner," I said, pushing my awkward body to my feet. "Thank you, Miss Warner."

Walking around the other girls, I made my way to the doorway. Over the weeks or months, my mindset had changed. I was less frightened by my upcoming assignment and more focused on the food. There had only been one time when I wasn't rewarded. The customer complained that I didn't satisfy his needs.

I wasn't given more information than that.

The next time I tried harder to be what I was supposed to be. I pretended it felt good. I made noises that seemed to encourage him. I kept trying from then on, calling them daddy or sir or whatever title they wanted.

It was demeaning and degrading.

Perhaps that was why that part was no longer my focus. Instead, as I climbed the narrow concrete stairs, I concentrated on the food. I so hoped it would be peanut butter and jelly.

Miss Warner didn't stop at any of the four doors. Instead, she nodded to the large man at the main door, who inserted his key and opened it.

Fear sparked to life like a match struck against flint.

Quickly, the spark ignited until my body trembled with each step. I wanted to ask if I were getting another shower. I wanted to know what was happening, but I knew better than to question.

If doing so wouldn't earn me a sharp swat with her crop, it would land me a full-face slap. One would think they'd avoid damaging the merchandise; however, some of the customers, even if they weren't into inflicting pain, enjoyed seeing the resulting bruising.

We passed the door to the room with the showers and came to another door.

Miss Warner had the key to open this one.

My steps stuttered as I closed my eyes to the light. In the rooms with the men, there were overhead lights. This was different, brighter. I turned my head and squinted as sunshine streamed through windows. After so long without it, its presence overpowered and even disoriented me.

Miss Warner stopped at another door and opened it, revealing a bathroom.

It was a real bathroom with a sink, toilet, and tub with a shower. The curtain hanging to the side was clear and on the counter by the sink was a towel. Inside the shower, I saw bottles of shampoo and bodywash. The only thing missing was a mirror.

Dumbfounded, I stood, my feet rooted in place.

"Well, be quick about it," she said. "Take off those rags, use the toilet, and get in the shower. I'm not leaving you alone. Clean yourself. If you don't do it sufficiently, I will."

I couldn't take my eyes off the bathroom. Not only was it real, it was bright and clean.

How could this be in the same building?

Pulling the dress from my head, I didn't hesitate as I pulled down the remnants of my panties, the same ones I'd put on from the department store. I'd stopped wearing the bra a while ago. With the pregnancy my breasts had grown and the wire in the bra was painful.

Miss Warner went to the shower and turned the knobs. "Use the toilet while we give it a minute to get warm. Collect those filthy rags and place them in the trash." Her nose scrunched as she looked me up and down. "Use plenty of the soap and shampoo. We can't have you smelling like a barnyard."

Toilet.

Warm water.

It was my focus.

"Yes, Miss Warner."

Staying true to her word, Miss Warner remained in the bathroom, watching and directing as I complied with her instructions. I should have cared that she was present. I didn't. After all, she saw us all naked multiple times a day as she arranged our positioning on the bed. After the customers left, we weren't allowed to dress until she entered and looked us over.

We were never told why she did that. I'd like to think she was assuring our safety, but even that was hard to believe. We were instructed to stand at the end of the bed until she approved our status.

The heat in the water brought tingling to my hands and feet. It was painful and also wonderful. The sensation was as if my extremities were finally awaking from hibernation, the blood circulating as it was meant to do.

My senses filled with the aroma of flowers as I lathered my long hair not once or twice but three times. Miss Warner directed my every move, and under the warm water, I was happy to oblige. She handed me a bottle of conditioner and instructed me to massage it in and leave it while I used the bodywash. The conditioner smelled like apples, tart and yet sweet.

I pushed the thoughts of apples and Patrick away, not allowing myself to be sad as I was experiencing this luxury.

The bodywash bottle said Spring Rain. Its scent was also

sweet but fresh. I applied it to the washcloth Miss Warner provided and scrubbed. Beginning with my face, I scrubbed over and over, down my arms and midsection. I gently ran the soft cloth over my now-protruding stomach, wishing I could speak aloud to my baby.

After my skin was red and cleaned to her satisfaction, Miss Warner turned off the shower and handed me a towel. For only a second, I stared up at the showerhead, sad it was over yet happy I'd experienced it.

As I stepped out onto the soft rug, Miss Warner opened a cabinet and removed a razor and shaving cream.

"Do you want me to shave?" I asked.

Her chin rose, letting me know I wasn't supposed to speak. She scoffed. "I wouldn't trust you with a razor." She pointed to the closed toilet seat. "Sit and lift your leg to the tub."

I did as she said.

The shaving cream was cool and tingled my skin.

How long had it been since I'd shaved?

It wasn't something I did on the street. I had at the mission. A memory returned of me excitedly showing Patrick how smooth my legs felt. With a shake of my head, I pushed that away, concentrating on Miss Warner's instructions and actions.

She left no surface untouched as she told me to spread my legs. I'd never before been shaved bare between my legs. It wasn't only there. At one point she told me to bend over the vanity and hold the cheeks of my behind apart.

I winced, holding back tears as the shaving cream foamed around my anus. Swipe by swipe she purged my body of hair until from the waist down I was as smooth as a baby's bottom. My armpits were next.

Once Miss Warner was satisfied, she produced a toothbrush and toothpaste.

While I was excited for the opportunity, the bristles were stiff and my gums bled. She made me rinse and rinse until the red was gone. Next, she instructed me to comb out my long hair. Even with the hose water showers, there were no combs or brushes.

My fingernails and toenails were then trimmed.

Finally, wearing only a towel, I was led by her to another room, following a step behind. At the threshold I stopped, my mind besieged by memories of Dr. Miller's office. Within the room was an examination table, complete with the stirrups.

"Up you go."

MADELINE

Present day

*M*arion laid his hand on the table, palm up. "Madeline, I apologize for the circumstances of your arrival."

I didn't lift my hand to his. "I agreed to come here. You said you could help me with Ruby. I didn't need to be drugged."

"It was a small dose of tranquilizer. I promise it was completely safe."

We stilled as Eloise returned with a cart. As she worked, place settings were set before both of us: a plate, a small glass, and a steaming cup of coffee. On the center of the table was a decanter with more of the caffeine-filled liquid with a small pitcher of cream, a larger pitcher of orange juice, and one of ice water. The next additions were various large dishes with silver lids. As she lifted the first lid, my stomach again revealed my hunger as the magic aroma of bacon saturated the fresh air. By the time she was done, our feast included eggs, potatoes, fruit, and an assortment of pastries.

"Thank you, Eloise," Marion said dismissively.

She smiled my direction. "Ms. Miller, if you would prefer anything else or want to request for future breakfasts, please don't hesitate to ask."

Marion looked my way as the small lines formed near his eyes and his cheeks rose. "Your comfort is our priority. We realize this could be difficult. Of course, I'm here, but know Eloise is also. She's been with me for a very long time and she wants only our happiness."

I looked from one to the next. "Thank you, Eloise. I'm good for today. I don't believe I'll be here for too long."

She glanced at Marion before nodding and backing away.

Once she was gone, Marion reached for the platter of meat and offered it my direction. "I certainly hope you're not a vegetarian. I thought I recalled you having steak in Chicago."

Yes, I was hungry. I wasn't starving. In that I had experience.

Instead of taking the food, I pushed back the chair and stood. "Marion, what is happening? Why is she saying things about clothes being delivered and future menu choices?"

He gestured toward the chair I'd just vacated. "Please sit and eat. You missed your dinner last night."

I spun toward him, my palms slapping my thighs beneath the long robe. "Your semantics are inaccurate. I didn't *miss* dinner. Per you, I was tranquilized. I was never given the opportunity to consume a dinner."

He placed an exorbitant pile of bacon upon his plate

followed by multiple scoops of scrambled eggs and fried potatoes. "I've waited for you to wake, but I am a busy man. I'll eat. You are free to do as you choose."

"As I choose? I'm not following along." I returned to the chair. "Marion, you said you'd help me with my situation with my daughter. I'm not staying here indefinitely. I'm here for your help."

He took a bite of his bacon.

"Are you going to help me with Ruby?" I asked.

"I am. I said I would." He tilted his head toward the plate. "Eat and we'll discuss this."

Shaking my head, I added eggs, fruit, and two pieces of bacon to my plate and filled the small glass with ice water. I couldn't deny it looked and smelled delicious. Marion was also right about the length of time it had been since I'd eaten. As I lifted a forkful of eggs, my stomach again growled. I would have liked to pretend it went unheard, but by Marion's quick glance and grin, I knew it hadn't.

"Tell me about her," he said, lifting his coffee. "You didn't mention her while we were in Chicago."

"Her? My daughter?" I didn't need him to nod. I knew who he meant. "She's beautiful."

"As beautiful as her mother?"

My cheeks filled with warmth, but I didn't address his comment. Instead, I went on, "I don't talk about her because she isn't part of my gambling persona. She's more important than that." I sat back and looked him in the eye. "She's everything to me. By not mentioning her, I can keep her away from the public eye. Marion, I miss her."

"What does she enjoy doing?"

"Everything. She loves to read and she's quite talented

with drawing. Her medium is charcoal. Her instructors even
agree that her work is impressive. And her smile..." I went on
talking, eating, and sipping coffee. The entire time Marion
listened, genuinely listened. It wasn't until my plate and cup
were empty that I sat back. "Please tell me what's happening."

"Let me tell you a story."

"Marion—"

He lifted his hand. "You told me something personal. It's
my turn."

"Okay." I refilled my cup of coffee, added cream, and sat
back.

"I'm sixty-seven years old."

Marion Elliott was in good condition for his age. While
his skin showed the signs of years in the sun, his body seemed
strong and healthy, as if it belonged to a man a decade
younger. I presumed it was the result of working on this
ranch. "I've googled you as I do all of my opponents."

"First, little lady, let's forget that label. I don't want you to
be in opposition to me or vice versa."

I sat taller. "Go on."

"What I'm about to tell you isn't on Google or any other
search engine. I've purposely kept it out of my biographies."
He exhaled. "I believe I did that for the same reason as you
with your daughter. What I'm about to say is also more
precious to me than all the money..." He tipped his chin
toward the corrals, barns, and stables. "...or possessions I
could ever accumulate. This isn't something for the public to
discuss or debate. It's mine."

Marion Elliott had my attention.

"Over thirty years ago my life ended, or should I say I
wanted it to." He took another drink of his coffee. "I lost my

wife and daughter in a small plane crash. They were on their way to meet me for a spontaneous vacation near the coast. It wasn't a long flight. Hell, I had made it the day before to meet with investors. My daughter was fourteen. I should have insisted they come the day before with me, but my daughter didn't want to miss school. I should have returned and traveled with them. There are many things I should have done. It's too late for every one of those things."

I heard his pain in each word and empathized with his thoughts. We all had things we wish we'd done differently. "Marion, I'm sorry. I had read where you had been married, but there was nothing..."

"There's a price for everything. One thing that money is good for is keeping certain things out of the public glare."

Ms. Miller, for a moment I thought you were a ghost. I recalled Eloise's greeting.

"Was Eloise with you when...then?" Thirty-plus years was most of my life.

"She was. As you can imagine, we all mourned."

"Do I...?" I wasn't certain how this would sound. "Did she look—?"

"Like you?" he asked, finishing my question. "Yes and no. Her hair was dark like yours, but in reality, you are more dissimilar than similar. She wasn't as tall as you and she carried herself in a different manner."

"Oh."

"I meant that as a compliment, Madeline. She would never have done what you do, going into the spotlight and making a name for herself in poker. If I'm honest, I was fascinated by you—I told you that I entered the Chicago tournament because you were there?"

I nodded.

"I've seen your photos and watched your career. I wanted to meet you because of this." His gaze moved over me. "You're incredibly beautiful and yes, you remind me of Trisha. That was why I wanted to meet you. However, after meeting you, seeing you play, watching you, and talking with you, I wasn't satisfied with a one-tournament introduction. I wanted more. You may recall I invited you here before the final round?"

"I do. Marion, I'm not in a position to offer you any kind of relationship. I like you." I did. "Currently, my priority is getting my daughter."

"I've been made aware of your situation."

"You have? What are you aware of?" I asked, sitting straighter.

"Mr. Ivanov and I have, shall we say, developed a business relationship. I know that the two of you have been..." His lips formed a straight line as he sought the right words. "I know you have history."

Beneath the robe, a chill peppered my flesh with goose bumps.

What did he know?

Did he know that Andros purchased me when I was pregnant with Ruby?

Like a rambunctious filly Marion might sell from one of his stables, I'd been bought to be broken, trained, and rode. I couldn't verbalize that. "It's complicated, Marion. Andros has my daughter, and I must get her back."

"I believe that deal has been made."

"What deal?" I asked.

Marion stood and as he did, he offered his hand.

At the gesture, my thoughts went to Patrick. As I accepted Marion's hand, my free fingers fluttered near my neck.

I needed to find the necklace.

"Madeline, I'm not sorry about last night. There were matters not yet finished that were better discussed without you present. I had hoped it would all be set by your arrival. Unexpectedly, you were able to catch a flight quicker than I imagined. Let me just say, allowing you the opportunity to rest was in your best interest."

Allowing me to rest was translated as tranquilized.

"Matters about me?" I asked. "About my daughter? With Andros?" I looked around. "Is he here?"

"He was, and yes, it was about you and Ruby. I won't lie to you. It's something you'll learn quickly. I'm a straight shooter. I am also not prepared to divulge all the details yet." He grinned. "I like to keep my cards close to my vest. I've already shared more with you than I have with anyone in a long time.

"I'm many things," he continued. "A cowboy at heart—perhaps we can go for a ride later today. An oilman—as you've no doubt seen the wells. I am also a businessman and a negotiator. When I set my mind on something, I go after it. My mind is set."

Retrieving my hand, I took a step back. "On what?"

"No, little lady. The question is *on whom?*"

PATRICK

An hour earlier

"A helicopter," I confirmed, watching the live satellite footage. "Follow it."

We'd been able to see that Ivanov and a pilot were the only passengers. His other associates had boarded a large car.

"It appears," Christian said, looking at security footage from a private airport near Elliott's ranch, "as though Ivanov's plane is being fueled. No flight plan filed yet."

"He's in a hurry if he isn't including his henchmen," Garrett said.

"We can't allow him to move Ruby again," I said. "We all know that the chances of saving a kidnapping victim decrease when they're transported."

"Kidnapping?" Garrett asked as we both watched the helicopter rise over Elliott's ranch. "Ivanov has custodial rights. Mr. Murray located the public records affording him those rights. He could argue in court. If we step in, we're guilty of kidnapping."

"Why?" I asked—not to the person I wanted to ask. Madeline's necklace and phone were both silent.

"Sir?"

"Forget the kidnapping," I said. "Why not adopt Ruby or marry Madeline? I mean, other than the fact that she was still married to me, something she said she never told him. I don't understand."

Garrett shook his head. "There's no record of Ruby's birth occurring in a hospital, nothing that can be found in either Illinois or Michigan. Romero is going through neighboring states, but the birth certificate was eventually issued in Michigan."

And birth certificates were issued in the state of birth. Garrett didn't need to say that aloud. We all knew how it worked. "What about Madeline? Any visual confirmation?"

"No, sir."

I paced back and forth within the suite. "If Ivanov boards his plane, he'll be to Padre Island before us. He already has a head start."

"I don't believe we have the manpower to storm his retreat," Garrett said. "The ranch has less security. Elliott is wealthy as fuck, but he isn't paranoid like Ivanov. His security is top of the line but not as secure as I would assume he believes. Ivanov has manpower, most likely armed. Hacking into computers and disabling alarms is easier and safer for Ruby and Ms. Miller."

"Once this is all over," I said, "I'll recommend that if Elliott wants to continue the company he's keeping, he should consider adding more men."

"My point is," Garrett said, "the ranch has more potential for a rescue."

I stopped and looked again at the helicopter on the screen. "What about Hillman? Is he still on the ranch?"

"We have no indication that he's left," Christian said. "Between here and Chicago, we've had eyes on both the ranch and the retreat consistently since yesterday. Until now, the only coming and going is from verified ranch employees."

"If Ivanov flies to his retreat, what guarantee do we have that he won't move her someplace other than the ranch?" I asked aloud. "He has to know Madeline is there. Why hide Ruby from Madeline only to deliver her?" I had more questions than answers.

"What are our options?" Garrett asked. "Detroit? Mr. Pierce believes he has the location of the bratva command center narrowed down to a few city blocks, but like ours, it's hidden in plain sight, in a populated area of the city."

"I'd like to blow it to ashes," I said. "But not at the expense of innocent people."

Using unsuspecting civilians as shields was part of the world in which we lived. That was why our command center was located near the top of a Chicago skyscraper. The building held thousands of residences as well as hundreds of offices and small businesses. Hell, there was a busy coffee shop on the street level.

The people who paid big money to rent space or who entered each day for a grande latte had no idea that they were in the same building where the Sparrow outfit ruled the city. It wasn't as if we had a neon sign or even etched glass as there was at Sparrow Enterprises on Michigan Avenue, the real estate side of Sterling Sparrow's portfolio.

That gave me an idea. "What about Ivanov Construction?" I asked. "Where are those offices?"

Garrett typed into his phone. "I don't know, but that's a good question."

I sat down near the dining room table and allowed my eyes to momentarily close. I couldn't recall the last time I'd had a good night's sleep. In the middle of the night last night, I'd succumbed to sleep for nearly three hours. Over the span of the last forty-eight hours, that wasn't much.

My mind went over what we knew and what I could learn. I opened my eyes. "I need one of the computers."

Christian stood, hitting a few buttons and pushed one of the many laptops my direction. "Can I help?"

I shook my head as I began accessing the Sparrow servers. "I need to save my wife and daughter and instead of doing that, I'm watching." I looked up. "That fuck is over."

"Sir, Mr. Sparrow—"

I cut Garrett off. "We're not storming the ranch or retreat. Everyone has their talents. Mine is simple and up until now, I've been letting others do their specialties."

Garrett's lips turned upward. "Money."

"Fuck yes," I said. "We need to locate that missing fifteen million, and on top of that, I want in-depth research on all the players here: Ivanov, Hillman, and Elliott. We know that back in Chicago, Leonardo's and Madeline's rooms were paid with shell corporations. Hillman's was too. Dig. Somewhere there's a flaw in their trail. You start on that, and I'm going to check out Elliott. Is he as wealthy as he acts? Where does his money come from, and has he spent any significant amounts recently?"

I lifted my phone and sent a text to Mason.

. . .

WE'RE ON THE MONEY TRAIL. I COULD USE YOUR HELP WITH THE DARK SIDE OF THE WEB. I CAN ACCESS, BUT IT APPEARS IVANOV'S DEALINGS ARE MOSTLY IN RUSSIAN.

For a man who started as a kid from the South Side of Chicago, Mason had an uncanny ability in linguistics—reading, writing, and speaking. He'd be a hell of a lot faster than translation programs.

Mason replied.

ON IT.

"Mr. Kelly?" Romero said. "Flight plan has been filed. Ivanov is headed to Detroit."

I sat back and took my eyes off the computer before me. "He's leaving both of them?"

"That's how it appears."

"Why?"

My phone buzzed with an incoming call. I looked at the screen: *SPARROW.*

"Hello?" I answered.

"Wanted to let you know there's been some action in Detroit."

I stood and walked toward the fourth bedroom. "Action—like what?"

"Distractions. Hundreds of thousands of dollars of damage to a construction site."

A smile came to my lips. "That sounds terrible."

"No casualties, but a crane fell this morning, damaging the structure under construction."

"What company had this bad luck?" I asked.

"Ivanov Construction." Sparrow said. "Would you like to hear the rest of the story?"

"Yes."

"The subcontractor was McFadden Construction. It was. The name was recently changed to Great Lakes."

I let out a sigh. "Yeah, most people don't want to do business with a corrupt politician's company, one convicted in human trafficking. They do have their limits."

"And a fire broke out in a warehouse," Sparrow said, "near the docks in Detroit. It appears that the crates were supposed to contain construction materials. ATF, the Bureau of Alcohol, Tobacco, Firearms, and Explosives, is on the scene."

"Why?"

"Construction materials shouldn't explode," Sparrow said. "It appears, according to the news outlets, that the containers were filled with firearms."

"Who owns the containers?"

"The same shell company that paid Madeline's hotel bill."

I let out a long breath. "No wonder Ivanov is headed back to Detroit."

"Diversions can work both ways. Get ready, Patrick. You have a family to collect."

"Thank you, Sparrow."

"Not yet."

MADELINE

*a*s Eloise showed me an easier way to find my room, I politely nodded and made small talk as Marion's promise gave me strength to take the next step. I recalled our last conversation.

"When I set my mind on something, I go after it. My mind is set," Marion said.

Retrieving my hand, I took a step back. "On what?"

"No, little lady. The question is on whom?"

I stood as tall as my bare feet would allow. "Marion, either you're going to help me get Ruby or I'm leaving."

The glass door opened and Eloise appeared.

"Where is my phone?" I asked her. "I need to call for a car."

Her eyes opened wider as she alternated her gaze between Marion and me.

"Eloise?" I questioned.

"Yes, Eloise," Marion said. "By all means, please assist Ms. Miller

so that she has all of her belongings." He turned back to me. "There is no lock on this ranch. You're free to come and go as you wish. However, I'm expecting a guest this evening, and I would suspect you'd want to be present." He took a step back. "However, little lady, I'm not making any assumptions. Perhaps you'd rather book a flight."

"Who is your guest?"

"I haven't met her yet, but I've been told she's a delightful young lady."

My mouth grew dry and eyes moist as I stared from one person to the other.

Eloise was the first to allow her smile to bloom, lifting her cheeks as her eyes shone in the morning sun. "Please let us know if there's anything particular we should have in Miss Miller's room. It's been a long time since this house has seen a young lady, and I know times have changed."

I focused on Marion as tension flowed from my limbs. I reached for the back of my chair for support. "Ruby? Here? How?"

"You should know," Marion said, "I enjoy keeping some secrets."

"You said you don't lie."

"And I don't." His blue eyes shone. "Keeping my cards hidden for now."

"Ms. Miller," Eloise said, "I came to tell you that your clothes have arrived. May I show you a bit of the house and a simpler pathway to your room?"

"Really, she's going to be here?" I asked Marion as my heart grew heavy with a feeling it was about to burst.

"I hope this is only the beginning of seeing you smile."

"Ms. Miller?"

I turned to Eloise. "Yes, please show me."

As we walked Eloise pointed out different rooms and amenities while constantly reassuring me that everything was available to me. Hardwood dominated the décor, giving it an authentic Texas feel.

Attached to Marion's large home office was an equally grand library with a grand fireplace and shelves that reached to the high ceiling. I recalled the shelves in my room. "Does Marion...I mean, Mr. Elliott...enjoy reading? There are so many books."

"He does. His love of literature came from Mrs. Elliott. They'd passed it on to McKenzie. How about you?"

McKenzie.

"I do. I usually read on my Kindle." I didn't know where it was. "However, I believe diving into real books would be an adventure."

"And Miss Miller?" Eloise asked.

"She loves to read, too. It was an activity that kept her curious mind working while at the same time keeping her from trouble."

Eloise reached out and took my hand. "I can't tell you what this means to us. We're so excited."

For us to visit?

"I hope we can return in the future. I'm thankful for Mr. Elliott's help."

"Let me show you more."

Before going upstairs, Eloise took me to the outdoor pool.

"It's heated, but I'm sure you'd rather wait for warmer weather."

I peered up at the blue sky as the sun shone down upon my face. "This is much warmer than Detroit."

She smiled. "I suppose that's true. I will be sure you have bathing suits delivered if they weren't in this first shipment."

"I'm really not comfortable with Mr. Elliott buying all of this."

"As I said, we're all elated. I promise he doesn't mind. And besides, there is also a sauna and hot tub in the pool house that can be used even in these winter months."

I followed along until we made our way upstairs. The stairway we used was three times as wide as the one in the back of the house. This one had curved architecture giving it a Southern plantation feel. As we walked the hallways, this time I lingered, looking at the photographs of oil wells and beautiful skies filled with oranges and reds of sunsets as well as others with billowing clouds of an impending storm. There were also photographs of horses and beautiful pastures.

"These are lovely."

"Mr. Elliott enjoys photography," Eloise answered.

Really? That was also not listed in his biography. There seemed to be much more to Marion Elliott than I'd realized.

When we entered the bedroom deemed mine, Eloise opened the closet to show me racks of clothes.

"This really isn't necessary."

Next she went to the chest of drawers and opened each one. No longer were they empty, but now each contained some items of clothing including undergarments and lingerie. The final drawer she opened was in the dresser. From its depths she pulled a small wooden box. Placing it on the top of the dresser, she opened it.

"Oh," I said.

Within were my necklace, earrings, and phone.

"Thank you."

She handed me the phone. "I'm afraid it isn't charged. I have a charger downstairs that I can bring up to you."

"Thank you again," I said as I held the necklace between my hands, remembering that Patrick said it charged via body heat. If that were the case, it too was most likely without a charge.

"May I follow you down to the kitchen and get the charger?" I asked. "And then I'll take a shower."

"Certainly."

With my necklace in place, I followed Eloise, this time down the back stairs. On my way back to my room, I found myself once again in the maze of doors when unexpectedly, one opened and a man stepped out.

Startled, I sucked in a breath as the charger slipped from my grasp. "Mr. Hillman?"

Before he spoke, Antonio Hillman unapologetically took me in, from my head to my toes, his dark gaze scanning. With each second, I was more and more aware that my only covering was the pale green robe.

"Ms. Miller."

My gaze scanned from right to left. "Is Andros...?"

"Is he here?" Antonio asked as he took a step toward me. "No. He was called away." Antonio bent down and picked up the charger. "I believe you dropped this."

Taking it from him, I nodded. "Yes, well, I need to change."

"You don't remember me, do you?"

I took a step back as instinct bid my feet to run. "I'm afraid I don't."

"We've actually met a few times. The tournament was the first time we were properly introduced."

"I'm sorry, I don't recall."

A closed-lip smile came to his face. "I never forgot you."

My head shook. "I do need to be going."

"Elliott thinks he has this wrapped up. He doesn't know that I have bigger plans than both of them."

Another step back. "Mr. Hillman, I really must pass through."

He stepped to the side with a grand gesture. "Do you know what piques my interest in..." He shrugged. "...anything?"

"I'm sure it's a fascinating story. Perhaps another time."

"Competition," he continued. "I thrive on it. You see I don't seize opportunities that no one else wants, even if they're ripe for the picking. I like to watch to see what is trending. I love to watch."

I clenched my teeth as he spoke, praying he wasn't insinuating a different kind of voyeurism. "Another time," I said again as I stepped past him, praying he wouldn't decide to reach out.

"Madeline."

I turned around, breathing easier since I'd made it closer to my room. "Yes?"

"Another time," he said with a grin.

Turning away, I hurried down one hallway and then another. By the time I reached the hallway with my bedroom —thank goodness I'd left the door open—I was running and nearly out of breath. A quick glance over my shoulder confirmed I wasn't followed.

Once inside, I closed the door and fiddled with the lock, hoping it worked.

As the mechanisms engaged, I took a deep breath and then another until my pulse found its normal rhythm. I couldn't pinpoint why Antonio Hillman made me so uncomfortable or why I'd had that reaction. I just knew he did.

Plugging in my phone, I stepped into the large bathroom and turned on the shower.

MADDIE

Seventeen years ago

ears filled my eyes as I looked at the examination table, yet I didn't argue.

Sometime during the last few months, my will to fight had died. I'd become a shell of a person who obeyed to be fed, no different than a stray dog begging for food or performing tricks for treats.

I sat on the edge in silence until the door opened.

The person who entered looked like a doctor—more than Wendy had at Dr. Miller's. This woman wore a white lab coat over her clothes and had a stethoscope around her neck. She didn't address me upon entry, mostly speaking to Miss Warner. The only exceptions were when she asked me a direct question.

"Any pain?"

I looked to Miss Warner.

"Answer her, girl."

"Sometimes during sex."

She seemed unconcerned. "How about regularly? Any tightening of your uterus or lower back pain?"

Other than that back pain caused by sitting on a concrete floor?

"No," I replied.

"Do you feel the baby move?" she asked.

"Yes."

"Lie back."

She laid the stethoscope on my midsection, moving it from one side to the other. "Strong heartbeat," she said.

My heart leapt as I longed to hear what she had. Of course, it wasn't offered to me and with Miss Warner standing guard, I knew better than to ask.

The doctor took a measuring tape and measured from my belly button down to I didn't know where. Then she measured from the top of my baby bump, again down.

"Scoot back and put your heels in here," the doctor said, pointing to the stirrups.

The conversation from that point on excluded me. I was present, the subject of their comments, but at the same time, I wasn't.

I listened as she spoke, poked, and prodded.

Using a cool gel, she placed something inside me; after removing it, she pushed her finger inside first my vagina, and then my anus.

"Malnourished," the doctor said, "but the baby takes what's needed. It doesn't leave much for her. The girl is measuring thirty-two weeks. Her cervix is healthy and there's no visible sign of disease, open lesions, or discharge. Still, we should run a panel. She does have various stages of lacerations and contusions. Some, like her anus, will take time to heal."

"How long?" Miss Warner asked.

"I recommend no anal and a topical medication. It would be good for a more hygienic atmosphere and an antibiotic for good measure. If you follow that protocol, I'd say a week or two and she can resume normal activity."

Miss Warner shook her head. "We don't have that kind of time. Can they be covered?"

What did she mean?

"The first option would be best for her."

"She isn't my concern," Miss Warner said. "Can the bruises and cuts be hidden long enough to withstand the auction?"

Auction?

The doctor sighed. "Yes, I believe so. Over there." The doctor pointed at the cabinets. "In that second drawer."

Miss Warner stepped away from my view. When she returned, she had what looked like a tray of makeup, containers with multiple shades of flesh tones.

"I'll apply a layer of antibiotic ointment first and we can cover most of the bruising. There's some on her legs and arms too. Do you want them all covered?" The doctor shrugged. "I suppose it depends. I've heard that some buyers like to know how much their purchases can withstand."

Miss Warner shook her head. "This is a special audience. Cover them all."

I gripped the edges of the table as the two women critiqued my body and all of its parts. They discussed shading as if I were a canvas, a piece of art. I supposed that was true. I was. Such as a piece of art at a show, I was about to be auctioned and sold to the highest bidder.

The more the idea settled, the less disconcerting it was.

I had no doubt. They'd totally broken me.

Yet in this unreal situation, I chose to see hope.

I hadn't given birth, and I was to be auctioned.

Did that mean I'd be with my child?

As I lowered myself from the table and continued to follow their instructions, I held on to that hope.

Once the doctor left, Miss Warner applied makeup to my face. I was certain it was to accomplish a similar goal of covering bruising—however, I hadn't seen my reflection in months so I truly didn't know. As she applied color to my cheeks, the last sandwich I'd eaten percolated in my stomach and threatened to reappear. Flashbacks of the department store caused my knees to weaken.

"Stand still, girl."

Inhaling, I complied, fully naked before her.

Girl.

Miss Warner knew my name, called it multiple times a day, and yet, when she addressed us personally, we were all *girl*.

"Close your eyes."

Eye shadow and liner were applied, followed by mascara. Lip stain was next and then a gloss.

I flinched as she ran her finger over the areolas of my breast. Whatever she was applying reminded me of the rouge I'd seen on my grandma and her friends when I was very young.

"Men like to see darker nipples and areolas. It makes them believe you're aroused." She looked up at me. "This is a unique opportunity. Behave or you'll end up back here. If that happens, that ass of yours will never heal. I'll make sure of it."

My eyes widened as her words settled in. If it went well, I could never return. If it didn't, I would.

"What do you say, girl?"

"Yes, Miss Warner. Thank you, Miss Warner."

The dress she provided was more of a drape, white, flimsy, and mostly transparent. It lay over my shoulders and was cinched at the waist by a gold rope-like belt. My hair was dried and wrapped into a bun or twist at the back of my head and secured with a clip. Lastly, she provided a long cape to cover the transparent draping slash dress.

"Follow me," she instructed.

I looked down at my still-bare feet, and then quickly followed to a waiting car.

As I stepped from the building, I expected the cold and snow I'd last experienced. Instead, I lifted my face to the dark sky. The breeze upon my skin was balmy. Above me, leaves rustled in the trees. My baby hadn't been the only change over time. The seasons had also changed.

I didn't even know what month it was.

An unfamiliar large man opened the back door of a car.

Miss Warner looked me up and down. "Make me proud, Maddie. You can do this. You're one of Dr. Miller's girls."

She used my name.

It was a small thing, and yet for some reason, it filled me with gratitude.

"Yes, Miss Warner. Thank you, Miss Warner."

I sat in the back seat. As the man closed the door, I heard Miss Warner's instructions. "The senator is expecting her for an important guest. Don't touch her. We have plenty here for that."

I didn't hear his response.

Once the man was in the car, I couldn't shake the feeling that he was watching me in the mirror. I tried to look around, to gather information on where we were or where I had been. My arrival to this place was fuzzy at best. After Dr. Miller's office and my introduction to hell, I fell asleep. I didn't know if I'd been drugged or simply exhausted from the four rounds of sex and abuse. When I woke, I was in a moving van and blindfolded.

From what Cindy told me, the blindfold was a pretty standard thing. Everyone's first memory of the place we'd been was being forced down the concrete stairs.

Scenes continued to pass by beyond the car windows. Although I'd lived most of my life in Chicago, I didn't recognize the area. It struck me as surreal that for as awful as the cell, work rooms, shower room, and everything was inside, that beyond its door, the world appeared completely normal. No one would know that girls and women were being held without their consent amongst these normal dwellings. There were no signs, and the area wasn't run-down.

All around us was middle- to upper-class standard fare.

Such as the men who used us, exteriorly everything appeared normal and unsuspecting.

Invisible.

That's what we'd been.

Cindy.

Jules.

Others.

Me.

No one saw us, though we were right under their noses.

I'd accomplished my goal. I was invisible.

For a moment, I considered speaking to the driver, asking for him to not carry out my delivery to this auction. I imagined begging him to help me escape. Even my imagination was now tainted, not in rose-colored glasses as I'd once heard. No, mine was tainted by reality. This man wouldn't help me and if he did, I'd be exchanging one hell for another. I knew what men were capable of doing. Maybe the auction was my best hope.

On the sides of the street, the sizes of the houses grew. And then as the streets wound around, houses were no longer visible. Tall hedges, wrought-iron fences, columns, and gates were all that was seen.

My empty stomach twisted as my pulse quickened. It was too late, and I was without choice. Sitting here was the waiting period—similar to being positioned upon the bed. This was the time questions filtered through my mind.

Who was the honored guest, and what would it be like to be auctioned?

Would he like me?

Would he take me with him or would I be returned back to the cell?

How sick was it that I was hoping for the first?

The car stopped. I tried to look out to see where we were, but all I saw was a tall wall with ivy and decorative lights.

It was normal from the outside.

The inside, invisible to the world.

When the door opened, the driver held a satin blindfold. He didn't tell me what he was going to do, but I knew.

Without a word, he placed it over my eyes and tied the back behind my head.

Voices came into range.

A woman.

"Thank you." I heard her say. "Here's a healthy tip from the senator. Have a nice evening, Jimmy."

"You too, ma'am. Glad to be of service."

"This way, girl," she said as she helped me from the car and led me by my elbow.

Girl.

I was back to girl.

"Steps."

I listened to her directions as if she were leading a blind person. Turn right. Take three steps. Through it all, I only stumbled a few times. When I did, I quickly regained my poise before actually falling.

Such as a person without sight, I had to use my other senses.

Based upon the change in sounds and lack of breeze, I surmised that we were now inside the house, behind the tall wall with ivy, into a world that many never saw. The surface beneath my bare feet changed as I was led by the elbow: cool tile, soft carpet, hardwood, and back to tile. The air was filled with the aromas of food, cooked and baked.

My stomach grumbled, remembering what it was like to eat anything warm.

"Do you need a drink of water?" she asked.

Water wouldn't quench my hunger, but it would help. "Yes, please."

"Polite. You've been well trained." She reached for my hands and placed a glass in my grasp. I lifted it to my lips. It was water. It shouldn't be spectacular, but it was. Each swallow was cool and clear, the freshest I'd ever had.

I couldn't stop drinking.

When the glass was empty I extended it toward where I believed she was standing, hoping for more. I must have been right about the location because she took it away.

"I'd offer you more, but it's better if your bladder isn't full."

The heaviness of the cape came off my shoulders as the chill of air conditioning permeated the sheer dress. The coolness caused my nipples to draw tight.

"Oh, I think you will do well." She again reached for my arm. "Come this way."

I heard the voices and smelled the aromas before we reached our destination. Unlike the stale cigarette scent often associated with many of the customers back at the cell, the fragrance permeating the air was rich. I recognized it as tobacco in different flavors, such as cherry and birch.

My feet stilled. The last time I'd smelled those scents were from the men at Dr. Miller's.

"This way," the woman said. Whispering close to my ear, she warned, "Keep your hands at your side and do as you're told."

Could I run?

Where was I?

I heard the opening of a door. The murmur of voices stilled as the woman took me across another threshold. The floor beneath my feet was again hardwood and then a carpet.

"Gentlemen," a man announced, "our attraction has arrived."

MADELINE

Present day

*T*hroughout my shower, I heard noises, sounds I couldn't identify. Were they real or was it my overactive imagination? I couldn't be certain; then again, my imagination wasn't simply make-believe. It had the benefit of real-life monsters to recall. They weren't the things of movies, TV, or books, but of real life. They were monsters who wore suits and expensive, spicy cologne. They were shape-shifters who appeared innocent one minute and became predatory the next.

I'd spent my life accepting whatever came my way.

A man with no name whose presence would reward me a small amount of food.

A transaction that reduced my worth to dollars and cents.

Andros Ivanov, a man who took the pieces of a broken girl,

ground them to dust, creating a pliable clay, and recreated a woman to his satisfaction.

I was tired of being who others wanted me to be.

In the short time I'd spent back with Patrick, I'd remembered what it was like to be loved for simply being me. He'd tended the spark that had nearly extinguished and brought to life a flame. I wouldn't let Antonio Hillman or Andros Ivanov threaten my future. After all, Andros abandoned me.

Looking in the mirror as water dripped from the length of my hair, I tried to recall seeing Antonio Hillman before the tournament. When I did, I'd had the feeling that he was familiar, but it was only a feeling.

Why couldn't I recall the time?

With a deep breath, I wrapped a plush towel around my body and willed my feet forward. I wasn't going to hide from these men. I'd spent too much time hiding and staying invisible. I reached up and touched the necklace. While in the shower, I'd done my best to not get it too wet. I didn't want to take it off again and even hoped the warm water would help the transmitter charge.

"I don't know if you can hear me," I said without too much volume, "but I'm safe." I hesitated with my hand on the doorknob. "And I don't care if your men hear. I love you, Patrick. Marion said Ruby will arrive here tonight. I can't leave as long as that's possible."

I turned the knob and pulled the door inward. Even though I knew I'd locked the door from the hallway, I looked in all directions. The bed where I'd slept caught my attention. It was made and neat with pillows upon the satin cover.

Was it made when Eloise and I entered?

I couldn't recall.

Step by step, I moved, my bare feet on the hardwood as I opened the closet. The racks were still filled and appeared untouched. The last place to look was beneath the bed. I was painfully aware of how silly I would look to someone else, yet I didn't care.

Holding my breath, I knelt down and lifted the bed skirt.

Nothing.

Standing, I rechecked the door. The lock was still in place.

I shook my head and bending my knees, I collapsed on the end of the bed.

I hoped the necklace was transmitting again.

There were so many things I wanted to say to Patrick. I wanted to tell him about how odd it was that Marion had bought me clothes—lots of clothes. And tell him that it seemed as though Andros wasn't here. I assumed he was on his way to get Ruby.

Who else would get her and bring her here?

I wanted to tell him that I wasn't the one who removed the necklace. And I wanted to tell him over and over that I loved him, that Ruby would soon be here, and tomorrow he and his men could meet us off the ranch. After all, Marion had said there were no locks. I'd reunite with Ruby tonight and spend the proper amount of time with Marion to thank him for all he'd done.

Standing, I reentered the bathroom.

My feet stilled as I stared at my own reflection.

It had been a long fucking road, but it was almost over.

I couldn't recall the last time I'd been so filled with optimism for the possibility of the future, for a family, a real family.

Thirty minutes later I'd applied a minimal amount of makeup, dried my hair and pulled it back into a low ponytail, and dressed in a pair of blue jeans and a sweater from the closet. It was as I was putting on socks and ankle boots that a knock came on the bedroom door.

In stocking feet, I walked toward the door.

Why didn't bedroom doors have peepholes?

Because most people aren't as paranoid as you are, I answered myself.

"Who is it?"

"Marion."

I hesitated.

"Are you decent?" he asked.

His drawl made me smile. Maybe he was the good man Eloise boasted. "I am." I turned the knob and opened the door toward me. "About to put on boots."

With his hands in the front pockets of his jeans, Marion stepped inside the bedroom, leaned against the wall, and looked around. "Is everything to your liking?"

I scanned the room. "It's beautiful. Your whole house is lovely."

His blue eyes gazed at me, from my head to my toes. "And the clothes?"

"It's really all too much."

Leaving his perch near the door, Marion came closer and reached toward me. When he did, I backed away. It wasn't conscious, more instinct.

His chin rose. "You know I think you're lovely."

"Thank you."

"I'm not a difficult man."

"I can't thank you enough for helping me, for helping Ruby."

He walked toward the closet and opened the door. "For now, this is best."

"What is best?" I asked, more confident with his distance.

"The two of you will have this wing to yourselves, for now."

"Marion, again, I'm not in a position to make long-term plans."

He took a deep breath. "Little lady, will you join me for a tour of the property. We won't cover the entire grounds, but I'd like to show you the highlights."

I recalled him inviting me here during the tournament, and now I'm here. "That sounds nice."

"Would you do an old cowboy the honor of allowing me to escort you?" He asked as he lifted his elbow.

A grin came to my lips. He wasn't that old, not really. However, if his family were alive he could be a grandfather. My hand stopped mere milliseconds before it landed upon his offered arm.

Memories stilled me, as they hadn't in years.

Fathers.

Grandfathers.

Older men.

All at once, I recalled the stench of their bodies and breath, their hands and touch as they violated me.

"Madeline, are you all right? You're white as a sheet."

I inhaled, shaking my head. "I'm sorry. I don't know what just came over me."

"Little lady, you're in good hands. I promise."

In hands.

There were only one man's hands I wanted to be in.

I stepped back. "I really do need to put the boots on first, if we're going outside."

Again, he leaned against the wall, this time with his arms crossed over his chest. "I'll have Beatrice pack us a lunch. After all you've been through, I'm sure you deserve to not be hungry."

Deserve?

A reward?

I looked up. "What do you mean?"

His forehead furrowed as his eyes opened wider. "I merely mean that we like to eat around here, and I like women with a bit more meat on their bones."

After the boots were on, I stood. "Excuse me?"

"Take no offense, little lady. You're perfect the way you are now. Lunch or no? It's up to you."

I pushed away my memories. Scattering away my clouds, as Patrick called them. It was ridiculous that Marion Elliott would know anything about my past. He wasn't one of those men. They were his age then.

Or did they appear older due to my youth?

I reached for his arm, forcing myself to comply. "While we see your property, please tell me a little about yourself. You said you knew Antonio's father?"

"That's boring, water under the bridge."

"Where did he live?" I persisted. "Here in Texas?"

"No. He lived in Chicago with his family."

"His son, Antonio?"

"Yes, and his wife, Ruth. She was always lovely."

"So you would visit them?"

Marion stopped walking as we neared the staircase. "Off

and on. After I lost Trisha and McKenzie, he would invite me to Chicago. Our relationship was mutually beneficial."

"How was that?"

"He worked with a politician who helped me with a few things. In turn, I helped them. All in all, he wanted to help me forget my loss."

"Help you forget? In what way?" I asked.

"That's enough of that. It's time to move forward." Marion gestured toward the stairs. "I didn't ask you if you ride— horses, that is."

"I don't, but I'd be willing to learn." I smiled. "And I would imagine that Ruby would love to try."

"About that, there's been a change in our plans."

I gripped the banister. "A change?"

"Mr. Ivanov was called back to Detroit to handle some business issues. He's no longer able to fulfill his part of the deal and retrieve your daughter tonight."

"What?"

"Thankfully, Mr. Hillman has agreed to take his place."

PATRICK

"Oh fuck no," I said, as the entire room listened to Madeline's transmission. It had begun broadcasting around an hour earlier. "No, Hillman is not to be alone with my daughter."

"Did you hear before that?" Romero asked. "That shit about Hillman's father?"

"It confirms what we already knew," I said, uncertain how well versed these men were on the details of our history. "Wendell Hillman was McFadden's consigliere. That position has landed him his current accommodations in a federal penitentiary."

"But we now have more," Garrett said, "a verbal confirmation that Elliott was involved with the McFaddens. They did favors for one another. We should go back in financials and determine when he was in Chicago. He could be more connected than we realized."

I shook my head. "Yes, we should and can. Tell me how that pertains to our number-one priority. Right now all that matters is Ruby. We need to watch for Hillman's departure."

"Mr. Elliott hasn't mentioned," Garrett said, "anything about Ruby's paternity, you, or the Sparrows. Does he know?"

Fuck.

I wasn't certain of who knew what or even what I knew. "Elliott," I began as I recalled, "was standing there in the poker hall when I learned the news. Ivanov had Madeline's bracelet wired. She said Ivanov gave her the bracelet on her way to the tournament that morning. That means he had access to her throughout the day. He also could hear everything prior to her taking it off.

"Elliott, Ivanov, and Hillman were together most of the day yesterday. I have no idea what they told one another." I began to pace. "Shit, I just remembered that I'd met alone with Madeline before the final round of the tournament."

"Met?" Garrett asked.

"Talked to."

"Was Ruby mentioned?"

"No," I replied. "I didn't know anything about her before Madeline dropped the bomb after the tournament."

"Okay. What did you talk about?" Garrett asked.

I tried to recall.

It was less than a week ago, but it felt like a fucking lifetime. "I had a suite for her at the Hilton. I told her to cash out of the tournament and go to the hotel suite. I said the tournament wasn't safe."

Garrett let out a whistle as he leaned back in his chair. "So Ivanov heard a Sparrow, a top Sparrow, offer his woman—"

Garrett's eyes widened as he hesitated. "...his *player*..." It was probably Garrett's best choice of wording. "...assistance and advice to leave. That means that Ivanov knew Ms. Miller somehow had, maybe even recently, made a connection with you. It also means that he knew the Sparrows knew something big was brewing."

Christian was still wearing the earphones.

I tapped his shoulder. "Anything new?"

He eased one off his ear. "It sounds like they're outside. Ms. Miller offered to go with Hillman, but Elliott insisted he had it worked out. Now, Elliott is rambling on about horses and when the new foals will arrive." He shrugged. "Stimulating."

I patted his shoulder. "Keep us informed."

"A car is leaving the ranch," Romero said. "Look here, it's our friend Hillman."

"Doubt he's visiting his pops in prison," Garrett said.

Rubbing the back of my neck, I continued pacing. "He's going to Padre Island. I can't decide if we stop him before or after."

"*After* would have Ruby out of the resort." Garrett volunteered.

"And with him," I added. The decision was made. "I'm calling Sparrow, and then we're headed down to Corpus Christi. Our best chance to get Ruby is at the airport when they make the transfer from the car back to the plane. They don't know we're even in the state. With the chaos Sparrows are causing in Detroit, they probably think we're there."

All three men looked my direction. I wasn't certain if I saw agreement in their expressions or something less.

Removing my phone from my pocket, I placed the call as I walked to the fourth bedroom.

Instead of being answered, it went to voicemail.

"Sparrow," I said, "Hillman has left the ranch on his way to one of Elliott's planes. We're watching the flight plan. If it's to Corpus Christi, we're following." I realized it didn't sound like a request. It wasn't. "Ivanov's fortress is too well guarded for our manpower." Even if we were successful there, it would result in the deaths of Ivanov's men and I didn't want Ruby to see that. "Our single best opportunity for obtaining Ruby is when they transfer from the cars to the plane at the airport in Corpus Christi. Right now Hillman's alone. His two goons may meet him, but even so, he doesn't have Ivanov's manpower. We also have the element of surprise. Call me if you can."

I hit disconnect and looked out the big windows of the fourth bedroom, wondering what was happening in Chicago, wondering what Elliott's plans were, why he was sticking his neck out for Ruby, and how his plans included Madeline.

"Mr. Kelly," Garrett called from the other room.

When I entered the larger area, Garrett handed me his phone. "Mr. Pierce is on the line and said he didn't want to leave this in a voicemail."

I took the phone. "Talk to me."

"I've been researching Ivanov's offshore accounts. There's no sign of the fifteen million. I've been thinking about that. Since that was cash, there's no guarantee he won't keep it in that form. Unfortunately, the bills weren't marked.

"Yeah, some serious changes are happening before Club Regal reopens."

"Anyway," he continued, "the reason I called is because yesterday Ivanov had a ten-million-dollar infusion."

"And you think it's separate from the cash?"

"I know it didn't come from Ivanov himself. I traced it back to Elliott."

I turned a circle as I blocked out the people around me. "So Elliott is helping to fund the Ivanov bratva, why?"

Garrett's eyes opened wide as he looked my way.

"Hold on," I said to Mason. "What?"

"Flight plan is filed. Hillman is minutes from the airport and the plane is fueled and ready to fly to Corpus Christi."

"Mason," I said back into the phone, "we're headed to Corpus Christi. Hillman's going to retrieve Ruby. I'm not letting that fucker near my daughter for any longer than necessary."

"Sparrow—"

"I left him a voicemail," I interrupted before more could be said. "Man, I need to trust my gut. I've been sitting still on this too long. Besides, the way I see it, we've got advantages here. They don't know we're here. Hillman doesn't have the manpower of Ivanov. And they won't expect us. I feel it...it's now."

"Keep us updated," Mason said.

I appreciated him not trying to talk me out of it.

"Take every precaution," Mason said. "We need you—all four of you—back here. We've got a war going."

"We will."

"Hey," Mason said, "for what it's worth, your gut's track record is pretty fucking good. I believe in you."

"Thanks. Can you keep Madeline's necklace monitored? Sometimes on the plane..."

It was more than that. I didn't want to hear anything that would set me off more than I already was. To pull off Ruby's rescue, my head had to be in the fucking present.

"Consider it done," Mason answered. "We have capos on one who can tag team." One was the floor of our glass tower where other members of the Sparrows came, went, and worked. "We'll inform you if there's something that can't wait. Otherwise, radio silence until we hear that you've succeeded."

"I'll call once we have the asset." Fuck, Ruby wasn't simply an asset. It was a title given in instances like this, and I presumed that my mind was moving away from paternal feelings to my job, what I did.

I had no idea if I could be a father. I knew I could do what we did and were about to do.

Feelings got in the way. I needed a clear line of thinking.

Leaving our computer equipment in the hotel suite with a do-not-disturb sign on the door—yeah, real high tech—and a slight adjustment to the lock mechanism, we hurried to the SUV in the parking garage.

As we did, I called Marianne and the rest of our flight crew. Garrett was mapping out our approach. Romero was going through a list of supplies, and Christian was driving. We were a team and together we'd get this done.

There were multiple airports in Corpus Christi. Garrett was ensuring that we'd land at one different from Hillman yet close enough to get to his by car, set up, and be ready for our ambush by the time he arrived back with Ruby.

By the time we reached the airport, our flight plan had been approved and we had two cars waiting for us in Corpus Christi.

As we boarded the plane, I spoke to Millie. "There are

certain cases kept in the luggage hold. I need them up here before we take off."

She nodded. "Yes, sir. All of them?"

"All of them. Christian and Romero will help. They're heavy."

I looked at my men. "You've got this."

"Yes, sir."

MADELINE

Seventeen years ago

H *ow many eyes were upon me?*
My body trembled as I was told to step up. The surface under my feet was smooth and cool.

Was I upon a raised platform?

"This young lady is ready for your bidding, sir," a man said, his voice very near.

The room filled with murmurs as my hair was released, the length cascading down my back. Next, he tugged at the belt, allowing the sheer drape to fall open.

"A lovely, willing specimen," the same voice continued. "She's eight weeks from her delivery, plenty of time to train her to your liking."

A deep voice spoke in heavily accented English. "Have you had her?"

The draping was removed, leaving me completely exposed as cool air rained down.

The first man continued speaking. "Look at her nipples, so responsive. Perhaps we could add a few clamps."

"Have you taken her?" the deep voice asked again.

The man beside me ran his hand over my midsection. His touch sickened me, just as the men upstairs from the cell did. As with them, I'd learned to not respond.

"Would you believe she's a virgin?"

The room broke out in laughter.

"To answer your question," the first man said, "Mr. Ivanov, yes, I have. I enjoy new merchandise. She had a little more fight in her then, but I'm sure you can mold her to your liking."

He had?

This was one of the men from Dr. Miller's.

My hands flinched as I made sense of this revelation.

The room hummed in agreement, yet I couldn't see what was happening.

The air around me moved as someone brushed against me. From the scent of cologne, I assumed another man.

What were they going to do?

Together, they gathered my hands and secured them behind me. I wasn't sure what they used. There was no click as there would be with handcuffs. The binding was secure yet soft.

With my hands behind me, my shoulders pulled back, making my breasts and midsection pronounced. The man who helped was gone. It wasn't that I knew by sight, but by the loss of warmth and lessening of the cologne.

"Lovely breasts," the first man said. "Mr. Ivanov, I'm sure

if you chose to pass on this one, someone else among us could find good use for her. Hell..."

My neck straightened and breath caught as his cold hand lowered to my breast.

"...I may need another go at her."

"Take off her blindfold," the man with the accent demanded. "I see her breasts. I want to see her eyes."

"Very well."

The blindfold slipped away.

My breath caught as I took in the vast number of eyes peering my way. Well-dressed men of all ages were spread around the room, focused on me. They were all different, some with gray hair, some with blonde, and others with dark. They had different skin tones, from light to dark. There were ones with wrinkles and others with the glow of youth. All were the same with their attention directed on me. My hands twitched to move, to cover myself, yet the binding reminded me of the warning I'd received, stilling my attempt.

Swallowing, I scanned their faces, searching for their distaste at this demeaning display. Searching for a sign of humanity, even for one with downcast eyes instead of ones filled with lust. I found none. Instead, with drinks and cigars in hand, their gazes simmered with amusement. They weren't seeing my discomfort or recognizing how wrong this was. No, they were bidders at an auction, buyers of art or perhaps a thoroughbred horse.

The reality hit me.

I wasn't an anomaly.

A naked woman poised in the midst of these men wasn't extraordinary.

In fact, it was quite possibly commonplace.

"Is the child yours?"

I followed the voice; it was the same one as before with the accent, the one who had told them to remove the blindfold. The possessor of the voice was tall and broad with dark hair and striking features. His stare was more discerning than the others, critical and decisive. Only his dark eyes moved as he scanned from my head to my toes. He appeared unaffected as if this were again a daily occurrence—with one difference. The longer he stared, the deeper his breaths became. It probably wasn't noticeable to those around him. It was to me.

"Is it?" he asked again.

"No, it is not," the first man said. "The father is unknown."

The tall dark-haired man's chin rose. "Turn, girl, show us your body."

There was no one to look to for direction and no one to encourage or discourage.

Do as you're told.

I peered down at my feet. The platform where I stood was round and probably four feet in diameter. The man who had been beside me was now among the silently waiting crowd. With my hands bound and all eyes on me, I focused on balance.

Taking a deep breath, I did as the man asked. Moving my feet, I turned all the way around once and then again. By viewing the room in 360 degrees, I discovered there were more men present than I'd realized.

"What is your name?" the same man asked when I stopped.

"Madeline, sir."

"Last name?"

"Miller," the first man said. "Madeline Miller. She's one of Miller's girls. He's a legend in my mind. Among the forgotten, he finds us the best and ripest, if you know what I mean."

More laughter from the crowd.

The dark-eyed man wasn't laughing. His gaze was on mine. I wanted to look away, to hide, but that wasn't possible. Finally, I lowered my lids and my chin, fearful of staring his way longer.

"Mr. Ivanov?" the first man asked.

That was the dark-haired man.

Mr. Ivanov lifted his glass to the crowd. "More cognac and cigars. Enjoy yourselves and the senator's generosity. Let the girl stand untouched for now as we admire her beauty throughout the evening. Later, I will make my decision."

Stand.

I did.

This time I could judge how much time passed by the hands of a large grandfather clock on the other side of the room. It had been near eight-thirty when the blindfold was removed. It was now approaching one in the morning. My bladder needed relief and my stomach was empty.

I continued to stand.

All around me, the men ate, drank, and smoked. Suit coats and ties were discarded, buttons undone, and sleeves rolled up. Some men played cards while others told stories with groups of eyes turning my way. Occasionally, one or two men would come close, their gaze simmering with lust as their erections grew beneath their trousers. Not one person spoke to me. It was as if I were an inanimate object for their viewing, a statue. It wasn't only the male guests who saw me.

Servers, men and women alike, came and went, either oblivious to my presence or uncaring.

As time continued to pass, the crowd began to dwindle, and still, I hadn't been released from my platform. My attention went from person to person, always landing back upon Mr. Ivanov. There was something about him that told me he was the honored guest. I watched as he whispered something to the man who appeared in charge. I'd come to know through listening that he went by several names: Rubio, Senator, and Senator McFadden.

The two whispered back and forth until Mr. Ivanov stood tall and offered his hand. Immediately after their handshake, Mr. Ivanov spoke to the crowd. "Leave us."

"Everyone leaves," the senator said. "Those who want to remain for the continuation of festivities are welcome to join me in my study. Mr. Ivanov is ready to interview Miss Miller more—intimately."

The remaining crowd murmured with sounds of approval as they filtered from the room.

It could have been the length of time I'd stood, hunger, thirst, or maybe it was the word: interview. Whatever it was, it was as if the temperature plummeted, causing my body to tremble and the room around me to sway.

I tried to move my feet.

Numb, they were lead weights from the hours of standing. Closing my eyes, I gave in, knowing I was about to fall.

A strong hand came to my side and then a presence.

My eyes flew open.

He was here—Mr. Ivanov—on the platform with me, keeping me steady.

Turning toward him, I was eye-level with the buttons of

his pressed black shirt. Cologne filled my senses. Unlike the men in the rooms, this wasn't stale or unpleasant. I looked up beyond his wide chest and broad shoulders to his stern expression.

"Miss Miller, may I help you down?"

Nodding, I tried to speak. "Yes, thank you, sir."

What was he going to do?

Moving wasn't as easy as I'd presumed. My feet had lost their feeling. My arms and legs ached. With the assistance and stability of his large hands at my waist, I managed to step from the platform to the rug below. As I did, I stumbled, falling against his solid chest. Immediately, I flinched back.

"Do I frighten you?" he asked, releasing my waist.

"No, sir."

His finger and thumb pinched my chin and pulled it upward. "I will accept no less than total honesty. Do I frighten you?"

I stared into his dark eyes. "Yes, sir."

He released his hold. "Now that was easy. Would you like me to release the ribbon?"

Ribbon.

Without my answer, he gently turned me around and reached for the binding upon my wrists. It slid from my skin. I hadn't realized how sore that position made my shoulders. Out of pure relief, I groaned as my wrists became free and arms fell to my sides.

"Better?" he asked as he tucked the red satin ribbon into the pocket of his trousers.

"Yes, sir."

He gestured toward one of the leather chairs. "Sit, you must be tired."

I was, but I was still nude and it seemed improper.

Mr. Ivanov must have sensed my unease. He walked to another grouping of chairs and came back with his suit coat. Though I hoped he'd wrap it around me, he laid it upon the seat of the chair and nodded.

Obeying, I sat upon his coat on the edge of the chair and he took the seat opposite me.

"Tell me how you became one of Dr. Miller's commodities?"

Commodity.

Not even a girl.

Commodity: a raw material that can be bought and sold.

That definition seemed accurate. I sat taller. "I was sold."

"How much?"

"I wasn't told."

His gaze narrowed. "You're a smart girl." He reached out and ran his finger over my cheek.

I fought the urge to flinch away, yet his action wasn't painful or demeaning.

"I can see intelligence in your eyes," he went on. "You weren't told your price, but you know. Tell me."

"I overheard them talking, three hundred dollars for me and five hundred for my baby."

He scoffed. "Is that a lot of money?"

"It is to me."

"One million," he said.

"What?" It was a number I'd heard only in fiction.

"I told Senator McFadden that I'm willing to pay one million for both of you."

"You did—both?"

"I said I was willing. The deal is contingent upon our discussion."

"You mean with me?"

"Yes, you."

This was an insane conversation. And yet it was a conversation. This man was asking for my input. "You are willing...a million...why?"

"Tell me, is that a sufficient amount?"

I couldn't compute his question. "Are you asking me?"

"Miss Miller, if you're unable to converse..."

"No, sir, Mr. Ivanov, I am able to converse. It isn't something I've been able to practice much lately, but, sir, I am capable."

Despite my nudity, his gaze was on my eyes, as if we were two clothed people having a discussion.

"Tell me your worth, Miss Miller?"

"My worth?" I took a deep breath. "I've never considered it." I looked down and then sat taller. "But the worth of my baby is more than a million." My head shook. "There's no price tag."

"I see," he said, standing.

I reached out for his hand. As I did, we both stilled.

My pulse raced.

Was this unacceptable?

Would I be punished?

Would I be sent back?

I pulled my hand back. Swallowing my fear, I spoke, "Please, sir, stay. To answer your question, I don't know my worth."

He sat again.

"I don't," I went on, "but as I said, my baby..." Tears

came to my eyes. "If you're offering a chance for me to stay with the baby—with you... If that's what you're offering and if I have any say in this transaction, I say yes."

He tilted his head from one side to the next. "You know nothing about me."

"I don't care."

"Tell me why?"

"You may be a bad man." I looked around the now-empty room. "I mean, what kinds of men do what was just done, leaving a nude woman on display?"

He nodded.

"I don't care," I went on. "The money is irrelevant. I won't see a penny. I didn't see any of the eight hundred or a penny that the customers paid." I took a breath. "I don't care about that either. I want nothing more than my child. Ever since...when I heard them discuss selling my baby, I've been terrified. Whether you're good or bad, if you'll take me *and* my baby, I will go." I shrugged. "I would suppose in reality, I have no choice. I didn't before, but I want you to know, I will go willingly."

"You get to be with your child. What do I get out of this transaction?" he asked.

I looked down at my naked form. "I realize I'm not..."

He again lifted my chin. "Not what, Miss Miller?"

"I'm used."

"Would I pay one million dollars if I didn't see your value?"

He saw value.

"What will I need to do?" I asked.

"What if I say this..." He gestured to the platform. "...what was done tonight? What if I say things you can't even imagine?"

My imagination was more experienced than he knew.

"Does it matter," he went on, "if you stay with your child?"

It didn't.

"No, sir."

Leaning back against the leather seat, he laid his arms on the armrests. "Stand, let me see you closer."

Relaxing my arms at my sides, I straightened my neck and stood. The tingling in my feet was still painful, yet I could stand. One small step and then one more, and I was standing before him.

He reached for one of my breasts and ran his thumb around the nipple before inspecting the pink upon his thumb pad. Next, he gently turned me, inspecting each bruise and cut as if he could see through the makeup Miss Warner and the doctor had applied. He even examined my most intimate areas. "You have been hurt. You need to heal."

"I understand if you don't want me."

Without responding, Mr. Ivanov stood and walked toward the door, the one where the others had left. With each of his steps, I imagined the cell, the men, the smell, and the hunger. This room smelled of expensive things. In this room, there were partially filled platters with all different foods. The leftovers could feed all of the girls in the cell for a week, and more than likely, these people would throw it away.

Tears filled my eyes. My hands and legs began to tremble as I wrapped my arms around my midsection and pictured my return to Miss Warner.

"A coat for Miss Miller," Mr. Ivanov said to someone beyond the door.

I stood, my chin down, knowing I'd failed and he was sending me away.

A moment later, he returned. I saw his shoes.

"Look at me."

I did. I looked up to see the cape I'd worn draped over his arm.

"You are appealing." He scanned me from my hair to my toes. "I believe you're worth the investment."

"You're not sending me away?"

"No. I'm keeping you."

I stared up at him.

"Trust me," he said, "I am not an easy man. I will not retain a broken woman beside me or allow her to raise a child in my home. You will heal. Physically because it's important for the baby. Mentally because I enjoy a challenge. Along the way, you will become strong, and all the while, bend only to me and my wishes."

"Yes, sir."

"I want you whole, and I will make you that way. In return you will owe me, not for the money for as you said, that isn't yours, though you will be taken care of. You will forever owe me for the gift of your child. Is that clear?"

My head bobbed as gratitude blossomed within me. "Yes, Mr. Ivanov. Thank you."

This transaction should be demeaning. I was a commodity and that reality should be mortifying. Compared to where I'd been, I wasn't humiliated. In a strange new way, I was elated.

I was being bought, not for hundreds of dollars but a million.

No, I was being purchased for the invaluable price of my child.

I couldn't comprehend or have any way to understand what my future would hold, but as long as it included my child, I would be all right—I wanted to believe.

"Do we have a deal, Miss Miller?" he asked.

Mr. Ivanov didn't need my permission. I was all too aware of the inequality of my position. Nevertheless, the mere fact he asked boosted my confidence.

"Yes, Mr. Ivanov. We do."

"You may address me as Andros. We'll work on the rules once we return home."

With his thick accent, I couldn't be sure of where he called home. "May I ask where home is located?"

"Detroit."

How different could it be than Chicago?

As he wrapped the cape around me, I said, "Thank you, I'm Madeline."

PATRICK

Present day

We had eyes watching everywhere. My current concerns were Ivanov's retreat as well as Elliott's ranch. The real-time satellite images were transmitting to Chicago. Reid's ability to multitask had never been more appreciated than it was now. Garrett had an open line of communication going with him. It would have normally been me, but I had enough voices in my head as we moved closer and closer to rescuing Ruby.

There were numerous choices for airports in the area. The four of us landed southwest of Corpus Christi at a private airport. It was less commercial, primarily used by corporations, the kind of airport that saw CEOs, CFOs, and the like, arrive with family—or perhaps mistresses—in tow for an investor-paid trip to the beaches of Texas.

January's temperatures were still cool enough to keep the

traffic down. Things became extremely busy once spring breaks rolled around.

Elliott's plane carrying Hillman landed at a small private airport inside the city limits of Corpus Christi. Though he didn't travel this way often, Marion Elliott was influential in this state and the airports capable of handling his planes vied for his business.

The Sparrows in charge in Chicago decided that while they were fighting battles there and in Detroit, I needed more manpower. To assist, Mason coordinated with some Sparrows near Houston.

After a situation we dealt with in Colorado about two years ago, Sparrow made it a priority to broaden the Sparrow bandwidth. Keeping small units of men around the major cities gave us an advantage when we were called to other locations, such as today.

The Houston Sparrows were our eyes at the airport where Hillman landed. Through them, we'd confirmed his landing, departure in vehicles, and that the aircraft was being refueled for a return trip to Dallas. We'd also learned that other than his flight crew, he had one other man with him.

Reid was still working on facial recognition of that man, as he wasn't someone that any of us recognized. That also meant that the three men with him in Chicago had gone elsewhere. The obvious guess was Detroit, but at this point, we had capos searching the Chicago area to ensure that they had left our territory.

As we arrived by car to the airport in Corpus Christi, I received a call from Sparrow.

"Hello," I answered, knowing this was the first time I'd spoken to him since deciding to leave Dallas.

"We're all here."

"Here?" I hoped he didn't mean Texas.

"On two. We're watching every way we can."

I let out a sigh. Two was our command center, a floor high in Chicago's skyline. I was thankful I wasn't getting an earful and also knew he deserved an explanation. "I left a voicemail."

"And spoke with Mason, I know," Sparrow said. "We trust you, Patrick. Above all, bring me back four Sparrows, and I don't want to lose the few extras you've picked up down there."

"We're prepared," I said, surveying my men. "Tell me you're watching the retreat."

"We are," he said. "Hillman's car entered not more than five minutes ago."

Did Ruby know to expect Hillman?

Did she know who he was?

Or would it take time to convince her to leave with him?

"The security at that airport is shitty," Sparrow said. "We can't see you in real time."

"That's because we have it running on a loop." That meant we couldn't be seen by anyone, in real time or if and when this was reviewed. "I'll call you once we have her."

"Witnesses?" he asked.

"These Sparrows are persuasive. The staff closed down, and our men reopened, including looping the security footage. No one is here but us and the crew on Elliott's plane. My plan is for it not to get that far."

"We're here for you."

I disconnected the call and went through our plan one more time.

The airport's size was to our advantage. Its small-scale

workload this time of year was the reason the employees were easily convinced that they were let go for the day. An email from one of the owners stating that since there were no scheduled flights—as far as they saw—the three employees could take the day off with pay.

It was an easy ruse. Never had I seen it fail. What employee working an hourly wage would argue with a paid vacation day?

The Houston Sparrows had taken over, appearing as employees when Hillman landed. He didn't have a clue.

To our advantage, access to the facility was also limited. There was one two-lane road for customer traffic going in and out and another one-lane road for larger trucks and machinery.

One of the Houston Sparrows was currently sitting behind the customer desk. The other was keeping guard near the initial entry gate. If things went right, Hillman's car would enter the grounds and as they exited the car, we would apprehend Ruby. As for Hillman or his man, my orders were Ruby first, Sparrows second, and the rest was negotiable.

In all reality, apprehending Hillman for questioning regarding his current or future role in the Ivanov bratva sounded appealing. However, putting a bullet between his eyes was a bit more tempting.

Garrett came to me. "Hillman's car left the retreat. It's a twenty-minute drive with current traffic. There's no way to be sure who is on board."

"Tell Reid to check with the capos listening to Madeline. Maybe she or Elliott has gotten word."

Garrett nodded as we all took our positions near the entrance of the airport's small terminal.

Garrett returned, his eyes wide and brow furrowed. "Sir, Ms. Miller's necklace is no longer broadcasting."

My circulation went south as I stared at him. "That doesn't make any sense. She spoke directly to me. She wants to cooperate."

"All I know is the signal has stopped."

"Try emailing her new email address," I suggested though there'd been no communication via her phone since she entered Elliott's car at the Dallas-Fort Worth Airport last night.

I ran my palm over my hair. "Distractions. We'll worry about Madeline later. First, we have to succeed. Ruby isn't spending any more time with Hillman than this drive, not without Madeline or..." I hated to say his name. "...Ivanov present."

I fucking hated Ivanov for crimes I'd yet to confirm. I knew Hillman, knew him and his father, and knew many of their multitudes of sins. That entire pack of McFadden trash deserved to be rotting in jail or six feet under.

Tension pulled the muscles of my neck as we waited. The eerie silence of the mostly empty terminal magnified as if a drumbeat were pounding out war signals. Breaking the silence, my phone vibrated.

Shit. I didn't want to talk anymore. My mind was set.

SPARROW appeared on the screen.

I could let it go to voicemail.

Begrudgingly I pushed the green icon. "What?"

"He's not using Elliott's plane."

"What?" I asked, my alarmed gaze drawing Garrett's attention.

"Listen carefully," Sparrow said. "He chartered a flight

from a local company. They're flying out of a rinky-dink airport west of your location. The flight is chartered for three people. Patrick, my gut tells me that he's double-crossing Elliott and Ivanov. That flight isn't going to Detroit. It's headed into Mexico."

My mind was spinning. My daughter was close, so close. It was one thing to think she was being taken to Madeline. It was another to have her taken out of the country.

"Send us all you have on the airport and the charter company," I said, louder than necessary. Looking around I said, "Cars now."

Our destination was fifteen minutes away. Taking off immediately would get us there mere minutes before Hillman.

"Three," I said aloud. "Hillman, Ruby, and the one man with him."

"Something's bothering me," Garrett said as Christian drove along dusty, isolated roads.

"What?" There were too many things bothering me to count.

"Where is her bodyguard?"

I turned to him. "Her bodyguard?" Yes, Madeline had mentioned someone.

"Think about it. Does Sparrow allow Mrs. Sparrow to go to the fucking bakery without someone?"

He was right.

"Mrs. Murray used to go out by herself, but that hasn't happened in nearly two years and what about Mrs. Pierce?" He sat taller. "I don't have kids, and I know Ivanov isn't her parent, but damn, I don't see him as the kind of guy who leaves a sixteen-year-old girl without someone."

"Madeline said Ruby would be safe." I tried to think back.

"When I asked about Ruby being alone, she said other than school, she never is. She mentioned the staff and named one man, Oleg or something."

"Then why are there only three on the charter? If Hillman and his man are present along with Ruby, where is Ruby's bodyguard?"

"Hurry," I said to Christian.

The land was flat and the sun high, allowing us to see. As we neared, the structures came into view. The small airport was barely an airport. From a distance, it looked more like a pole barn surrounded by a chain-link fence. There was one small plane near the makeshift terminal.

Our two cars were approaching from the east. Coming from the southwest, a large SUV could be seen kicking up dust.

"Sir, that has to be them," Romero said, directing all of our attention.

"So much for the element of surprise," I said. We'd make it to the airport entrance first. However, if we went in, they wouldn't. "Forget the airport, this is going down now."

The landscape was empty and dry for as far as the eye could see, fields waiting for their next planting and harvest. It was more open than I'd like, but sometimes we didn't get what we wanted. Sometimes we took what we got.

"Pass the airport, Christian," I said. "We're going to play a good old-fashioned game of chicken. Guns out and ready."

MADELINE

*W*earing the same pale green robe as this morning, I stood against the wall in Marion's home office listening to both sides of a conversation as he spoke fast and furiously to Andros. It was the magic of speaker phones. It was as if we were all in the same room.

My thoughts were scattered—as erratic as the men's conversation.

Ruby.

Antonio Hillman.

Ruby.

Andros was on his way back to Dallas, and for once, I wasn't upset to see him.

What I didn't understand was why Marion trusted Antonio Hillman. I'd asked to go with Antonio to retrieve Ruby. It wasn't that I wanted to spend time with Antonio. It was that after our little confrontation in the hallway, I had a gnawing feeling about him, one that lingered throughout my morning shower and beyond. The entire time Marion and I were out and about the ranch, I felt it remaining in the back of my mind.

Marion dismissed my concern, telling me I didn't know him.

I didn't.

That wasn't the only reason I didn't trust him. His proclamation of our earlier meetings and comment about *watching* had me on edge. I definitely didn't feel comfortable having him with my daughter. The only reason I didn't protest more was that I believed no matter what, she'd be accompanied by one of Andros's trusted men. I hoped it was Oleg.

Since Ruby had been little, we never left the bratva or traveled without a guard. Even alone, it was why I traveled with Mitchell.

I knew the men were Andros's way of keeping track of us and me, a pair of eyes to report our every move. I also knew that if necessary, those men would protect us. Their devotion had less to do with me and more to do with their respect for Andros and admiration of Ruby. Even men with stone-cold hearts were influenced by a precious child.

As Ruby grew, I worried that they'd see her as a woman and not the child they knew. I was led to believe it was why Andros didn't assign new men to her detail, but ones who had known her most of her life.

Marion was listening to Andros as he simultaneously spoke on his cell phone. "Holy hell," he said, stilling Andros's speech. "Antonio never returned to the plane. I've just been in contact with my flight crew. They're still waiting." His head shook. "The pilot said the airport is a ghost town. No one is there. The crew, everyone, is gone."

My circulation thumped within my ears as my heart beat at untold speed beneath my breastbone. "That doesn't make sense," I said softly. "Where is he? It's been too long." The temperature around me seemed to cool, my bare toes and fingers filling with ice.

The last report Andros had received was that Hillman was on his way to the island retreat. It was when his entry had been authorized. The expected report alerting Andros that they'd left never happened. It was then when Andros called back to the house staff.

Why had he allowed Antonio to enter?

It wasn't a question I could ask without meeting Andros's current wrath. To say he was enraged was an understatement. I understood. I felt the same. My rage, however, rarely erupted; instead, it festered inside like a cancer eating away until gaping holes remained. If anything happened to Ruby, there would be nothing left.

I'd be empty.

Andros's speaking echoed off the walls, coming in bouts of English and Russian.

That was why I was summoned. Not to tell me what was happening with my own daughter, but to translate when Marion couldn't understand.

I'd been literally seconds from entering a freshly filled bath when Eloise banged upon my bedroom door. After all the time outside in the wind and dust, I had wanted to soak, relax, and cleanse myself for dinner and mostly for Ruby's arrival.

It wasn't unusual for me to shower and bathe multiple times a day. It was just something I did, finding a sense of solace under a spray or soaking. I felt rejuvenated under the sensation of warm water and invigorated by the scents associated with the ritual: bodywashes, soaps, shampoos, conditioners, and gels. In Detroit I had an entire shelf dedicated to lotions of all scents. It was a love I'd instilled in Ruby at a young age. After her baths, we'd pick a scent. When she was a child, strawberry was her favorite. Apple had always been mine.

All Eloise said was that something had happened that had to do with Miss Miller. That was all the information I needed. Without question, I turned off the tap, wrapped the robe around me, and hurried down to Marion's office.

Now that I knew the emergency, I wasn't thinking straight. I hardly noticed the language of Andros's rant. I'd heard him lecture before in both Russian and English, and more frequently, in a mixture of the two.

Therefore, it wasn't Andros who would cue me to translate but Marion.

"What did he say?" he'd say softly as Andros yelled.

With my arms wrapped around my midsection and tears teetering on my eyelids, I replied, soft enough that Andros didn't think I was interrupting and yet loud enough for Marion to hear.

We listened as Andros received updates from Padre Island.

"They left the grounds over fifteen minutes ago," he said.

"Fifteen minutes ago," I repeated.

"That isn't right," Marion said. "They should be to the airport."

Andros continued.

"Oh my God," I muttered.

Marion's brow furrowed as his blue eyes came to mine. "I don't know what he said."

I could barely form the words as my cold fingers began to tremble. "Oleg is dead."

"Who is Oleg?" Marion asked.

Sobs racked my chest as I slid down the wall, pulling my knees to my chest. I smoothed the soft robe over my legs as the world around me faded. I was back in a dim room. The stench of human waste hung in the air, yet there was no way to escape.

"Madeline?" he whispered.

The only sounds were the occasional crying of the other girls.

A memory came back with a vengeance.

Her name was Patty, or was it Patsy?

I saw her face, ashen under the dim lighting. We all were pale, yet this was different. Girls began to gather around her. We weren't allowed to speak, yet the others were, saying her name over and over.

It was as I knelt beside her that my knees came into contact with the warm, sticky liquid.

Had she been injured or was her miscarriage the result of our situation?

We'd never know or be told.

The next time Miss Warner opened the door, the girl she called informed her of our fellow cellmate's demise. The men who helped Miss Warner entered as we all sat like obedient statues with our backs against the wall. A few minutes later she was gone. We were given two buckets filled with cold water and each handed a rag. Our instruction was to clean the floor.

Under the single light bulb, I recognized the rag I'd been given. Moments earlier it had been Patty's dress.

"Madeline."

No. I wouldn't lose my baby. I didn't then. I won't now.

I shook my head as the stench faded and Marion's office reappeared.

Andros's voice continued to reverberate through the office, yet Marion was in front of me, crouched down, with his gaze even with mine. "Madeline, talk to me. You're white as a ghost."

I blinked as the memory evaporated, leaving me in a similar hell.

Would I too lose my child?

MADELINE

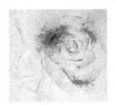

"*W*ho is Oleg?" Marion asked again.

"He's been with...as long as I..he..."

Andros's voice stopped, filling the space with silence as if he expected a response.

We both turned toward the speaker.

Taking a deep breath, I slowly stood and walked to the speaker, to where Andros could hear me. There was no need to hide my emotions. Andros had seen them all. I purposely spoke in Russian. "How?" I spoke between sobs. "I'm so sorry. Oleg was always good."

He had been. More of an anomaly amongst the dangers of the bratva, he'd been patient and kind to a little girl and even more patient as she grew, testing the limits of her independence.

Shot.

Point blank.

Back of the head.

"Did she see?" I asked, imagining Ruby's fear and shock.

For only a moment, Andros and I spoke, the two of us. What happened at Club Regal no longer mattered. There were too many things that didn't matter. Our relationship wasn't one that little girls dreamt of having. It wasn't always pretty and at the same time, it wasn't always ugly.

It was sometimes colorful and other times devoid of color.

White and black were both capable of erasing the hues of life.

Our one connection, from the night we met, was Ruby.

"Andros, please find her. I'll do anything."

"Madeline." There was uncharacteristic emotion in his utterance of my name. Not rage as he'd been spouting, but remorse—an uncharacteristic show for him. "Michail and Leonid were out by the shore," he said. "They didn't hear or see. It wasn't until my call..."

I settled into Marion's chair, aware he was listening— wanting to know what we were saying—and at the same time, not caring. "Everyone else?" My mind went to Annika, an older woman who'd shown me kindness from my first island visit. Her job was the retreat's cook, and she always enjoyed making Ruby her special pastries.

"Five," he said. "That fucker murdered five of my people."

They were *his*, and in a way also *mine*.

Seventeen years was a long time.

More tears came. "Please, tell me that Michail and Leonid are following Antonio."

"They are. If they'd have heard, but they didn't. They're too far behind. The car, it has a tracker... but..."

"What happens if he takes her away?" I asked, my

stomach knotting upon itself as I spoke. "How will we know where they've gone?"

"I'm getting something," Andros said. Before I could ask, the phone disconnected.

Silence settled as Marion sat across his desk, his blue eyes set on me. "You didn't want me to understand?"

I shrugged. "Andros isn't a good man. I know that. But he's been there for me and Ruby since the night we met."

"What did he say?" Marion asked.

"Five people, members of his staff, are dead. They weren't all bad people. Oleg has been around since I first went to live with Andros..." I leaned back against the tall leather chair as pleasant memories surfaced, suddenly uncaring what Elliott knew of mine and Andros's history. "He deserved better."

"What about Ruby?"

More tears streamed down my cheeks. "Two men from the retreat were out of the house. Antonio probably didn't know the number of staff or he and his man would have searched for them."

"His man? Antonio was alone when he left here."

"Andros has closed-circuit surveillance. There was someone with him." I remembered what I'd told Patrick about dissension in the ranks. My fingers fluttered to my neck.

My necklace.

I closed my eyes, remembering that I took it off for the bath. I was afraid if I soaked, it would affect the transmission.

"Madeline, I want you to know, I never expected this. I told you that I've known Antonio since he was a teenager. I trusted him to do as Andros and I wanted."

The phone on Marion's desk rang, its old-fashioned jingle rattling the large wooden desk. Our eyes met.

"It's probably him," Marion said. Lifting the receiver, he spoke, "Yes?"

My eyes widened as he continued to talk through the receiver, prohibiting my hearing of Andros. This was his way to pay me back for speaking in Russian.

Oh hell no, he was not going to do to me as I'd done to him.

The telephone system wasn't that advanced. I reached forward and hit the speaker button. Andros was already speaking as his voice filled the room. "...dead."

"What are you saying?" I asked.

Marion responded. "What about Ruby?"

Ruby.

She wasn't who was dead.

I exhaled.

"She's not there," Andros said, "but I fucking swear, we will find her."

"She's part of our deal," Marion said, his gaze going to me. "You're not reneging. Find her." He hung up the phone.

"You just hung up on Andros." It wasn't a question, more of a statement of shock.

Marion paced before his desk, his posture growing straighter as he took deep breaths. "Madeline, I wanted to ease you into this. But now, Antonio and his man are dead along with members of Andros's staff. Along with that, Ruby is missing. We need to be honest with one another."

"Were we not?"

"I know what I said earlier, but you're not leaving, and I'll spare no expense to find Ruby."

Could she be with Patrick?

The thought superseded whatever Marion had said. It gave me a dawn of hope. I didn't care that Antonio was dead. I was happy he was dead. It was Ruby who was my concern.

Was she safe?

Recalling the secret email on my phone, I stood, not engaged in whatever Marion was saying. "Marion, we can talk about this later. I need to get upstairs."

He inhaled, his chest expanding. "Andros is on his way, and I think he should know that you know."

I was near the door when I turned back. "That I know what?"

Marion came closer, reached into the pocket of his jeans, and removed his hand. His fingers were balled, and then they began to open.

My world stopped as his palm flattened, revealing a faded red satin ribbon.

There was no way he could know about the auction. This was some strange head game planted by Andros.

"What is that?" I asked.

"Wear it tonight, in your hair or maybe as a bracelet."

I took one step away. "Where did you get that?"

"I think you know. It was stunningly erotic laced on your wrists."

My head shook. "Why would Andros give that to you?" His last sentence penetrated my disbelief. "You saw it?"

His lips curled upward. "I'd so hoped we could discuss this in a different setting. I have thought about it constantly since seeing you again at the tournament. You were...spectacular."

Acid bubbled upward from my stomach.

I'd dined with this man, stayed at his home, played poker

with him. Today we'd had a nice time on the ranch including a picnic lunch...

And he had been there. One of those men. One of the men staring at me.

"I was a child."

"You were eighteen and it wasn't as if you were a virgin."

My feet moved and hand came out faster than I planned as my palm connected to his cheek. Immediately, I pulled it back, holding it to my breasts. "I'm leaving." I spun on my heels only to have my arm seized and I was spun back.

"You heard my story," he said, his hand grasping my arm. "I had suffered."

"You?"

"My wife and daughter, I told you."

"I won't minimize your loss," I said, my pulse racing. "It was tragic, but don't you ever talk to me about suffering."

His grip didn't loosen. "You enjoyed it. We were all talking about it, watching as your nipples hardened and you fidgeted, trying to find relief. I was the second highest bidder that night."

My eyes narrowed as I pulled my arm from his grasp. I could tell him that I was cold up there, standing naked for hours, or that I fidgeted because my bladder was full and I had a baby sitting on it. However, I refused to credit this conversation with more of my input.

"Marion, I'm leaving before Andros arrives. I want your help, but by God, I will find my daughter. I, however, want to make it very clear that I never want to see you again."

He smoothed the front of his shirt and looked back up with a grin. "I wanted to tell you another way, but I can't say I don't enjoy your fight. Little lady, who you see and who you don't is not at your discretion. I didn't have the high bid that night. The senator accepted Andros's as you're aware. Yesterday, I made him an offer he couldn't refuse." He lifted the ribbon again, handing it my direction. "With you and Ruby came the ribbon. You could say it was to seal the deal. You might like to know that like a fine wine, your price has increased with age, and I'm content to pay every penny."

I couldn't think, move, or speak.

Marion came closer and reached out to my cheek.

Closing my eyes, I flinched, yet his touch was soft. "Madeline, you and Ruby now belong to me. And if I find out that Andros pulled something to steal her out from under me, he will end up like Antonio."

PATRICK

I stepped into the cockpit and eased myself into the copilot's chair. Muting the phone, I spoke to Marianne. "How much longer?"

"We should land in just over two hours," she said. "I wish I could go faster."

"I wish you could too. I'm supposed to take this call in private. Every room in the plane is occupied. Pretend you can't hear." The only person not on the plane was Garrett. He'd made his way back to Dallas with the Houston Sparrows to empty the hotel suite of its contents.

She smiled and hit a switch on her earphones. "What?"

I unmuted the phone. "Are you there?"

"Are you alone?" the deeply pissed-off voice asked.

"I'm in the cockpit. Marianne has headphones. I should have brought a bigger plane."

"I'll keep my voice low. Fucking listen," Sparrow said. "You went over my fucking head. I can't believe you did that. After all these years..."

A genuine smile came to my lips. It felt amazing to allow myself the luxury. There'd been very few real smiles since this crazy nightmare began. "I can't believe you admitted that," I said, still smiling. "I thought there was no 'over Sterling Sparrow's head.'"

"I didn't admit that there was, and if Marianne says differently, she's fired."

There was no way he'd fire Marianne. She was as true as they came. I was probably closer to the guillotine.

"Tell me what I was supposed to do," I asked. "Perhaps keep a sixteen-year-old girl in a hotel room against her will? Maybe in a hotel suite with three to four grown men? That wouldn't set off any alarms around the hotel or city. Sparrow, once Ruby was in my grasp, I knew those weren't options."

"Two fucking options ruled out out of how many? Say...a million."

I shook my head. "You and I both know that there's no place safer in this world than our tower. Araneae offered her mother's house, and while I'm certain the good judge would be thrilled to help hold a young adult—who may or may not try to run—captive indefinitely, I thought it may be a lot to ask. Until we have Madeline back, this is technically kidnapping.

"The paternity test is happening first thing."

"I'm fine with that, but I don't need it. This girl is my daughter. No fucking test will tell me otherwise."

"It's not negotiable."

"I don't give a shit as long as she's safe. As we both know, security and safety work two ways. In our tower, no one can get in, and if we set the elevator locks, no one gets out."

"I said no. Do you remember that?" he asked. "The first fucking night, I said no."

Though he was giving me hell, I heard the resignation in his voice. I can only imagine the conversation he had with his wife.

"I do. You said no to Madeline. This is Ruby. Would you believe me if I said this whole thing with Araneae was an accident? You see, I *accidentally* hit Araneae's number instead of yours."

"Accidentally?"

"Yes, and you know how she is. I told her that I meant to call you but that in all my confusion with finding my lost daughter and all, I hit the wrong number. I offered to let her go and call you. She said this thing about telling her what was happening. I believe she mentioned that you'd once said—"

"Shut the fuck up."

Leaning back in the copilot's seat, I continued my momentary state of contentment.

Calling Sparrow's wife's number instead of his wasn't done in confusion. On the contrary, it was done in desperation. Once we had Ruby on the airplane and Millie reassured her that despite the numerous scary-looking large men, she was safe, I knew I couldn't allow the plane to stop in Dallas. I couldn't keep Ruby hidden in the city that Elliott practically owned and where Ivanov would soon arrive.

We knew Ivanov rushed out of Detroit the moment Hillman double-crossed him.

We had eyes.

In killing Hillman, we possibly did Ivanov a favor,

stopping Hillman's plans for a coup. That said, it was also a favor to the Sparrows. Hillman had been the one who had been networking our men. Also, wars were easier won between two factions, not three or more.

The reality hit me as Marianne prepared to take off. My options with Ruby were limited. Unlike Sparrow who had a cabin in the middle of the wilderness of Ontario and Mason who owned a massive ranch in nowhere Montana, I was fresh out of alternative housing.

A quiet house in the suburbs with a picket fence continued to come to mind, but no matter the future, that wouldn't work. The only neighbors I was willing to live nearby were the ones I already did.

What *would* work, what was feasible, was the safest place I knew. The place my family and neighbors called home.

The scene from a few hours ago came back to me.

An SUV headed toward us as Christian, Romero, Garrett, and I approached in one car and the two Houston Sparrows followed closely behind.

"Don't back down," I said as we passed the entrance to the airport that held Hillman's chartered plane. We braced ourselves as we continued full speed toward their oncoming SUV.

At the last possible second, Christian spun the wheel; the SUV clipped our back fender sending both of us into a spin. The driver of the SUV slammed on his brakes as the second car of Sparrows came at it.

The next few minutes will replay in my head for years to come.

The cars came to a squealing halt.

Airbags deployed.

Doors flew open.

Men screamed profanities.

Bullets shattered glass and ricocheted off metal.

When it was done, when Hillman and his man were dead, and only one Sparrow was wounded—Romero, and he's currently on the flight with a bandaged arm assuring us he's fine—I approached the SUV.

There'd been a short but steady firestorm of bullets. My heart fell to my stomach and my mouth lost all moisture as I stepped closer.

What if Ruby was hit by one of the bullets?

After all of this, she couldn't be hurt.

How could I tell Madeline?

The front two doors were open with deployed airbags. I reached for the handle of the back door.

Holding my breath, I opened it.

Crouched in the back seat was my daughter.

Of course, she didn't know that. She didn't know anything of what was happening.

"Ruby," I said calmly. It took three times. Finally she looked up.

They say there are moments when the world stops spinning. It's often associated with love at first sight, a carnal, physical type of love. As my eyes met hers, my world stopped spinning. The overwhelming emotion was unlike even that I'd felt for her mother. It wasn't romantic but agape—an unconditional love that knew no bounds.

Blue eyes such as I saw in my own reflection peered up beneath a beautiful head of dark hair.

The young lady before me was Maddie.

She was me.

She was both of us.

And for the first time, I was staring into her eyes.

Holstering my gun, I slowly reached out my hand. "Ruby, I can't imagine what you've been through. I know you're scared. We're here to take you to your mother."

"My mother?"

"Yes," I said, nodding. "She is very worried about you."

"But Andros said my mother would be gone for a while."

My lips moved upward—despite what she was saying, despite that she was more familiar with Andros Ivanov than me—at the sound of her voice. "He was right. Things have changed." I opened and closed my fingers. "Please come with us."

Her wide eyes peered around the windows, some shattered and the others riddled with bullet holes. "Who are you?"

"I'm a friend of your mother's," I replied.

She tilted her head as she looked me up and down. "My mother doesn't have friends. Are you a friend of Andros?"

"No, I'm afraid I'm not." I couldn't lie to her at our first meeting.

"Did you...?" She peered around. "Is Mr. Hillman...dead?"

"I'm afraid so, Ruby. I'm sorry that had to happen with you—"

"He killed Oleg," she blurted out.

It was then that she began to cry, sobs bubbling from her chest as she laid her head on the back of the seat in front of her.

I didn't know Oleg, but I knew genuine grief when I saw it.

"I-I saw him do it." She turned my way. "I-I was afraid he'd kill me."

My hand was still extended. The Houston Sparrows were shielding the bodies of Hillman and his partner as best as they could. "I'm sorry about Oleg. Your mother said he was a good man. Come with me, Ruby. Hillman can't hurt you now."

She began to move and stopped. "How do I know that you know my mom?"

"You choose to believe me," I offered.

"You killed them. You're murderers."

I nodded. "We did and are, to save you."

"Tell me my mom's name."

Any other question. I took a breath as I considered the real answer, Madeline Kelly. "When I met your mother," I began, "her name was Madeline Alycia Tate. Today she goes by the last name Miller."

Ruby sat taller. "You know her middle name?"

"Yes, her middle name is after her mother."

Ruby scooted from the car, still apprehensive. "Are you going to take me back to Andros?"

"No," I said as she came closer. I wanted nothing more than to reach out and hold her, but I knew it wouldn't make sense. "No, we're going to take you someplace safe, and if I have my way, your mother will be there very soon."

She stopped and narrowed her blue eyes. "You knew Mom before I was born?"

"I did."

"And since?"

"We lost touch for a while. I'm happy I can be here to help you and her."

"How can I believe you?" she asked.

"I don't know. Ask me something else about her. I'll try to answer."

She thought for a minute. "Do you know that she has a tattoo?"

A rush of heat ran up my neck to my cheeks. "An apple. Now will you come with us?"

She looked around the empty road. My men were standing by our cars. Romero had a t-shirt wrapped around his arm, saturated with blood. The Houston Sparrows were standing in front of the bodies.

"What will happen to them?" she asked, nodding her chin toward what she could see of the bodies.

"We'll leave them."

"Won't someone find them?"

Madeline was right. Ruby was smart and inquisitive. However, I would have preferred that our first question-and-answer session didn't involve the proper disposal of dead bodies. "We're not far from the border. It won't take much digging on the part of ICE or the police to learn that at least one of these men has a questionable past. It was probably a drug deal gone bad."

She looked from them, to my men, and back to me. "I believe it was a kidnapping. I just hope this still isn't one."

"I will get you to your mother. I promise."

"How is she doing?" Sparrow asked, still on the phone.

"Decent but scared. She's strong. I was able to get a message to Madeline. Madeline sent one back. Ruby's been better since then."

"One at a time."

"Sparrow, I'm getting Madeline, too."

"Give me some time."

"I don't know how much time we have. There's no reason to suspect she's in danger with Elliott, but damn, I don't care. I need her in Chicago. Ruby will too."

"Come back," he said, "get the test, and we'll go from there. When you arrive, take her to one."

My neck straightened. "Two."

One was the floor of the Sparrow outfit that was the least secure. It was where our workers and capos came and went. It was where we held meetings with members of other factions. Two was where only we, the top of the Sparrow chain, frequented. The three men with me on this assignment had never been to two.

"Fuck," Sparrow replied. "Apartments then. Dr. Dixon will be in the common area. I'll try to keep the crowd to a minimum, but the three women are...just get here."

I could only imagine how Sparrow, Mason, and Reid's

wives were reacting to the news that I was a father, news their husbands had known for a few days. "Why Dr. Dixon?"

"She can check Ruby out, be sure Hillman didn't...do anything, and initiate the DNA test. She'll do a saliva quick test, but the blood test is more accurate."

"Fine," I said. "We're on our way."

MADELINE

I'd stalled as long as I could. The sun had set, filling the sky above the ranch with a twinkling of stars. Andros had arrived to the ranch hours ago, and he and Marion were waiting for me downstairs. Eloise had come to my door three times now. The first time, I informed her that I was too distraught over Ruby to go to dinner. She returned a quarter of an hour later with a tray, insisting that I try to eat. The last visit was to inform me of Mr. Elliott and Mr. Ivanov's location and impatience.

I didn't give a shit about their impatience. If I didn't believe Andros would come after me, I would wait until tomorrow. The truth was that I wasn't actually distraught over Ruby. I had a myriad of things to cause me distress. Ruby wasn't one of them, not since I'd received Patrick's message and briefly corresponded with my daughter.

Her email asked if Patrick was really my *friend*. That must be the description he gave her. My reply was truthful. He was my very first friend and was still a dear friend. After I sent the message, I reflected on that reality.

The most important thing to me was that our daughter was safe. They were on their way back to Chicago and away from here.

Would I ever be with them?

My reasoning for my lack of appetite wasn't Ruby but the bombshell revelation that engulfed my life in flames. For only a few days it appeared as if Ruby and I had made it to the other side. I'd lived through hell and survived in the flames of purgatory only to be thrown back into the furnace.

I'd said thank you to Andros the night he purchased me; Marion was not receiving the same gratitude. The memory of the night I met Andros twisted my stomach as I recalled the room full of eyes. I now knew for certain the names of three of those sets. I'd never forget the name of the senator. Recently, I saw a news story about him being associated with a human-trafficking ring. For weeks I searched the news for updates as I wondered how many of his victims knew his name.

I wouldn't have known if I'd have given birth in the cell or upstairs or whatever they did. I wouldn't know if I'd been placed back down in that cellar, or in a similar hell, after Ruby's birth. I probably would have died.

How many had?

Why hadn't I?

The longer I paced the bedroom at Marion's home, the more questions I had. They were questions I'd never before sought to answer. Perhaps it was my knowledge that Ruby was safe. Maybe it was my utter disgust for the men downstairs. Or there was the possibility that I was done.

Ruby was safe and with her father.

I was tired of fighting.

I was tired of living as a commodity.

I'd willingly die before I took on that role with Marion Elliott.

As I perused the clothes hanging in the closet, I made a decision.

"Fuck you both, you all..." I said, thinking of the other numerous men in that room and the men who found sick pleasure in screwing filthy young girls. I supposed it gave them a real rush of superiority. They were better than us. They could dominate a child.

"Fuck you," I said aloud to no one.

It was cathartic. I said it again and again until I was doubled over in a fit of laughter.

Perhaps the real assessment was that after all this time I had gone mad.

If I were mad, I was going to share my newfound mental freedom.

The closet contained an assortment of dresses—short, middle length, and long. It was as if whoever had made these clothing choices believed that I'd willingly accompany my *new owner* to his social engagements. My fingertips brushed the different materials as I surveyed the various styles.

Removing a hanger from the rack, a smile came to my lips. "My name is Madeline Kelly and I'm done being invisible."

Thirty minutes later, I descended the grand staircase, the one I'd been shown earlier this morning. My head was held high. My hair was styled back with crystal combs I'd found in the bathroom drawers. Upon my feet were jewel-encrusted high heels complete with the designer name under my sole. It was the dress that I was certain would garner my audience's attention.

What neither of the men realized was that their bargaining chip was gone. In this game of poker, they were out of aces. Andros held me in my place for seventeen years with one ace in his pocket.

They had no idea how far I would go to fuck them both over.

My high heels tapped across the tile of the entry as I recalled Eloise's instructions.

"Mr. Elliott and Mr. Ivanov are in the library. If you don't remember, it's down the hallway to the right at the bottom of the stairs, next to Mr. Elliott's office."

His office—the place where he told me the truth, the place he declared his proprietorship. Yes, I knew that room.

Marion's and Andros's voices came into range as I neared. The door was slightly ajar. I stopped as I approached, my stomach knotting as my nose scrunched. The scent of rich cigar smoke wafted from the room.

Willing the memories away, I moved forward, opened the door, and stood in the threshold. "Good evening, gentlemen. I believe your attraction has arrived."

The red dress I'd found was brighter than the ribbon. Of course, the ribbon was old and faded. This dress had a skirt whose hem fell above my knees and a bodice that scooped low, revealing the rounded tops of my breasts. The sleeves were capped and the back dipped low, forbidding the wearing of a traditional bra. The ribbon was secured around my wrist, tied in a large bow.

Their discussion stalled as they both stared my direction.

Marion was the first to stand—as if I believed either of these men were gentlemen.

"You...look," Marion stammered, "I-I expected—"

Me to be broken?

No, motherfucker, I'd been broken. Now I was visible.

Each man held a small tumbler of an amber liquid.

If we were going to relive our past, I was rewriting the script. Walking across the wood flooring near the roaring fire, I found the crystal decanter. With a brightly painted grin, I poured myself a glass and took a healthy sip. The bourbon coated my tongue and throat in warmth, giving me liquid strength. With a feigned grin, I sat in one of the leather chairs near the fire and crossed my ankles. "Tell me where my daughter is. Tell me how you plan on rescuing her."

"Madeline," Andros began, "Hillman brought assets to the bratva. I believed..." His dead eyes came to mine. "I was wrong about him. He's dead. And my men are tracking all flights from the area. We'll learn something soon."

"Dead? At your doing?"

"All that matters is that he's dead."

I took another drink. "No, what matters, *who* matters is Ruby. She has always been all that mattered." I placed my drink on the table beside the chair. "Gentlemen, I believe we're all gamblers."

They both stared.

"I have a wager."

The rumble of nervous laughter filled the air.

"I wager me," I said.

"You can't wager what isn't yours," Elliott said.

"Oh, you see, but I can. We live in a brand-new world.

Gentlemen's agreements involving forced servitude are frowned upon. As a matter of fact, that same little issue has brought down those wealthier than either of you as well as royalty. I believe it would be a misjudgment on your part to suppose you're immune."

Marion sat back and crossed his ankle over his knee. "Remember the story I told you about my wife and daughter?"

"Yes."

"I told you what it takes to keep things from the press. Social media is no different."

"Hmm," I said. "It is. The press thirty years ago was dominated by news outlets. Today one tweet can go viral in seconds."

"I'm offering you more than the agreement," Marion said. "I'm offering more than what Andros did."

Offering me, as if he were giving me a choice.

I turned to Andros and shrugged. "We had our ups and downs, but I can honestly say that my and Ruby's needs never went unmet." I turned back to Marion. "What exactly do you propose you can offer above what Andros did?"

As I spoke Andros's one cheek rose—his amused expression. That wasn't necessarily a good thing, but I had his attention.

"Marriage," Marion replied. "As I said, I had plans for a more gentlemanly approach to the subject. The unfortunate business with Ruby caused a detour in those plans."

I fiddled with the faded ribbon, tied into a bow on my right wrist. Pulling one end, I released the ribbon. Lifting it between my thumb and finger I allowed it to dangle. Only looking up with my eyes, I said, "Gentlemanly." Wadding the ribbon into a clump, I tossed it into the fire. The flames grew as the symbol of my servitude disintegrated before our eyes.

"Marion, most men who are interested in marriage offer a ring, not a seventeen-year-old ribbon. The ribbon is ashes and so are your plans, I'm afraid."

It was as if I didn't speak. He continued, "You will have whatever ring you desire—ten carats or more."

"So let me get this straight. Instead of binding me with a ribbon, you want to bind me with a diamond. Will I be clothed when I'm introduced to your friends?"

Marion's face reddened. "This isn't—"

"The deal is complete," Andros said. "His use of the word offer is merely for conversation. An offer was made to me and I accepted. Your fate was sealed a long time ago. Marion has known your secret as long as I. He's kept it. I respect that."

"He's kept that I was bought after being on display—"

Andros's head shook. "No. That wasn't a secret. The secret was your worth, but more importantly, your child's worth that has remained unknown to most."

I sat forward, no longer as confident in my wager. "My worth is that I'm done being owned. I don't care what deal the two of you made. I refuse."

The two men looked from one to the other. It was Andros who sat forward with his elbows on his knees. "Did you ever wonder why I would pay one million dollars for a damaged, pregnant, and uneducated commodity?"

With each of his descriptors my neck straightened and the small hairs on my neck and arms came to life. It wasn't that his depiction was inaccurate, but more that hearing the truth was painful.

When I didn't reply, Andros went on, "I gambled on a son."

"Why? My child wasn't yours. You have never even suggested Ruby take your name."

"It was about her parentage," he said. "Sometimes the most valuable weapon is one that stays hidden."

"Parentage," I repeated. "Her father? I never told you."

Andros laughed as he sat back and lifted his tumbler to his lips. Once he set the crystal down upon the table, he smiled. "I didn't care. Now that I know, it's humorous."

"I don't understand."

Marion stood. "Little lady, it isn't Ruby's father we care about. The senator didn't care about him." He came closer and lifted his glass. "It's *your* father."

My head jerked back as my skin tingled. "My father was no one. My mother was no one. They were everyday people with nowhere jobs. They didn't even have a will or make provisions for their daughter."

"Their daughter wasn't meant to survive. According to the senator, you were supposed to be in the car."

I began to speak, but Marion continued, "After that, you were lost in the foster care system. As soon as you were found, you would run away or move. The belief was that you'd died, and then one day you completed the paperwork for Dr. Miller. You used Tate as your last name, and listed your mother with the unique name of Alycia."

I lifted my hand to my throat as my eyes closed. The necklace was upstairs. It was better; this wasn't a conversation I wanted overheard. Images came back from seventeen years ago. I remembered those forms. Kristine had told me to not add Patrick. I hadn't. I'd completed them as Madeline Tate.

"Why would my father want to kill us all?"

"The man who was married to your mother, Will Tate,

wasn't your father," Andros said. "This was why I valued you that night. And if your child had been a son...there would have been no limit to the value and possibilities." Andros shrugged. "It was a gamble and I lost." His eyebrows rose as a grin came to life. "No, I didn't lose. I made an investment. I had my turn and Marion has paid handsomely."

I stood and walked toward the fireplace, yet I couldn't feel the heat. I spun toward the men. "The man who raised me wasn't my father? How do you know this?"

"Senator McFadden assured us that a DNA test had been performed at Dr. Miller's. There was too much potential to not bid on you."

I recalled that horrible night. The senator had said he'd had me. He was one of the men at Dr. Miller's. I looked up at Marion and Andros as the meal Eloise delivered churned in my stomach. "Are you saying that he, the senator, is my father?"

"No," they said in unison.

I let out a long breath. "Who then, and why and how did the senator know?"

Marion's eyebrows rose as he tilted his head. "If there's one rule in this world it's to learn all you can about your opponent."

"It's the reason I sent you to Marion in Chicago, remember?" Andros said. "You were to learn all you could."

My head shook. "But that wasn't the truth. You sent me to Marion so he could meet me, so this..." I gestured between us.

Andros shrugged. "I have a war to finance. Ruby isn't a boy and you're unable to conceive. However, in time, Ruby will."

"Wait."

Marion lifted his hand. "We're not suggesting with one of us. The who in that equation is her choice. As your husband, I will adopt her. She will be my daughter."

I tried to make sense of this riddle. "My biological father was an opponent of the senator? Did my biological father know about me?"

"Men like him don't appreciate the appearance of bastard children or grandchildren making a claim on their empires."

"They arrange car accidents," Andros said with a sneer.

"Perhaps they should choose mistresses with more common names," Marion added.

"My mother was some rich guy's mistress?" I shook my head. "I don't want a claim—" The truth before me hit me. "*You* want to make a claim."

"That was the plan," Andros said.

"Who is he? Tell me."

"He's deceased," Marion said.

"So there's no claim," I replied. "Let me go. Let Ruby go. This is over."

Marion retook his seat. "No, your father's empire still exists, and it's stronger than ever."

PATRICK

I'd awakened to a text message from Reid to meet immediately on two. After all that had happened, I'd been anxious to get upstairs to the penthouse, the place where Ruby had spent the night. While I agreed that having her alone with me in my apartment would be questionable to the world, in our tower, we weren't in the world. She was my daughter, my flesh and blood.

The reason Ruby slept in the penthouse wasn't only to avoid the appearance of impropriety or out of concern that Ruby would be uncomfortable. It was her immediate taking to Sparrow's wife, Araneae.

It was Sparrow's plan that upon arrival, Ruby and I would take the elevator to the apartments, the floor that held Mason and Laurel's, Reid and Lorna's, and my residences. Then we would meet with the doctor, directly off the elevators in our common area. It was similar to what you'd see in a hotel lobby

—stupid and wasted space—but it came in handy once in a while.

As the two of us took the elevator higher and higher into Chicago's skyline, I explained to Ruby that there would be a doctor waiting. I told her that her mother wanted to be certain that she was unharmed.

When the elevator doors opened, Dr. Dixon was present and thankfully alone. After introducing the two of them, they went into my apartment. Before I knew it, the elevator doors opened and I was joined by my three best friends. It wasn't five minutes before their wives also joined us.

While the men were more reserved, the ladies buzzed with excitement. If I'd ever been concerned about how they would react to my long-kept secret, I needn't have.

When the door to my apartment opened, Ruby was met with a seven-person greeting party.

It made me smile that she came to me.

"Are they all my mom's friends too?" she asked.

Before I could answer, Araneae Sparrow came forward and reached for Ruby's hands. "We will be."

My lack of sleep was evident as I turned away and cleared the accumulating moisture from my eyes.

Later that night, with all eight of us in Sparrow's kitchen doing our best to make Ruby comfortable while Lorna plied her with sweets and other foods, Araneae came to me.

"I was sixteen."

"We all were."

"No, Patrick, I was sixteen when my world changed. I lost the only parents I ever knew. I needed friends. I know we don't have the test results yet, but I don't care. I know what it's like to be lost in this big world at Ruby's age. I will do anything to help her through that."

I also knew what it was like to be alone, but my story was different. In many ways Araneae's and Ruby's held similarities I'd never considered. "I don't know what to say."

"You could say that she may stay up here in the penthouse."

My gaze went to Sparrow who was watching us from the other side of the room. "I think you should discuss that with your husband first."

Araneae's brown eyes sparkled. "I promise, I've got it covered. Besides, we have, like, a trillion bedrooms upstairs, ones that are only used when we..." She smiled. "Never mind that. The sheets are clean and Ruby will be my first official guest."

Now, the next morning, I was waiting for the elevator to open so I could answer Reid's call. When the door opened, I was met with Sparrow's dark glare.

"Good morning," I said as I stepped in.

"Hmm."

"How did she do?"

He shook his head. "Fine, I think. Araneae checked on her about ten times. It's not like anyone can leave the tower. I swear my wife was up more last night than I was."

I gave him a sideways glance. "Sorry."

Sparrow laughed. "That's not what I meant. What I mean is that if Reid has the results and she's not your kid, I'm going to have to deal with my wife. This is why we can't have a cat. She's easily attached."

The elevator came to a stop on two.

"She's Madeline's daughter," I said as we both stepped from the elevator. "I believe she's also mine, but if somehow we learn she isn't, that doesn't change the fact that I want to help Madeline and Ruby escape whatever hold Ivanov has on them."

We walked across the hallway to the sensor beside the steel door. A quick scan of my hand and the door slid open.

"It's about time," Reid said.

Mason was sitting on a nearby chair with a coffee mug in his hand. Shrugging, he said, "I got the text too."

"Is this about the paternity test?" Sparrow asked. "Or is it bigger? Is this something with the bratva?"

Reid took a deep breath. "Yes, it's about the paternity test. Yes, it's bigger. I don't know how it relates to Ivanov."

"You're making me nervous," I said.

"Everyone, sit down," Reid instructed. "As you know we asked for a rush on the saliva test. The blood one should confirm the findings but will take another forty-eight hours."

"Fuck, man, just tell us." I didn't need a preamble.

With the rest of us sitting, Reid stood. "The way this works—"

"We have a war," Sparrow said decisively.

"This will only take a minute," Reid said. "We all have DNA segments called alleles. We get one DNA segment from our mother and one from our father. These segments vary in length. It's the length of the alleles that is compared for paternity testing. The best possible test includes the mother's DNA. As you know we didn't have Madeline's. The recommendation then is to have a contrasting test subject, one you know won't register as a possible paternity match."

My nerves were ready to snap. "Reid, fucking please."

"Okay, well." He spoke faster. "We didn't have Madeline's

DNA so Dr. Dixon used DNA from the three of us for comparison—you know, to show that you, Patrick, are a better match than any one of us."

"And?"

"And with a possibility of paternity at 99.98 percent you are not excluded as her father."

My eyes opened wide. Even though math was my thing, I wasn't ready for an equation. "In plain fucking English."

"Ruby is your daughter."

It wasn't the same as announcing a pregnancy or a birth. There were no cigars with pink bands to pass around. Nevertheless, it was fucking surreal. Springing from our chairs, I was met with hugs, back slaps, and genuine words of congratulations. "I'm not shocked," I said. "I'm confirmed."

"Let's go upstairs and eat breakfast," Sparrow said. "Lorna was cooking when I left. Now we can get our heads straight and concentrate on Ivanov."

"And Madeline," I said.

"Do you plan to tell Ruby?" Mason asked as the three of us headed toward the door.

"Stop."

The three of us turned back to Reid.

"I know we're busy," he said, "but could everyone sit down for one more little thing?"

Exchanging glances, we all slowly retook our seats.

"You said she's my daughter?" I questioned. "The blood test won't reverse that?"

"She's your daughter," Reid confirmed. "Dr. Dixon was certain of that. However, she was perplexed by another result that she found." He had our attention. "She was so surprised that she ran the test three times."

"What test?" I asked.

"Mason's and my counter tests came back with no statistically significant number of similar markers." Reid said.

"Yours and Mason's," Sparrow repeated a bit slower.

"Yes," Reid said with a nod. "I'm just going to say it."

We all waited.

"While Mason and I share a statistically insignificant number of genetic markers with Ruby..." He took a breath. "Sparrow, you share just under twenty-five percent of the genetic markers—a statistically significant amount."

Sparrow stood and lifted his hands. "I never met Madeline before the other night."

"No," Reid said. "You're not Ruby's father. Dr. Dixon and I consulted Laurel..." He looked at Mason, took another deep breath, and turned back to Sparrow. "...we are all in agreement that while you're not Ruby's father, genetically you're related —statistically, closely related."

"That isn't possible."

MADELINE

Last night

"*D*oes this mystery asshole who didn't want to be bothered with bastard relations have a name?" I asked.

"His name was Allister," Marion said. "Your *father's* name was Allister."

"Is that supposed to mean something?"

"You might be more familiar with his son," Andros said with a fucking shit-eating grin on his lips.

"Tell me."

"I believe you've met your brother," he said, "Sterling Sparrow."

Thank you for reading *FLAME*. Patrick and Madeline's story

concludes in *ASHES*. You're not going to want to miss a moment of *WEB OF DESIRE*. Preorder *Ashes* now by tapping on the titles.

And if you haven't read *WEB OF SIN*, Sterling Sparrow and Araneae's story, begin the **completed trilogy** today by clicking on *SECRETS*. Keep turning the pages for a sneak peek.

Lastly, if you haven't read *TANGLED WEB*, Mason/Kader and Laurel's story, begin the **completed trilogy** today by clicking on *TWISTED*. Check out a sneak peek of *TWISTED* after the glimpse into *SECRETS*.

HUMAN TRAFFICKING RESOURCES

Human trafficking is a real and horrible crime happening throughout our world today. Madeline's story was not meant to portray her experience as romantic.

If you know or suspect someone is a victim, or if you yourself are a victim, please call:
National Human Trafficking Hotline

Call 1-888-373-7888 (TTY:711) or Text 233733

The National Human Trafficking Hotline connects victims and survivors of sex and labor trafficking with services and supports to get help and stay safe. The National Hotline also receives tips about potential situations of sex and labor trafficking and facilitates reporting that information to the appropriate authorities in certain cases.

The toll-free phone and SMS text lines and live online

chat function are available 24 hours a day, 7 days a week, 365 days a year. Help is available in English or Spanish, or in more than 200 additional languages through an on-call interpreter.

If you would like to help in the fight against human trafficking here are but two recognized organizations:

Durga Tree International

Mission: Durga Tree International's mission is to raise funds that support global initiatives to heal, protect, educate, and economically empower survivors of Modern Slavery. We bring together qualified partner organizations in the spirit of collaboration to support their individual and collective strengths, create a support network for modern abolitionists, foster a variety of programs around the globe effectively dealing with the many facets of modern slavery, and educate local US communities about their relationship to Human Trafficking and how it effects every person's life.

Polaris Project
Donate today

Mission: Polaris is a leader in the global fight to eradicate modern slavery. Named after the North Star that guided slaves to freedom in the U.S., Polaris systemically disrupts the human trafficking networks that rob human beings of their lives and their freedom. Our comprehensive model puts victims at the center of what we do – helping survivors restore their freedom, preventing more victims, and leveraging data and technology to pursue traffickers wherever they operate.

A PEEK AT SECRETS, BOOK #1 WEB OF SIN

Araneae

PROLOGUE

*M*y mother's fingers blanched as she gripped the steering wheel tighter with each turn. The traffic on the interstate seemed to barely move, yet we continued to swerve in, out, and around other cars. From my angle I couldn't read the speedometer, though I knew we were bordering on reckless driving. I jumped, holding my breath as we pulled in front of the monstrous semi, the blare of a truck's horn filling our ears. Tons of metal and sixteen wheels screeched as brakes locked behind us, yet my mother's erratic driving continued.

"Listen very carefully," she said, her words muffled by the quagmire of whatever she was about to say, the weight pulling them down as she fluttered her gaze between the road ahead and the rearview mirror.

"Mom, you're scaring me."

I reached for the handle of the car door and held on as if the seat belt couldn't keep me safe while she continued to weave from lane to lane.

"Your father," she began, "made mistakes, deadly mistakes."

My head shook side to side. "No, Dad was a good man. Why would you say that?"

My father, the man I called Dad for as long as I could remember, was the epitome of everything good: honest and hardworking, a faithful husband, and an omnipresent father.

He *was*.

He died less than a week ago.

"Listen, child. Don't interrupt me." She reached into her purse with one hand while the other gripped tighter to the wheel. Removing an envelope from the depths of the bag, she handed it my direction. "Take this. Inside are your plane tickets. God knows if I could afford to send you away farther than Colorado, I would."

My fingers began to tremble as I looked down at the envelope in my grasp. "You're sending me away?" The words were barely audible as my throat tightened and heaviness weighed down upon my chest. "Mom—"

Her chin lifted in the way it did when her mind was set. I had a million visions of the times I'd seen her stand up for what she believed. At only five feet three, she was a pit bull in a toy poodle body. That didn't mean her bark was worse than her bite. No, my mother always followed through. In all things she was a great example of survival and fortitude.

"When I say your father," she went on, "I don't mean my husband—may the Lord rest his soul. Byron was a good man who gave his...everything...for you, for *us*. He and I have always been honest with you. We wanted you to know that we loved you as our own. God knows that I wanted to give birth. I tried to get pregnant for years. When you were presented to us, we knew you were a gift from heaven." Her bloodshot eyes—those from crying through the past week since the death of my dad —briefly turned my direction and then back to the highway. "Renee, never doubt that you're our angel. However, the reality is somewhere darker. The devil has been searching for you. And my greatest fear has always been that he'd find you."

The devil?

My skin peppered with goose bumps as I imagined the biblical creature: male-like with red skin, pointed teeth, and a pitchfork. Surely that wasn't what she meant?

Her next words brought me back to reality.

"I used to wake in a cold sweat, fearing the day had arrived. It's no longer a nightmare. You've been found."

"Found? I don't understand."

"Your biological father made a deal against the devil. He thought if he did what was right, he could... well, he could *survive*. The woman who gave birth to you was my best friend —a long time ago. We hadn't been in contact for years. She hoped that would secure your safety and keep you hidden. That deal...it didn't work the way he hoped. Saving themselves was a long shot. Their hope was to save you. That's how you became our child."

It was more information than I'd ever been told. I have always known I was adopted but nothing more. There was a promise of *one day*. I used to hope for that time to come. With the lead weight in the pit of my stomach, I knew that now that *one day* had arrived, and I wasn't ready. I wanted more time.

The only woman I knew as my mother shook her head just before wiping a tear from her cheek. "I prayed you'd be older before we had this talk, that you would be able to comprehend the gravity of this information. But as I said, things have changed."

The writing on the envelope blurred as tears filled my sixteen-year-old eyes. The man I knew as my dad was gone, and now the woman who had raised me was sending me away. "Where are you sending me?"

"Colorado. There's a boarding school in the mountains, St. Mary of the Forest. It's private and elite. They'll protect you."

I couldn't comprehend. "For how long? What about you? What about my friends? When will I be able to come home?"

"You'll stay until you're eighteen and graduated. And then it will be up to you. There's no coming back here...ever. This city isn't home, not anymore. I'm leaving Chicago, too, as soon as I get you out." Her neck stiffened as she swallowed her tears. "We both have to be brave. I thought at first Byron's accident was just that—an accident. But then this morning...I knew. Our time is up. They'll kill me if they find me, just as they did Byron. And Renee..." She looked my way, her gray eyes swirling with emotion. While I'd expect sadness, it was fear that dominated. "...my fate would be easy compared to yours."

She cleared her throat, pretending that tears weren't cascading down her pale cheeks.

"Honey, these people are dangerous. They don't mess around, and they don't play fair. We don't know how, but they found you, and your dad paid the price. I will forever believe that he died to protect you. That's why we have this small window of time. I want you to know that if necessary, I'll do the same. The thing is, my death won't stop them. And no matter what, I won't hand you over."

"Hand me over?"

We swerved again, barreling down an exit until Mom slammed on her brakes, leaving us in bumper-to-bumper traffic. Her gaze again went to the rearview mirror.

"Are we being followed?" I asked.

Instead of answering, she continued her instructions. "In that envelope is information for your new identity, a trust fund, and where you'll be living. Your dad and I had this backup plan waiting. We hoped we'd never have to use it, but he insisted on being prepared." Her gaze went upward. "Thank you, Byron. You're still watching over us from heaven."

Slowly, I peeled back the envelope's flap and pulled out two Colorado driver's licenses. They both contained my picture—that was the only recognizable part. The name, address, and even birth dates were different. "Kennedy Hawkins," I said, the fictitious name thick on my tongue.

"Why are there two?"

"Look at the dates. Use the one that makes you eighteen years old for this flight. It's to ensure the airline will allow you to fly unaccompanied. Once you're in Colorado, destroy the one with the added two years. The school needs your real age for your grade in school."

I stared down at one and then the other. The name was the same. I repeated it again, "Kennedy Hawkins."

"Learn it. Live it. Become Kennedy."

A never-before-thought-of question came to my mind. "Did I have a different name before I came to you?"

My mother's eyes widened as her pallid complexion changed from white to gray. "It's better if you don't know."

I sat taller in the seat, mimicking the strength she'd shown me all of my life. "You're sending me away. You're saying we may never see one another again. This is my only chance. I think I deserve to be told everything."

"Not everything." She blinked rapidly. "About your name, your dad and I decided to alter your birth name, not change it completely. You were very young, and we hoped having a derivation of what you'd heard would help make the transition easier. Of course, we gave you our last name."

"My real name isn't Renee? What is it?"

"Araneae."

The syllables played on repeat in my head, bringing back memories I couldn't catch. "I've heard that before, but not as a name."

She nodded. "I always thought it was ironic how you loved insects. Your name means spider. Your birth mother thought it gave you strength, a hard outer shell, and the ability to spin silk, beautiful and strong."

"Araneae," I repeated aloud.

Her stern stare turned my way. "Forget that name. Forget Araneae and Renee. We were wrong to allow you any connection. Embrace Kennedy."

My heart beat rapidly in my chest as I examined all of the paperwork. My parents, the ones I knew, were thorough in their plan B. I had a birth certificate, a Social Security card, a passport matching the more accurate age, and the driver's license that I'd seen earlier, all with my most recent school picture. According to the documentation, my parents' names were Phillip and Debbie Hawkins. The perfect boring family. Boring or exciting, family was something I would never have again.

"And what happened to Phillip and Debbie?" I asked as if any of this made sense.

"They died in an automobile accident. Their life insurance funded your trust fund. You are an only child."

The car crept forward in the line of traffic near the departure terminal of O'Hare Airport. A million questions swirled through my head, and yet I struggled to voice even one. I reached out to my mother's arm. "I don't want to leave you."

"I'll always be with you, always."

"How will we talk?"

She lifted her fist to her chest. "In here. Listen to your heart."

Pulling to the curb and placing the car in park, she leaned my direction and wrapped me in her arms. The familiar scent of lotions and perfumes comforted me as much as her hug. "Know you're loved. Never forget that, Kennedy."

I swallowed back the tears brought on by her calling me by the unfamiliar name.

She reached for her wrist and unclasped the bracelet she always wore. "I want you to have this."

I shook my head. "Mom, I never remember seeing you without it."

"It's very important. I've protected it as I have you. Now, I'm giving it to you." She forced a smile. "Maybe it will remind you of me."

"Mom, I'd never forget you." I looked down to the gold

bracelet in the palm of my hand as my mom picked it up, the small charms dangling as she secured it around my wrist.

"Now, it's time for you to go."

"I don't know what to do."

"You do. Go to the counter for the airlines. Hand them your ticket and the correct identification. Stay strong."

"What about those people?" I asked. "Who are they? Will you be safe?"

"I'll worry about me once I'm sure that you're safe."

"I don't even know who they are."

Her gaze moved from me to the world beyond the windshield. For what seemed like hours, she stared as the slight glint of sunshine reflected on the frost-covered January ground. Snow spit through the air, blowing in waves. Finally, she spoke, "Never repeat the name."

"What name?"

"Swear it," she said, her voice trembling with emotion.

It was almost too much. I nodded.

"No. I need to hear you promise me. This name can never be spoken aloud."

"I swear," I said.

"Sparrow, Allister Sparrow. He's currently in charge, but one day it will be his son, Sterling."

I wished for a pen to write the names down; however, from the way they sent a chill down my spine, I was most certain that I'd never forget.

WEB OF SIN is completely available: *SECRETS*, *LIES*, and *PROMISES*.

A PEEK AT TWISTED, BOOK #1 OF THE TANGLED WEB TRILOGY

Kader

The conference hall shimmered with the light from the oversized chandeliers. The atmosphere was set, the enticement dangling like a baited hook, and the gullible fish swimming about, ready to open wide while the sharks lurked in the depths.

I didn't belong here, that sentiment as obvious to me as to the others in my presence.

I wasn't an eager fish, willing to follow the school wherever the masses led.

Extending the analogy, I also wasn't a fisherman.

I was a hunter, standing motionless in knee-deep water, spear in hand, ready for the kill. Bring on the sharks. I was ready for them to show me their rows of teeth.

Dressing in a custom suit, shaving my face, and taming my hair didn't hide the truth beneath. All around me, the prey sensed the danger. A formal announcement of my presence or boast of my wealth, power, and abilities wasn't necessary. As one who truly possessed all three, the declaration preceded me, coming in silent waves radiating through the air and transmitted wordlessly.

One by one, fellow attendees moved about me, glasses of champagne in hand and their eyes averted, unable or unwilling to meet my gaze. Their only outward acknowledgments that they'd had an encounter with me were their whispers and mumbles as they uttered meaningless apologies under their breath.

"Excuse me."

"Sorry."

I didn't respond. There was no need to leave memories of my attendance other than a passing shadow.

The suit I'd worn was meant to allow me to fade into the crowd. In reality it showcased the gaping difference. My custom designer original was crème brûlée amongst a tray of Twinkies—lobster amid fast food.

Many of the people in this banquet hall were here to add their names to research, research few of them came close to understanding. Their riches were primarily on paper, their names listed in *Forbes* magazine for the world to lay prostrate at their feet. The truly wealthy didn't require a magazine to substantiate their worth. With our riches spread throughout the world, we did our best to keep its presence beneath the radar.

Scanning the faces of the invited guests, their attempts of deception and pretense were as clear as a neon sign. This room was filled with impostors consumed by the need to fulfill their lackluster lives—lives devoid of true accomplishment—with the praises of those their money can buy.

Money—in most cases it wasn't an asset but the expandable depth of their credit.

Acknowledgments.

Recognition.

Their names on a plaque.

I had no more desire to fit in with these imitations of wealth than to dine on the cheap catering being offered or consume the basement-bottom bourbon in my hand.

Fitting in wasn't my thing or my goal.

I was here for one reason.

An assignment.

A job I agreed to fulfill.

Offers came and went.

I only took the assignments I wanted.

The decision was always mine.

I worked for no man but myself, on my schedule, as I saw fit.

My work had made me a wealthy man, taking me into the shadows and leaving me in the dark. Rarely did I accept an offer that brought me into the light.

However, even I could make an exception.

There was something about this assignment, this target...something that superseded my usual rules. I didn't need the money. I could spend the rest of my life hidden away on my ranch or sailing the seven seas. I vastly preferred my own company to those currently in my presence.

The door near the back of the room opened as more guests arrived.

I stood taller, taking her in.

She had arrived.

My *exception*.

She was the reason I was here.

At the sight of her, the small hairs on the back of my neck stood to attention. It was as if she was electricity and I was the rod. My reaction was visceral, much as it had been the first time I'd seen her.

The first time wasn't in person. It was her likeness that appeared on my computer screen and inexplicably, I was mesmerized. Her blue eyes stared at the camera, staring at me through the screen—seeing me in a way that even I was incapable of doing.

That thought was ludicrous and I knew it. Nevertheless, I was drawn.

As she accepted a glass of champagne, her head turned my direction. Instinctively, I took a step back, away from her gaze and into the shadows. I wasn't ready to meet those blue eyes in person, not yet. From the distance, I watched as I took in each inch of her.

A natural beauty, she seemed unaware of her effect on the men around her. Unlike her usual hairstyle, currently her dark hair was pulled up on the sides, the front styled in sweeping waves as long curls cascaded to the middle of her back. The softness of the style showcased her sensual neck and the simple pearl necklace. Under the lights from above, her gaze shone and lower lip disappeared as she nervously scanned the crowd.

The long black dress she wore hugged her breasts perfectly, yet the skirt flared outward, hiding what I knew was a beautifully curved body beneath. I'd done my research, bided my time. No, I hadn't seen her as up close as I desired; however, I'd observed. Despite the cool spring weather, at least three times a week she'd don skintight athletic apparel and run a local trail.

From my observation, Dr. Laurel Carlson wasn't a woman who thrived on being the center of attention—not like the room of potential donors, many vying for her attention. Her unease was evident in the lines around her eyes and the straightness of her neck. And yet still she was here, a testament to her dedication to this project.

If only I'd moved faster, done my job, this would have been avoided.

I hadn't. I'd been too enthralled in a way I found unusual yet fascinating. It was a twisted, gnawing feeling I didn't recognize.

I wanted to understand it.

In that search for comprehension, I'd taken too long.

Now, the stage was set for this show, and it was too late to lower the curtain.

For that, I was responsible.

Now was the time to move.

I leaned against the far wall, yet my mind stayed on her— my exception, the one who fascinated me in a different way.

Maybe it was more than her outward appearance. It was her intellect along with her doctorate in pharmacology—she also had a doctorate in applied mathematics with a focus on computational neuroscience and pharmacology. The combination intrigued me. Rarely did I encounter a woman like her. Most were different, satisfied to be a physical outlet for me or other men. They concentrated on appearance, keeping their knowledge level hidden. Admittedly, my sample was skewed. I paid those women for their services, thus reducing the variables.

Laurel was different; she was unaware of her beauty and unapologetically confident with her intelligence.

Despite my obvious fascination, she was my assignment.

I'd never failed at a job.

In that regard, Dr. Laurel Carlson wouldn't be my exception.

It was time to get this done.

Download **TWISTED** today, book one of the Tangled Web trilogy, entire trilogy is COMPLETE. Get your copy today by clicking on the title.

WHAT TO DO NOW

LEND IT: Did you enjoy **FLAME**? Do you have a friend who'd enjoy **FLAME**? **FLAME** may be lent one time. Sharing is caring!

RECOMMEND IT: Do you have multiple friends who'd enjoy my dark romance with twists and turns and an all new sexy and infuriating anti-hero? Tell them about it! Call, text, post, tweet...your recommendation is the nicest gift you can give to an author!

REVIEW IT: Tell the world. Please go to the retailer where you purchased this book, as well as Goodreads, and write a review. Please share your thoughts about **FLAME** on:

*Amazon, **FLAME** Customer Reviews

*Barnes & Noble, **FLAME**, Customer Reviews

*Apple Books, **FLAME** Customer Reviews

* BookBub, **FLAME** Customer Reviews

*Goodreads.com/Aleatha Romig

BOOKS BY NEW YORK TIMES BESTSELLING AUTHOR ALEATHA ROMIG

THE SPARROW WEBS:

WEB OF DESIRE:

SPARK

Releasing January 14, 2020

FLAME

Releasing February 25, 2020

ASHES

Releasing April 7, 2020

TANGLED WEB:

TWISTED

Released May, 2019

OBSESSED

Released July, 2019

BOUND

Released August, 2019

WEB OF SIN:

SECRETS

Released October, 2018

LIES

Released December, 2018

PROMISES

Released January, 2019

THE INFIDELITY SERIES:

BETRAYAL

Book #1

Released October 2015

CUNNING

Book #2

Released January 2016

DECEPTION

Book #3

Released May 2016

ENTRAPMENT

Book #4

Released September 2016

FIDELITY

Book #5

Released January 2017

THE CONSEQUENCES SERIES:

CONSEQUENCES

(Book #1)

Released August 2011

TRUTH

(Book #2)

Released October 2012

CONVICTED

(Book #3)

Released October 2013

REVEALED

(Book #4)

Previously titled: Behind His Eyes Convicted: The Missing Years

Re-released June 2014

BEYOND THE CONSEQUENCES

(Book #5)

Released January 2015

RIPPLES

Released October 2017

CONSEQUENCES COMPANION READS:

BEHIND HIS EYES-CONSEQUENCES

Released January 2014

BEHIND HIS EYES-TRUTH

Released March 2014

STAND ALONE MAFIA THRILLER:

PRICE OF HONOR

Available Now

THE LIGHT DUET:

Published through Thomas and Mercer Amazon exclusive

INTO THE LIGHT

Released June, 2016

AWAY FROM THE DARK

Released October, 2016

TALES FROM THE DARK SIDE SERIES:

INSIDIOUS

(All books in this series are stand-alone erotic thrillers)

Released October 2014

ALEATHA'S LIGHTER ONES:

PLUS ONE

Stand-alone fun, sexy romance

Released May 2017

A SECRET ONE

Fun, sexy novella

Released April 2018

ANOTHER ONE

Stand-alone fun, sexy romance

Releasing May 2018

ONE NIGHT

Stand-alone, sexy contemporary romance

September 2017

INDULGENCE SERIES:

UNEXPECTED

Released August, 2018

UNCONVENTIONAL

Released January, 2018

UNFORGETTABLE

Released October, 2019

ABOUT THE AUTHOR

Aleatha Romig is a New York Times, Wall Street Journal, and USA Today bestselling author who lives in Indiana, USA. She has raised three children with her high school sweetheart and husband of over thirty years. Before she became a full-time author, she worked days as a dental hygienist and spent her nights writing. Now, when she's not imagining mind-blowing twists and turns, she likes to spend her time with her family and friends. Her other pastimes include reading and creating heroes/anti-heroes who haunt your dreams!

Aleatha impresses with her versatility in writing. She released her first novel, CONSEQUENCES, in August of 2011. CONSEQUENCES, a dark romance, became a bestselling series with five novels and two companions released from 2011 through 2015. The compelling and epic story of Anthony and Claire Rawlings has graced more than half a million e-readers. Her first stand-alone smart, sexy thriller INSIDIOUS was next. Then Aleatha released the five-novel INFIDELITY series, a romantic suspense saga, that took the reading world by storm, the final book landing on three of the top bestseller lists. She ventured into traditional publishing with Thomas and Mercer. Her books INTO THE LIGHT and AWAY FROM THE DARK were published through this mystery/thriller publisher in 2016. In the spring of 2017, Aleatha again ventured into a different genre with her first fun and sexy stand-alone romantic comedy with the USA Today bestseller PLUS ONE. She continued with ONE NIGHT and ANOTHER ONE. If you like fun, sexy, novellas that make your heart pound, try her UNCONVENTIONAL and UNEXPECTED. In 2018 Aleatha returned to her dark romance roots with WEB OF SIN.

Aleatha is a "Published Author's Network" member of the Romance Writers of America, NINC, and PEN America. She is represented by Kevan Lyon of Marsal Lyon Literary Agency.

facebook.com/aleatharomig

twitter.com/aleatharomig

instagram.com/aleatharomig